The Grass is Always Greener

A Novel

C.L. Johnson

Rebirth Publishing
1989 Nashboro Blvd.
Nashville, TN 37211

For ordering information visit www.CLJohnson.com

Cover art design by Svidenovic via www.dreamstime.com

ISBN: 978-0-578-00028-2

Dedication

God, I dedicate this book to you. I give it to you
as my first fruit offering, just as I promised. I
give you all the glory and praise for this gift and
I know that you have placed me in this position
I also thank you for your grace and mercy along this
journey. Without you I am nothing and I
could do nothing. Thank You.

Acknowledgements

First of all I have to acknowledge my wife. Erica, this book is as much your work as it is mine. I appreciate all the support and encouragement you gave during this process. I also appreciate you reading the manuscript time after time and letting me know when I *went a bit too far.*

Also to my two boys, Jontez and Micah, hopefully with me writing this book, you will see that books *are* actually cool and cool people write them. That is of course, given that when you are old enough to read this, you still think Daddy is cool.

To my mother, Linda, what can I say? There would be no book, no me, or anything else if it were not for you. I appreciate everything you have done for me, including sending me to college for something that I'm not doing right now. With God's blessing, this will become a much better alternative. Also to Eric, thanks for taking care of my mother. I know it's not easy to come into a blended family and it takes a real man to stick it out.

To my sister, who at the time of me writing this is preparing to be deployed to Iraq, your courage amazes me. Nikkie, not only do I need to thank you for being a great sister, but also for fighting for Americans to have the freedom that we enjoy everyday.

Courtney, thanks for the instrumental for the book trailer. Just like everything in life, the music industry is about determination. If you keep your persistence up, you won't have any choice but to make it.

Also to my extended family, every one of ya'll, thanks for everything. I wish I could name everyone individually, but with all my aunts, uncles, and *first through eighth* cousins, I would have to write an entire book just dedicated to that. Just know that each one of you has been very instrumental in my life and I thank you from the bottom of my heart.

To my Mt. Zion Baptist church family, thanks for being the best church home I could ever imagine and as Bishop Walker always says, for being *the best church this side of heaven.* Bishop thanks for being a true man of God and feeding my spirit with nothing but the Word.

To every author that's gone before me, no matter what genre, I have nothing but respect for you. If it were not for you I wouldn't be able to dream of anything like this. A special thanks is due to those that are writing African American Christian Fiction. This is an area that I am passionate about and I am merely trying to follow along side your footsteps while making my own. To name a few: ReShonda Tate Billingsly, Kimberla Lawson Roby, and Jacqueline Thomas. I'm a huge fan and I appreciate every one of you.

Last but not least, to everyone who bought this book, thank you for the love and support. There are no words that can describe how much I appreciate you investing in me. I promise that I won't loose track of the mission that God has given me which is to reach His people by telling stories they can relate to. With your support this is only the beginning.

Chapter 1

The beautiful woman confidently strode into the coffee shop. She wore a gray business suit with five inch black pumps. She was tall for a woman and had the face of an angel. Her skin glistened in the sunlight and the perfectly applied make-up she wore made her skin appear to be flawless. Her form fitting suit accented her almost perfect body and she carried a Gucci brief case with matching sunglasses to let you know that she liked the finer things and had the bank account to pay for it.

"Can I have a double latte," she asked and grabbed a seat at a nearby table to wait for it to be prepared.

As she waited she briefly scanned the room. It was pretty dull for a weekday. Around that time the shop was normally filled to the brim with local businessmen and women taking a break from their daily grind to grab a cup of coffee.

She took notice of a group of guys sitting two tables down from her. Two of them were pretty attractive and the other was not unattractive, but a little too close to fat for her taste. One guy was light skinned and had a detailed fade with a razor trimmed mustache and goatee. He wore a two piece outfit that looked like it was expensive. He wasn't as rowdy as the other two, so she guessed he had a couple of years in age on the others.

As he took a sip of his drink, she noticed the light gleam off of the wedding ring on his left hand. She thought, *if he wasn't married I would go over and introduce myself right now.* The second guy was sitting back mostly listening. He was the chunky one. He had a dark ebony skin tone and she surmised that if she were in to big men then he would be a cute guy, but chubby chasing just wasn't her style.

He also wore a fade and a neatly trimmed beard. He wore a long-sleeved Dallas Cowboys tee-shirt with a pair of blue jeans and sneakers. His demeanor as he sat back and took in what the other two were saying let her know he wasn't the dominant male in the group. Every time he tried to open his mouth one of the other two would cut him off. She also saw that he was married because of the glistening platinum wedding ring on his finger.

The last guy, who seemed to be doing most of the talking, was equally attractive as the first. He was also dark skinned. She noticed right away that he wore a Rolex wristwatch, an expensive looking black and white pinstriped suit, and had on a costly looking pair of dress shoes. He looked like some sort of businessman. She could not miss the fact that he did not have on a wedding ring. *Jackpot*, she thought as she got up to go to the bathroom.

She made her way past the table that sat the three men. She made sure to go out of her way to brush past the one without the wedding ring. As she, gently bumped up against him she placed a sweet smelling hand on his shoulder and seductively whispered, "Excuse me."

"No problem," he said as they made eye contact. She pulled down her glasses so she could reveal a pair of hazel eyes that would stop any man in his tracks. She also made sure to give a sensual nibble to her bottom lip to emphasize the sense of attraction. He didn't say anything else verbally. Instead, everything was said in the exchange of glances. She continued on her path to the bathroom and knew that her point had come across nicely.

"Did you see the butt on her," Mark asked as his eyes followed her to the bathroom. "Man, if I was single I would be all over that."

"Yeah right," Austin said in retort. "The only thing you would be all over is a jelly doughnut. Me, on the other hand, I'm going back there to get that number. She practically begged me to. You saw how she was biting her lip."

Mark shook his head in disgust. He looked down at the Dallas Cowboys shirt he was wearing and brushed off the doughnut crumbs he had spilled. "What about Jules, man? Did you forget about what you promised her?"

"Dude, you know what? I'm gonna get you a skirt and a pair of pom-poms for your next birthday. Don't you worry about what I told Julie, she's taken care of. You just worry about your wife and we'll be straight."

"Why you getting defensive, bruh? I was just asking," Mark snapped back starting to get a little angry. Austin never wanted anyone to check him on his mess ups.

"That's the problem. You're always *just asking*. When are you gonna learn? I'm a grown man and I do what I want to do," Austin said staring Mark down.

"Grown men handle their responsibilities and they treat their women like queens."

"It don't seem like that's good enough for Terri, does it? Being treated like a queen isn't enough to keep her happy."

"All right, ya'll need to chill out," Quincey said as he finished the last bite of his croissant. "It's starting to get too serious in here."

Quincey, or Q as his friends called him, was always playing the mediator between Mark and Austin. He was the oldest in the group by a couple of years, so it was almost mandatory that he took the role of older brother. Truth was he was growing extremely tired of all the childish arguing.

"Well just tell dough boy to stay off my back," Austin said as he got up to start towards the rest room. As he walked off he threw a thumbs up to his two friends seated at the table and flashed a quick smile. He walked back toward the restroom area like a man on a mission.

"So what's up, Big Mark," Q said trying to change the subject a little. "How's everything going at home? How are Terri and the kids doing lately?"

"They've been doing pretty good. The kids are active as ever and it wears me out just keeping up. My girls are growing so fast, they'll be eighteen before I know it. Terri's been spending more and more hours down at the hospital. It's cool though, because after I lost my job she buckled down and really took care of things."

Mark purposely withheld information because he didn't want to tell Quincey everything. There was more trouble brewing on the horizon than with Terri working too many hours. Terri acted as if she hated Mark and everything he said to her led to an argument. On top of all that, they had not been intimate in the last six months. All this along with the small amount of time they got to spend together was taking a toll on their marriage.

"That's cool, man. Don't forget you can come down to the law firm and I can always find some work for you to do.

Mark snorted at the idea. "Man, what do I look like? I don't need hand outs and further more I can't fit in at some stuck up law firm. I just couldn't do it."

"Pride goes before destruction and that's exactly where you're headed with that mentality. Besides I'm not offering any hand outs, I'm offering to pay for a service."

"Well, don't worry about me I'll manage. Anyway, what's up with you and Kim? I haven't seen her in a while?" Mark said changing the subject.

"She's been doing better. I've been working a lot of hours lately, so she's been having some difficulties with me being gone so much. I've just really been praying that she can come to terms with it."

Quincey was one of the top attorneys in Nashville and his star was constantly growing. He was getting all the top cases and was thinking about starting his own law firm. Kim was his beautiful wife of five years and on the outside they couldn't seem happier. Their problems started when Quincey announced his calling to preach. He had already been preoccupied with work, but when he added going to seminary school to get a degree in ministry he started spending even less time at home. When he did get some time at home, all he wanted to do was sleep.

All three men were raised in church, but somehow went astray. Quincey was the first one to rededicate his life to Christ. Since he assumed the roll of the responsible one in the group, he felt he needed to lead by example. How could he tell the others anything if his life wasn't at least remotely lining up with God's plan? Mark had just recently started attending church again. Austin, on the other hand was still a work in progress. He attended church whenever he felt like it and even then couldn't pay attention for checking out the women in the service.

The waitress finally showed up for the last refill on the drinks and placed the bill on the table. She placed one in front of Mark and Quincey and one in front of Austin's still empty seat.

"Man, I don't know why Austin is always fooling around with these women," Quincey said while angrily scanning the room. "My lunch hour is nearly up and I have a lot of work to do. I've been working on this big case and I gotta put in as much leg work as possible today."

Mark didn't respond he just smiled and shook his head. He knew how Austin was. He didn't mean to be hard on him. He just could not get over how some people overlooked their blessings and the way Austin treated Julie sickened him.

Austin was quickly becoming the most well known small business man in the state of Tennessee, and with that recognition came as many women as he could stand. Mark never would've had a problem with it if Austin had been single, but when you *do* have a good woman in your life you cherish her, especially one like Julie. Not only was she faithful to Austin but she was loyal. She had been with him since the time when he didn't have two cents to his name.

Quincey picked up his ticket and took a look at it. "Whew, this is a little more that I expected. It seems like the price changes every time I come in here." Quincey was rather well off, but his philosophy was you stay wealthy by saving money where ever you can.

He then reached over to grab Mark's ticket. "Don't worry about this one, big man. I got it."

"Bruh, what did I just tell you." Mark said quickly. "I don't need any handouts. I can handle my own bill."

Just then Austin came around the corner. He had a paper towel in his hand wiping lipstick from his lips. "Ya'll ready," he said while picking up his portion of the bill. "I gotta get outta here, I have a big meeting."

"No, we're not ready," Quincey said with a smile on his face. "I think you need you wait on us for a while. I believe I'll have another round on my fruit tea.

"Well, I can tell ya'll this. If you want to ride in the pimpmobile, then I suggest ya'll come on. If not I believe ya'll can afford to pay bus fare. Well, at least you can, Q," Austin said taking another shot at Mark.

That was the last straw. Mark stood up like he was about to attack Austin right there in the coffee shop. Quincey stood up too, so he could stop it from getting out of hand.

Just then the woman rounded the corner looking as collected and well put together as before. They all stopped when she passed by their table again. Austin's eyes were stuck on her as if she were an oasis in the middle of the desert. She peered over her glasses at him and flashed a smile. She then picked up her now cold latte and exited the shop.

"Dude, she was too hot," Austin said still looking at her as she exited the building. His eyes followed alone the brick wall as if he had some sort of x-ray vision. "Ya'll don't have to agree with what I do, but you gotta understand.

"Well, I don't understand," Mark said with a disappointed look on his face. "Julie is like a sister to us, Q. How right is it for us to just sit here while this *player* dogs her out?"

Austin just threw his money on the table and started toward the door. "Man lets get out of here before I have to hear anymore crying. I've seen ten year olds that were manlier than this dude."

"Man, Mark, just chill," Q said. I know where you're coming from, but you can't just get upset if someone doesn't take your advice. No matter how you feel about it, it's his life and he's not gonna change until *he's* good and ready."

"That's right, Mark. You should listen to the Rev because right now I'm not ready. When I am, I'll let you know."

Mark didn't say anything in response because he didn't feel as if that comment deserved one. Sure they had been friends since junior high school, but that doesn't mean you had to like everything the other one does. He stood, threw his money on the table, and exited the coffee shop.

Chapter 2

Mark awoke to the sound of the shower going in the master bath. He rolled over and felt for Terri but no one was there. Her side of the bed looked undisturbed so it was obvious she hadn't been there all night. Through blurred vision from the sleep that was still in his eyes, he looked at the clock. In giant red letters it flashed 3:30 a.m.

He turned back over and decided to wait until she got out of the shower. Normally he would have promptly drifted back into dreamland, but they hadn't had much time with each other lately. Terri had been spending a lot of hours at the Hospital to make up for his loss of income. He felt horrible about it, but jobs were scarce for a man without much education. Whenever he did get a call back, he flunked the interview process with flying colors.

Mark heard Terri's cell phone ringing over the sound of the running water. Just as he expected he heard the shower shut off and the ringing stop.

Mark rolled over onto his back and propped his head up with his hands. He could hear Terri's muffled voice barricaded by the bathroom door. He could not quite make out what she was saying but it didn't matter. He was quite sure that it was someone from her job, asking some nursing question.

The door to the bathroom swung open and Mark couldn't help but watch Terri walk out in just a bath towel. He checked out her shapely thighs as the towel couldn't do much of anything to cover them. She was still slightly wet from the shower and he couldn't deny how much this turned him on. He had to steal a look as she reached down to put on her bra and panties. Her butt protruded from the towel and that had to be his favorite feature on her.

Terri then got into the bed with him and Mark drank in her Passion Fruit Bath and Body Works scent. His engine was already running and he hadn't even spoken to her yet. He couldn't help it. It had been about six months since they last were intimate. Between her working so many hours and him being busy all day job hunting and tending to the kids, they just didn't have the energy. Well he did, but he had to be respectful of her.

He snuggled up behind her. As he moved closer and wrapped his arms around her waist, he felt her black lace panties brush against his abdomen. "What's up baby? How was your day?" He said trying to remain composed. His whole body yearned to make love to her. It was late but his hormones were wide awake.

"Long," she said in an exhausted voice. "Today we had to see patient after patient."

"I'm real sorry to hear that."

"I'm sure," Terri quipped. Mark tried with all his might to ignore the smart tone in her voice. He could tell she meant that comment exactly how it sounded.

"You know I've missed you over the past few weeks. It just hasn't been the same around here with you working so many hours."

"Well, somebody has to do it," Terri said sarcastically. "We still got bills to pay and if I don't work then they don't get paid."

"Whoa, where's all this coming from," Mark said feeling really hurt that she would even say things like that. "It's not like I haven't been looking for a job. You know that the economy ain't doing so hot and for someone with just a high school diploma the pickings are slim.

"I just feel like you're not looking hard enough. You should be willing to flip burgers to have some income coming in. I just don't think you're going that extra mile."

"Extra mile?" Mark asked angrily. "Was I going the extra mile when I worked to put your butt through school? I was the *only* one working and I didn't seem to hear any complaints then."

She laughed mockingly. "What? Do you want somebody to pat you on the back for something that a man is supposed to do anyway?"

"That's not something that I'm *supposed* to do. I did that because I love and care about you. I want to see you doing something that makes you happy. How many other men do you know would do that?"

"I can think of plenty," she said and then stopped all of a sudden like she was about to say something she would regret.

"Well... Who?"

"Just working in my field, I meet all kinds of men that do what they need to do to take care of their families."

Mark sat straight up in the bed. He felt like leaving the room before he grew too angry. It was just like Terri to look at a man's bank account and think because he was rich that he was any better than the next.

"Look, babe." Mark said determined not let a stupid argument get in the way of him getting some for the first time in six months. "I didn't have any intentions of starting an argument. I just miss the way things used to be. So, why don't you just turn over and let big daddy give you a back rub and soothe your pain."

She hesitated for a moment and then said, "That's okay. Tonight is not the night, Baby. I'm just not feeling up to it."

"Tonight is not the night?" Mark demanded now furious. "Just when will it be the night?"

"When you get a job," she said and turned her back to him.

He was so upset that he couldn't think of anything else to say. She had some nerve. *As much as I've done for her*, he thought, *how could she be turning on me when I need her the most*? He just grabbed his pillow and went to sleep on the couch.

The next morning, Mark was stirred from his sleep when someone climbed onto his chest. He knew exactly who it was but was not quite ready to open his eyes. He decided if he left them closed he would not feel the urge to get up. This trick worked for all of five minutes because all of a sudden he felt a pair of fingers prying his eye lids apart.

"Daddy," the little voice said. "Are you up?" Stephanie was six years old and the older of Mark's two children. She was normally the first one out of bed. No matter where Mark was sleeping she always jumped on his chest and woke him up. Jessica was only three years old and looked just like her mother. Mark adored the both of them.

"Well I wasn't, but now I am. Good morning, sweetie, did you sleep well?"

"Yes, Daddy, I slept okay," she said while turning the T.V. on and tuning into her favorite cartoon.

"That's good, sweetie, get your sister up and help her brush her teeth while I get your breakfast made."

Mark got up and went into the master bath to brush his teeth. As he passed the bed he noticed it remained unmade and Terri, as usual, had made her unannounced early morning exit. As he walked into the bathroom he grabbed the towel off the floor that she had dropped there the night before. She typically didn't pick up behind herself anymore since she was the only one working.

As he brushed his teeth, he reminisced on how things used to be between them. He thought about when they first met. He was just a young punk trying to be cool, still in high school but wanting to act like an adult. She was walking down the street and he knew he had no choice but to approach her. He was extremely nervous because she was so beautiful and seemed out of his league.

He just stood there and watched her for a while. Those beautiful legs sprouting out of a short tennis skirt. He watched how her hips swayed from side to side when she walked. She was only sixteen but had the body of a twenty year old. Then, there was her gorgeous face that was almost blemish free and was set off by the most amazing pair of dark brown eyes you would ever see. He was instantly stricken with the love bug. He knew that people said there is no such thing as love at first sight but that had to be the first case.

From that very moment they spent every waking second together. Quincey and Austin just didn't understand. He ate, slept and breathed Terri and he knew she felt the same way. Their relationship was so exhilarating that they couldn't get enough of each other. That's the reason they wed right after high school. Q and Austin at that point, still didn't understand. After all, women came a dime a dozen for them.

He just longed so much for the way things were and how in love they used to be. Since he lost his job he didn't know where the love went. He still loved her but wasn't so sure about her feelings.

He had a plan to make things right, though. All he had to do was find a job and things would go back to the way they were. He knew that deep down inside, Terri had to still have a glimmer of that love for him. He just had to make her believe it again. His first step was that day with his interview at the American Parcel Service.

He finished putting on his black slacks with a white button down collar shirt. He struggled a bit with tying the black neck tie because Terri always did that for him, but he finally got it.

He then got the girls dressed and poured them bowls of Lucky Charms. He smiled as he took care of his daily *cooking* duties. He rather enjoyed caring for them everyday because they were the best thing to ever happen to him. That's the reason he could not let his marriage slip away. He and Terri had been at odds lately, but she had given him the gifts of two beautiful children and He could not just let that slip away.

He grabbed his resume off the counter, loaded the girls in the car and was off to make his first efforts in saving his marriage and family.

Chapter 3

Terri sped down I-40 going 85 miles an hour. She always drove fast when she was upset. Her green Dodge Caravan only had 85 on the dash but it felt like she was going much faster. The steering wheel vibrated steadily in her hand and she blazed her favorite comfort song, *I'm Not Your Superwoman*, on the radio.

She was very furious with Mark and had been for a long time. The very thought of him made her get mad because she was sick of being married to a lazy man. *Why can't he just find a job?* She thought angrily to herself.

Her cell phone rang and vibrated against the dash board.

What is he thinking? He has a family to take care of and I'm the queen of the castle. The Queen is not supposed to work this hard.

She was so deep in thought that she didn't look before merging into the left lane and nearly ran into the eighteen wheel truck that was riding next to her. She struggled to gain control as she swerved back into her own lane. Her heart was beating furiously.

"See, this is all *his* fault," she mouthed aloud angrily. "If I wasn't working so many hours, I could be more alert."

Her cell phone rang and vibrated again.

My mother always told me that if I allowed a man to lay up on me for free then he'll do it forever. That's all Mark is doing in my opinion. That's why he ain't getting any. I'm not about to pass my cookie out for free.

Her cell phone rang and vibrated a third time.

She finally reached over and picked it up. It was Mark. *What could he possibly want?* Terri thought to herself. *Didn't he get the point? We are not on speaking terms right now.*

She answered on the sixth ring. "Hello?" Terri said trying to sound as mean as possible. She didn't want Mark to think anything had changed.

"Hey, babe," Mark said sounding like he hadn't noticed her attitude. "After last night I felt we should clear the air."

Clear the air, she thought. *Didn't I make the air clear enough? He needs a job. If he's not telling me he found a job, then we don't have anything to talk about.*

"Well, start clearing."

"Look, you know I'm doing everything I can to support this family. I know I haven't had a job in a while, but I have a few promising situations coming up."

"How many times have I heard that before, Mark? I'm tired of getting my hopes up and then getting crushed."

"I know and I'm sorry," he said sounding as if his feelings were genuinely hurt. "Look, just hang in there with me and I promise this situation will be turned around. We just learned at church the other week-"

"I don't feel like hearing any *spiritual truths* right now," Terri said cutting him off. "Besides, you're the *last* person I would hear it from anyway." Ever since they started going to church again, Mark was always trying to shove the bible down her throat.

"I'm not trying to preach at you. I just really feel like God has a plan for our family."

"Well, if God had a plan for *our* family, then he would help you get a job."

"You know what? I don't expect you to understand right now. I pray that you can grow into it. The only thing I'm asking for is patience," Mark said. Deep down Terri was surprised that he didn't explode. She was trying to push his buttons, but it just wasn't working.

"Look, I can't promise you anything except that I'll try. We'll have to continue this talk later, though. I'm pulling into work."

"Okay. I love you"

Terri hesitated. She didn't know what to say. She still cared for him deeply but the love she once felt was fading fast. Money wasn't everything but she was betting that it was a lot easier to buy into that statement when you had some. She didn't want to hurt Mark in any way, but the past six months had been hard and it had been enough to take a toll on any marriage.

"I love you, too," Terri said weakly. "Bye."

Terri pulled into the parking lot of Southern Hospital. She had been working there for two years and was almost more familiar with that place than her own home.

She hopped out of the car and was in such a rush that she didn't notice the black Mercedes Benz that was rounding the corner. She stepped off the curb and froze like a deer in headlights when she heard the horn blow and the brakes squeal as the car tried to grind to a stop. She was only able to fumble out one word. "Jesus!" she yelled in a high pitched squeaky voice. It seemed as if time slowed down because Terri had enough time to think, *Mark has that religious stuff stuck in my head.*

The car stopped so close to her that Terri could feel the heat rising from the hood of the car. She jumped back onto the curb and was shaking uncontrollably. Had the car been going any faster she would be a patient in the hospital instead of going to work there.

She felt overwhelmed. It was so warm out that it seemed as if the tears that began to fall from her eyes started drying against her skin instantly. She didn't know why she was crying, she just was. She tried to stop but couldn't.

She walked to her minivan and leaned against it while she gathered herself. The man driving the Mercedes leaped out and started walking toward her. He picked up speed when he saw how upset she was. She didn't know if he recognized her right away but she knew exactly who he was.

He was still just as handsome as she remembered. He was tall and wore a low fade. His hair was charcoal black with a few grey hairs sprinkled throughout. She didn't mind the grey because it made him look distinguished. He had no facial hair which revealed great skin complexion for a man. He wore an all black suit with a white collarless shirt underneath. Even through the suit she could see his chiseled frame. She was upset but all that started to go away when he grew closer.

"Miss, are you okay?" He said once he reached her. He walked up and placed a hand on her shoulder. That's when she finally looked up and made eye contact with him.

"Yeah, I'm okay. I'm just happy to be alive," she said forcing a laugh.

"I'm sorry but do I know...," He said trailing off at the last word. He was studying her as if she were someone he had seen before. "Yes, I do know you. Your name is Terri, isn't it?"

"Do I know you?" She said, pretending as if she didn't already know.

"You were one of my best students in the class I taught a couple of years ago. You're also easy to remember because you were one of a few non-conventional students I had that year."

"You got me. Do you remember all of your students like that?"

"Nope, I only remember the smartest ones and of course the beautiful ones."

After that she didn't know what to say. He just stood there looking at her with his brown eyes sparkling. She imagined that her face must be red as a cherry because she could feel the warmth begin to grow in her cheeks. Contrary to popular belief, some black folks blushed too. If nothing else she felt flattered.

"Well, I guess I should say thank you, Mister..."

"Thomas, Cedric Thomas. You mean you really don't remember me?

"I think it's coming back to me slowly," she said with a small smile forming on her face."

"Well, perhaps I should refresh your memory a little over dinner. I know a wonderful place where we could sit in a quiet area, talk, and uh... discuss some medical issues.

It had been a long time since anyone had talked to her in a flirtatious way. Maybe it wasn't right, but she was enjoying it a little. Actually, she enjoyed it a lot. She didn't know how she would get away from Mark for a night, but she would find a way. A fine man with money was inviting her to dinner and she was going to treat herself.

"Well, I guess it wouldn't hurt anything, Mr. Thomas."

"Please, we're both adults. Call me Cedric."

He stuck his hand out and offered her his card. She reached out and gladly took it. Even his card was expensive, she determined from rubbing her hands on the intricate letters that rose above the card's surface. She then shook his hand and started walking toward the building. With her back turned she could finally smile like a giddy little school girl.

"I'll call you later to get all the details," she shouted over her shoulder as she entered the building."

For the first time in a long time, she thought, *I'm going to enjoy myself.*

Chapter 4

Mark went to drop the kids off with Austin's fiancée, Julie. She was a real saint when it came to babysitting the kids and Stephanie and Jessica loved the time that they spent with "Aunt Jules". She was a nurse and only worked three days of the week which allowed her to present herself for babysitting just about whenever Mark and Terri needed it.

When he walked through the door of her and Austin's behemoth of a house, Mark could feel the negativity in the air. Before he researched the problem, he had to take time to stop and admire the house. Now matter how many times he visited, Mark couldn't help but think that maybe he would live in a house like that one day because it was he and Terri's dream home. It shook him from his daydream when he heard Julie sobbing deeply from the living room.

"How you doing, baby girl?" He asked as he walked around and took a seat on the couch. "Are you okay?"

Her mascara was running in two steady black lines down her chubby cheeks and she was looking like she'd had the worst day of her life. He didn't know why Austin treated her the way he did. Sure Julie was a big girl, but she was still attractive. She didn't have the body of a supermodel like some of the girls Austin had cheated on her with, but she was still good looking in her own right.

"Nothing, just fighting with your ignorant friend again."

"Ah, man. What about this time?"

"Where do I start? First of all, he's been working late a lot. It seems like every night when I call to check on him he just says, *Baby, I'm going to be late getting home. Don't wait up.*"

"Really? Where is he now?"

"He just left to go out of town for some business."

Mark followed her into the kitchen. Julie was plainly upset and she looked as if she were about to start crying again. It was this very reason that Mark didn't have a lot of respect for men who dogged women out. They did unbelievable damage to the woman's self-esteem and just made it harder for the next brother.

He looked at the kid's who were listening intently since they couldn't help but notice she was crying. "Go into the den and play, girls. I need to talk to your Aunt Julie in private."

Stephanie huffed as she grabbed her sister's hand. She had a sad look on her face as she turned to walk down the hallway. Mark didn't feel sorry for them, though. There were some things children didn't need to be exposed to.

Julie continued, "Then, there have been these strange calls lately. The phone rings all times of the night. When I answer, I just hear heavy breathing and then get a dial tone. Of course I can't say he's cheating just based on that, but why would anyone be calling and hanging up? 'm telling you, Mark, I'm not getting any younger. I'm getting tired of going through these same old games."

Mark felt so sorry for her, but he didn't know what to say. "Look, I'm sure it's nothing. After he promised you he would be faithful from now on, I'm sure he's honoring that."

Mark knew he was lying, but he had to tell her something to calm her down. He knew Austin had broken that commitment right after he made it and was also one hundred percent sure that it was another woman calling throughout the night. And what's up with the late night business meetings? He'd heard of meetings running late but not that late.

"Look," he said. "I can see if I can drop the kids off with my mother, or if not there at Q and Kim's. I can see you need a little time. I wouldn't wanna impose."

"What? And miss spending time with my two favorite girls in the world? I wouldn't dream of it." She wet a towel and started drying mascara from her face and faked a smile.

"You sure? I don't want to put you at any inconvenience."

"No inconvenience, I promise we'll be okay. We'll watch *The Lion King* and eat some Rocky Road ice cream. It'll be fun."

"A'ight. Oh, and please don't mention my interview to Terri. When I get this job, I want it to be a surprise."

"Don't worry about it. My lips are sealed. You're a good man, Mark. I wish Austin could be more like you. I can hardly believe you guys are friends."

Mark let out a loud laugh. "Sometimes I can't believe it either.

As he headed to the door, he stopped and said, "Don't give up yet. I'm working on him. I'll get some sense in him if it's the last thing I do."

"I sure hope so," she said smiling softly.

Mark pulled into the parking lot of APS. His stomach had a queasy feeling and his legs shook with nervousness. This was one of the biggest interviews he had been on and the results could determine if he kept his family or not. If he got the job, it would go a long way toward him winning back the affection of his wife.

He hadn't said many prayers but decided that he would try and stumble through one the best he could. "Lord, you already know what I need," he prayed sincerely. "I don't have to go into detail except to tell you that you know how much I love my wife and kids and if it's your will, please bless me to get this job. You know that my desire is to be a provider for them. Thanks in advance."

He got out of the car and hoisted himself up onto legs that wobbled like a bowl of Jell-o. He started toward the building and gained a little confidence with each step he took. By the time he reached the building, he had confidence that things would soon turn around in his life.

Mark went into the office and sat in a waiting room where three other applicants awaited an interview for the same delivery job that he applied to. One of the applicants was a white male in his mid-twenties. He was clean cut and dressed professionally. Mark thought he looked overqualified for a delivery position. The next applicant was a black man that appeared to be in his early thirties. The guy dressed more like he was going to the club than to an interview, as his Phat Farm sweater and matching jeans were out of place for someone seeking a job.

The guy got up and walked over to the water cooler. When he passed by, Mark couldn't believe his eyes. The guy's jeans were sagging and there was a huge brown stain on his white briefs. Mark had to choke back a laugh. He knew if he started laughing, he would not be able to stop. He had to divert his attention elsewhere.

I can't wait to get out of here and tell Q about this one. He's going to laugh so hard, Mark thought still stifling his laugh.

The last guy was also black. He dressed professionally and looked to be in his early twenties. He looked more than capable of doing the job, but didn't look like he had the experience.

Mark figured his chances of getting the position were pretty good. The most threatening competition he had was the white guy. His dad had always taught him about the rules of corporate America so he believed that because of race alone, the guy was in the running for the position.

Mark's dad, Nate Baxter, was employed as a janitor at Mark's school. One day when Mark was about fourteen years old, Nate came into his room and sat on the edge of his bed. Mark didn't know what to expect. He figured he was in trouble or something.

Nate sighed heavily. "Son, it's about time we had a talk about some fundamental rules of being a black man in America. Number one is you have to take care of your family. If you don't take care of them, no one else will. Secondly, you have to beat the white man at his own game. If you want to make it in this life, you have to be that much better than him at whatever you do," Nate had said gloomily. That was one of the last conversations Mark remembered having with his father because Nate passed away not long after that.

Growing up and living in the south, Nate had seen plenty of instances of racism. Mark, on the other hand, had been fortunate enough to not see any, but he never discounted his father's sayings on the subject. He didn't remember much else of what Nate had told him that day, although the first two rules were imbedded in his head. That's exactly why he felt so strongly about providing for his family and so nervous about this job interview.

"Lester Smith," a fat balding man came into the office and said. Sweat beaded on the man's shiny head. The air condition wasn't working well in the office so the temperature was scorching. The white guy rose and gathered his briefcase and followed him into the back room. The bald man shut the door behind them so that it left a small crack. Mark could just barely see the chair that Lester was sitting in.

It gave him an idea. He thought that if he could just get a little closer, maybe he could hear some of the interview questions and be a little more prepared when it was his turn to go in the office.

He got up and walked over to the water cooler which was located right next to the room. They could not see him because it was positioned behind the door.

"Okay, Lester," Mark heard what must have been the voice of the balding white man say. "I really appreciate you coming in for the interview. This is mainly just a formality. Your dad told me all about your little situation when we went fishing on Sunday. I'll have you sign the new hire paper work while you're here."

Mark grew angry. He tried to give them the benefit of the doubt and consider that maybe he had misheard. After all, the door did provide somewhat of a sound barrier and their voices were a bit muffled.

"Great, I really appreciate you helping me out," he heard Lester saying. He could tell that he wore a smug little smile on his face by the way the words rolled off his tongue.

"It's no problem. I just want to hurry up and get out of here, because it's too hot with the air condition being out. If I could cancel the rest of these interviews, I sure would. No need to worry, though, no matter what these other guys say the position is yours. When I'm done with you, I'm gonna rush through the interviews with their black tails and get them out of here so I can go swimming," he said and started chuckling. Lester chimed in on the laughter.

On that note, Mark walked back to his seat. He felt anger welling up inside of him. He couldn't believe what he had just heard. It was exactly what his father tried to warn him about. Other people had talked about the racism that existed in corporate America, but he never knew he would come face to face with it.

He stood up to walk to the door and leave but his head began pounding from the anger. Everything in his vision turned red as he let his rage overtake him. This was supposed to be a happy day. It was the day he was supposed to save his family. He just dropped his bags and marched back toward the room.

"Hey it's not your turn to go back there!" The lady sitting at the desk shouted.

"You'll sit down and shut up if you know what's best for you. I don't have to have permission for this."

He burst open the door and the two sitting in the room jumped up. "What are you doing?" The bald white man said.

"Don't worry about what I'm doing," Mark shouted. "You'll find out soon enough."

Mark pointed his finger in Lester's face and said, "Don't move or I'll put your lights out."

Lester just sat there looking scared and pleading "Please, just don't hurt me!"

He walked around the desk and grabbed the fat man by his polka dot neck tie and snatched him out of his seat.

"What do you mean you'll rush through the interviews and get our *black tails* out of here?"

"I don't know what you're talking about," the man insisted.

Mark couldn't take anymore he balled his fist up and socked the man right in the nose. Red trickles of blood ran down the man's upper lip.

"Do you remember now?" Mark demanded.

The man didn't respond. Mark socked him again and squeezed his eyes closed as the man's blood splattered all over his face.

"I'm going to ask one more time! Do you remember?

The man said, "Okay, I'll admit it but look how you're acting now. That's why we feel the way we do about you people."

"You people? That's the last thing you should have said."

Mark punched him in his face two more times and dropped the bald man back in his chair. Just as he was turning around he caught Lester trying to be a hero, like people in the movies always did.

Lester lunged at him. Mark just stepped aside and Lester stumbled and fell on top of the desk. He grabbed Lester around the neck and punched him one time. He was out with one shot. *This guy could have never been a boxer*, Mark thought.

He walked out of the office and the other two guys there for the interview just stared at him. Their eyes were wide with horror, but he could tell they appreciated what he had done, even though they would have never had the courage to speak up themselves.

He saw that the secretary was on the phone. She had to be on the phone with 911. It didn't matter to him at that point because he had expected her to do so. Mark did feel bad about the way things went down. The last thing he needed to do was add some jail time onto the problems he and Terri already had. He gathered his belongings and walked out of the building.

As he exited the last door to the building he saw that there were three police cars waiting on him. As they closed in and ordered him to the ground he thought, *Man, its funny how fast they respond in the white neighborhoods.*

Chapter 5

The sun peaked through the blinds and shined on Austin's face, stirring him from his sleep. He got up and walked to the rest room, stepping over a pink pair of thong panties and a matching bra along the way. He began his morning ritual by brushing his teeth to get rid of any trace of morning breath. As he opened the toilet top to take a leak, he noticed that the protection he had used the night before was lying on the floor. When he was finished relieving himself, he picked it up and flushed it.

He walked out of the bathroom and took a look out of the window. *Man, this is a beautiful view*, he thought to himself as he pulled the curtains together.

As he was about to get back into bed, he heard his cell phone ringing on the nightstand. "Who could possibly be calling so early in the morning," he thought aloud as he picked it up to view the caller id more clearly.

The ID read Jules and he hesitated a moment before answering. She had to have assumed that he would still be sleep at six o'clock in the morning.

"Hello?" He said in a still groggy voice.

"Hey baby," Julie said on the other end sounding full of vigor as if she'd been up for hours. "I was just calling to let you know that I miss you.

"What are you doing up so early?" He said trying as best he could to hide his aggravation.

"Well, I normally *am* up this early, but this particular morning Steph and Jessica woke me up. Mark dropped them off yesterday right after you left."

"You guys have a sleep over or something?"

She sighed briefly and said, "It wasn't intentional. I was only supposed to keep them for a couple of hours but it kinda didn't work out that way. Your boy, Mark, got in a little trouble yesterday."

"What do you mean a little trouble?" He asked now sitting up so he could hear a little better.

"Well, he beat up a guy that interviewed him for a job with APS, which landed him in jail."

"You think I should leave right now? If I have to, I'll come and bail him out."

He knew that he and Mark had their differences about a lot of things, but Mark would have done the same thing for him. They had been friends as long as Austin could remember and that was just what you did for your people you care about.

"You don't have to worry about it. I was able to get in touch with Terri about two o'clock this morning, which was odd because Mark told me that she would pick up the girls at about six o'clock that evening. It seems like she had a late night. Anyway, you don't have to cut your trip short."

"I knew something like this was going to happen soon. He's been under a lot of pressure lately, with him being out of work and the issues between him and Terri. You can only take so much before you just snap."

"Well from what he told me, it wasn't the fact that he just cracked under pressure. There were some racial things said, which no matter how wrong he was for doing so, made him loose it."

"See, that's the reason that I don't necessarily buy all into the religion thing. Everything I have now, I have because I worked hard to get it. Mark on the other hand has been working hard his whole life and that brotha can't catch a break."

"What does that have to do with whether you are into religion or not. It seems like you should be more grateful than the man that doesn't have anything," Julie said. The tone in her voice let Austin know she was ready for a good debate.

"That's my point though. I have more than a brotha that's dedicated his life to God. We've worked equally as hard in different aspects. I go to church simply because *you* make me….."

"What? I can't *make* you go to church," Julie said cutting him off.

"That's right. You can't make me, but you won't stop nagging if I don't."

"Whatever," Julie said sounding irritated.

"Mark goes because he feels like *God* has done so much for him. Can you give me one example of where *God* has been so good to Mark, because I just don't see it?"

"I'll tell you a couple that you're obviously overlooking. Number one, he has two beautiful children that are smarter than some adults I know. Number two, he's walking in good health. And I'll even give you a third one for free. No matter what problems he and Terri have, he has a wife that loves him. It seems like God has done plenty for him."

"I can't tell. Not the way Terri's been acting lately. Besides, I would rather live in my big house, drive nice cars, and have more money than I know how to spend. Whether you admit it or not, you would to," Austin said arrogantly.

"Is that what you think? That I'm that shallow?"

"Shallow, no, but a lover of fine things, yes."

"So you think I'm with you for your money?"

"No, I don't believe you're with me for my money, at least not consciously."

"What is that supposed to mean?" Julie demanded.

"What I'm saying is that all women seek some sort of financial stability as a qualifier in the man they choose. They need to know that they will be taken care of and their home will be stable. I *more* than provide those things for you."

"If that's what you think about me then you don't really know me at all. I'm with you because I love you. I don't care anything about the money, the house, or the cars. I would give all those things up for a chance to truly be loved. That's why I told you that if you ever cheat on me again, I'm done. I don't need those things to survive."

"I hear you," Austin said lying back down on the bed. He didn't feel like going into that argument. It seemed like Julie threw his cheating in his face every time the opportunity presented itself.

"Anyway, babe, when are you coming home? I tried calling you last night but I couldn't get any answer? I thought something was wrong. Had you not answered this morning, I was going to send a search and rescue party," Julie said.

She laughed but Austin didn't think anything was funny. He knew she was dead serious. Ever since she caught him cheating on her, she was overly jealous.

"I might be another couple of days. I still have a little more business I've gotta take care of."

"Another couple of days? I knew this was a last minute thing, but I had no idea you would be gone that long."

Here we go, he thought. "Yeah, and since I didn't give you a definite time frame, then there is nothing for you to complain about. When I get done here, that's when I'm coming home," he said as sternly as possible. It was too early and he did not feel up to arguing.

"That's fine, but if you're cheating on me its over," Julie said for the three thousandth time.

"A'ight, whatever."

"I love you, Austin."

"Ditto," he said and quickly hung up the phone.

He knew he would hear about him not saying I love you too, but right then wasn't the time. Besides he had better things to worry about.

He rolled over and pulled back the covers. He just admired the body on the woman lying next to him. He was so happy he took a chance and followed her to the bathroom at the coffee shop that day. Since that evening he had been enjoying some of the best sex of his life. Not only did she give it to him whenever he desired it, but she knew exactly what to do when she did.

He glanced to see if she was awake. It didn't seem as if she even budged during his entire conversation with Julie.

He reached out and caressed one of the naked cheeks of her butt and her skin felt warm to his hand. He nudged her just a little and then started slowly kissing her back. "Monica, I need my morning dosage," he said in between smooches. She rolled over and started wiping her eyes.

"You're in the mood again already?" She said and began to yawn. "I thought I put it on you pretty well that last time."

Austin didn't say anything as he leaned over and started kissing her soft lips. He rose up just for a second to look into those hazel eyes that he couldn't stop thinking about since that day at the coffee shop. Austin didn't completely lie. He did have some business to take care of, it just wasn't the kind that Julie thought it was.

The Cheesecake Factory was spilling over with people. It was Austin's favorite restaurant, so he was thrilled when his clients suggested it as the place to meet. When he checked in his reservations, he was given some bad news. Under normal circumstances he would not have minded the two hour delay, but since this was the most important meeting of his career, it was not acceptable to wait that long.

He walked back to where Monica was sitting with a disappointed look on his face. He decided to bring her along just as an arm piece. If there was one thing he was sure of, it was that men appreciated something nice to look at. He never could have brought Julie along because not a lot of other men saw her in the same light he did.

"What's wrong, sweetie?" Monica said showing genuine concern.

He loved when she called him sweetie. "Nothing, other than I may be missing out on one of my biggest clients because I can't get a seat at this stupid restaurant. I'm supposed to have a little pull and waiting two hours doesn't show that."

"Don't worry about it. Let mama take care of it," she said with a sly smile. She took off the jacket to her cream business suit to reveal a pair of fitted pants that accented her curves nicely. She then unbuttoned the top two buttons of her black satin blouse to show off a little more cleavage.

She walked away from Austin in the direction of the host who looked like he had to be about seventeen years old. As she walked, Austin couldn't help but stare at the way her butt shook with every step in the tight fitting pants. He noticed how the other guys sitting in the waiting area stopped and stared as she walked by. He couldn't help but feel somewhat jealous about it. One lady slapped her husband because he was staring so hard. The slap obviously didn't help, because when she started reading her menu again the man's eyes strayed back to Monica.

As she got closer, the host looked up and did not break his gaze at any other point during the conversation. She grabbed him around his

collar and pulled him in close. Austin could not hear what was being
said but he could tell that it was something mind-changing. All the
host did was nod several times. As she spoke to him, he looked down a
couple of times at her cleavage. He nodded one more time as she
placed a big kiss on his cheek and then she walked away with a
satisfied smile on her face.

"What happened?" He asked as she sat down and started
buttoning her shirt.

"He just needed a little coaching to make the right decision.
Nothing I couldn't handle."

"Well... what did you coach him into doing?"

"We'll have a seat in about fifteen minutes," she said and let
out a small giggle. "What would you have ever done without me?"

"I have no idea. You're a lifesaver," Austin said and he really
meant it.

When Monica finished tidying her clothes she slid in really
close to Austin, so close that he could feel the warmth of her thigh
against his. He was so caught up admiring her beauty that he didn't
even notice when his potential client arrived. He was so nervous he
could hardly stand to greet him.

"Mr. Green," Austin said rising to his feet and extending his
hand. "I'm glad you made it."

"I almost didn't. Almost got trapped in the three o'clock
Atlanta traffic," Mr. Green responded.

"Well," Austin laughed. "While I'm not happy for the traffic, I
am happy you were slightly delayed because as you can see, by the
number of people here, even I couldn't get a table on time. We'll have
one in about five minutes, though."

Mr. Green was a tall, husky man in his late forties. He was
extremely rich but you couldn't tell it by the way he dressed. He wore
a simple brown polyester double-breasted suit that you could get from
any cheap store in the mall.   Austin believed that was probably Mr.
Green's ticket to maintaining his wealth.

Mr. Green owned the Black Pride line of beauty products
which was taking Black America by storm. If Austin could land this
deal, it could mean more money that he had ever dreamed of.

After they were seated and ordered their food, they made with
small talk until dinner was done.

"So, Austin," Mr. Green said as he slurped down his final glass of wine. "I'll just get straight to the point. We're looking to expand out marketing efforts in the south and we were impressed with your company. I'm already seeing an increase in business in Georgia and I'm looking to increase our efforts in the South. How can we be guaranteed that we won't be sorry for choosing your business to handle our marketing?"

"Well…..um…..um….," Austin said. His words came out a little slurred because of his overwhelming nervousness. It was the moment of truth for him that could launch his career to another level or set him back a few years. He was thinking so hard about what to say during dinner, that he forgot what to say when it was time to.

Monica quickly took over for him. "Look, Mr. Green, our company has been responsible for phenomenal growth in business for all of our clients. Using our patented and unique form of marketing, our clients have seen their revenue increase in some instances as much as fifty percent. We also found that the average client company revenue increased by thirty percent. I said all that to say this, Mr. Green, Black Pride should have no reservations, what so ever, about choosing Barton Marketing."

She reached into her briefcase and pulled out some reports and charts that Austin had never seen before. She moved the plates and glasses to one side of the table and spread the information out before Mr. Green. Over the next few minutes, he and his business partner pored over the documents and mumbled amongst themselves.

Austin opened his mouth to say something but was speechless. The only thing he could do was smile. He was impressed. Monica must have really done her homework before coming to the meeting. It seemed as if Mr. Green was speechless as well. He just smiled and stroked the hair on his chin.

"What position does this young lady have with your company Mr. Barton?" Mr. Green finally said.

"Well… she's my *personal* assistant."

"You should be giving her a raise, because thanks to that dynamic information she just gave me, I'll be doing business with your company."

Austin looked over at Monica, who was smiling from ear to ear. Not only was she beautiful, but she was intelligent too. Where else could you find a more perfect woman?

"Don't worry Mr. Green. I'll be giving her all the thanks she deserves after this meeting convenes," Austin answered as he stood and shook Mr. Green's hand.

Julie could never have gotten him out of a jam like that. He was a go getter and that's the type of woman he needed in his life. He needed a woman that knew what she wanted and how to get it. Of course this was just his mistress, but if she stayed on that path she would become his misses.

Chapter 6

Quincey pulled into his driveway after a long day of work. He was exhausted. He was normally full of energy but he had taken on a larger workload at the firm. The most notable case was Mark's. He really didn't have any extra time as it was but he wasn't left any other choice in the matter. There was no way Mark would be able to afford a *real* attorney and, because he was Quincey's best friend, Mark being represented by anyone else wasn't an option.

Quincey had been in meetings all day with APS' attorneys. Then when he was done with all of the legal politics of the day, he had to rush straight to class. He went to school three nights a week on top of all the other obligations he had in the church. After a long stressful day, he just wanted to relax. He walked into the house and all the lights were turned off. "Kim must be in the bed," he thought aloud.

He went upstairs and stopped by the guest room where his 12 year old son, Jeffrey, was sleeping. Jeff was born when Quincey was only sixteen and in his third year of high school. The parents of Jeff's mother, Janet, urged her to abort the pregnancy, but Quincey begged her not to. After long nights of debating, she decided to keep him. Quincey was excited then and still loved the fact of having someone that was just like him running around in the world.

It was Quincey's weekend to keep Jeff, but unfortunately he had to work most of the weekend. Kim was usually pretty good about babysitting Jeff whenever Quincey had to work late. He really appreciated Kim's efforts in helping him raise his son in spite of her and Janet wanting to kill each other most of the time. A lot of times if it were not for Kim pitching in, he would not be able to see Jeff at all.

He walked into the room and kissed Jeff on the forehead. He just stood there and looked at him for a while. He loved that little boy so much. He never imagined that it was possible to love another male so deeply. He turned to leave, but right on cue Jeff turned over and opened his eyes.

"Hey, Dad," Jeff said wiping his eyes. "I missed you today."

"I missed you too. Did you have fun with Kim?"

"Yeah we had a lot of fun. We went to the zoo and then to get ice cream after we left there," Jeff said in the midst of a yawn. He sat up and slid to the edge of the bed.

"That sounds like fun. Too bad I missed it. We'll have to out-do your day today and have even more fun tomorrow."

"We'll see, Dad, but I bet that'll be hard to do."

"Okay, we'll see. Go back to sleep so we can get an early start on tomorrow. I love you."

"I love you too, dad. Goodnight," Jeff said and slid back under the covers. Quincey tucked him in tightly and kissed him again on his forehead.

Quincey walked out and shut the door. "Kim." He called as he walked down the hallway. He thought just for a moment he heard water running.

"I'm in our bathroom." He heard her call out in a muffled voice behind the closed bathroom door.

He walked into the bedroom. It was so dark that he could barely make his way around the large king size bed. When he opened the door he saw Kim sitting on the side of the tub striking a sexy pose.

She was adorned in a black two-piece lingerie set. When she bent over to run her fingers through the water he saw that she wore the black lace boy shorts that he loved so much. She looked amazing and the recessed lights above the tub made her ebony skin tone glow.

"Are you about to take a bath?" he asked. His eyes were concentrated on her beautiful body.

"I'm not, but you are," she said with a seductive grin. "This bath is for you."

"For me? What did I do to deserve this?"

"This is for you being who you are. I appreciate all the hard work that you do to take care of me.

"Well, you know that's what a man is supposed to do."

"I know but I just want you to relax. You're gonna take off your clothes and get into this tub so that I can bathe you. Once I get done pampering you here, you're gonna lie across the bed and I'll take care of you in there too."

Quincey didn't respond, he just did as he was told. In what seemed like two seconds, his clothes were off and he was in the tub. He was smiling from ear to ear as if he had just won the lottery.

Kim started by washing his back and his neck. She slowly wiped back and forth with the sponge. She then moved to his chest and his abdomen. Quincey felt like he was in heaven. With each stroke of the sponge, she completely erased all the thoughts of their lack of time together and all the baby mama drama with Janet. The only thing Quincey could think of at that moment was how much he loved his wife.

"Lie back," she said.

Quincey still didn't say a word. He just did as he was told. He liked the idea of her taking charge. She started rubbing the sponge on his lower abdominal area. "Whoa, baby, you've been working out hard lately, huh?" she asked as she dropped the sponge and started rubbing his rippled stomach.

Quincey felt like he really wanted to make crazy love to her right then. There was one problem. The soothing water and Kim washing his body was quickly sucking the energy out of him. He was extremely attracted to his wife, but he didn't know if he had the energy to go there.

She then grabbed him by the hand and pulled him from the tub. Next, she guided him into the bedroom. Water was dripping from his body, as he didn't take the time to dry off but it didn't seem to faze Kim at all. He could tell she was ready to make love from the time he walked into the room.

She laid him across the bed and climbed up and straddled him. She bent down and started kissing him and he felt her tongue part his lips.

He really was trying to pay attention but he felt himself getting sleepier. He didn't know why, but his body was about ready to give out. Quincey was so embarrassed. He had heard of men ruining their relationships because they had too many things going on in their lives but no matter how he tried, he couldn't equate that scenario to his life. One of the many things he had going on was the work of the Lord.

He felt himself drifting off.

"Baby!" he could hear Kim shouting. She started shaking him when he didn't respond. "Baby, please don't do this to me."

It was killing him but he still didn't move. He even caught himself snoring. It was a terrible situation but he would more than make it up to her the next time. He knew that this would possibly add to the problems they already had, but when she saw all of his plans come to fruition she would understand.

Kim slid off of him and Quincey heard her drop down on the bed with a huff next to him. It seemed like she was pretty mad and he didn't want to hear any part of it that night. So he just allowed himself to drift into a deep sleep, thinking about all the apologizing he would have to do in the morning.

Chapter 7

Terri fastened the last button on her Black Baby Phat blouse and then pulled in down to cover the top of her matching fitted hip hugging jeans. She stood there and admired herself in the mirror. She had always thought that she looked good in dark colors because it accented her fair skin so well and since she'd been out a couple of times with Cedric, she was starting to feel a little more confident about herself. He always told her how beautiful she was and how he admired her body.

She was putting on the last touches of her make-up when she heard Mark and the kids come into the house. She was hoping that she would be gone by the time they made it home, so she wouldn't be bombarded with a barrage of Mark's questions.

"Baby?" she heard Mark yelling as he came down the hallway.

"I'm in the bedroom," she yelled back attitude reeking in her voice. It bothered her that he had to call her like something was wrong every time he walked in the house.

The door burst open. "Mommyyyy," Stephanie and Jessica yelled in unison as they ran in the room.

"Where have you been? We tried to wait for you before we went out to McDonald's." Stephanie asked as she took her turn hugging Terri.

"Mommy was at work, honey. I tried to get home as soon as I could."

Jessica didn't seem to mind either way. She was just sitting on the bed eating her chicken nuggets. Nothing else mattered in the world as long as she had her nugget fill.

"That's okay, mommy. Just don't forget you promised to take us to the movies. I can't wait."

"I won't baby. I promise. We are gonna leave first thing in the morning."

"Okay," Stephanie said while leaving the room. Jessica just followed her. She still didn't say anything. She just looked up long enough to wave and then exited the room still concentrating on the nuggets in her bag.

After they left, Mark shut the door and started walking her way. *Here we go again*, she thought as she caught a glimpse of the sexual look on his face. Hadn't he gotten the picture yet?

He walked up and hugged her from behind and started kissing her on the neck.

"You smell good," he said in between smooches. "Where you going looking all good?"

"I'm going out with Shannon."

"Going out with Shannon where?"

"I don't know yet. We're just gonna ride for a while and maybe stop by a club."

"You know I don't agree with you going to a club. That's no place for my wife to be. Besides I hoped we could spend this night making up for lost time, if you know what I mean," Mark said sounding a little disappointed.

"Look, Mark. Please don't make me say something that will hurt your feelings tonight. I'm not staying at home tonight because I need this night to unwind after a long week at work."

"Well, I was hoping I could help you a little with your unwinding process. Please don't shoot me down tonight. I really want to spend some time with you."

"I can't believe I'm even talking to you after you embarrassed me by going to jail like some hoodlum. My mama still can't stop talking about that. I'm not staying home tonight and I'm *not* giving you any."

He let out a long sigh. "How many times do I have to apologize for that?"

"I don't care how many times you apologize. I'm not gonna forgive you until I'm good and ready."

"That's a shame. I've come to you as sincerely as I know how."

"I know, and it doesn't matter how sincere you were. Beating that man up was so stupid, I don't even know where to start describing my anger."

He didn't respond. He just sat down on the edge of the bed. The more Terri looked at the dumb look on his face, the angrier she got. She was so sick of him behaving like a child. If something didn't go his way then he just pouted and got angry. What she needed was a real man, not some little boy.

"Anyway, I thought you were all in to church now. How do you think God feels about that?"

"You of all people shouldn't be throwing that up in my face. You're getting ready to go to the club as we speak."

"Well, it doesn't matter to me one way or the other. I was just saying."

"Look, it may not be as bad as you think. As wrong it was, some good may come out of it."

"What good could come out of this stupidity?"

"You know what? Don't even worry about it. I'm so sick of your attitude that I don't even feel like talking about it anymore."

"Whatever. I was hoping I would be gone before you got here anyway. Don't wait up because it'll be a late night."

With that she just grabbed her jacket off the bed and walked out the room. She heard him calling after her and saying something about not forgetting about church, but she didn't turn back. She had a date to meet Cedric that night and she was not about to be late.

Chapter 8

The line at The Joke Joint wrapped around the corner. It was not the type of place Terri normally frequented so she stood in the long line impatiently. If it were up to her, she would never set foot in a place like that but since Cedric, her ex-professor, had invited her she felt the least she could do was humor it.

"This bouncer need ta hurry up," A loud ghetto girl was saying. She was standing just behind Terri, so she inadvertently heard all of the woman's conversation. The lady had light blond hair, which contrasted with her dark skin, and two big gold teeth right in the front. She wore a red dress and shoes to match that were the loudest colors Terri could remember seeing. "It look like it's bout to rain out hea, an' I ain't tryn' ta get my hurr wet. Know what I'm sayn'?"

The chubby lady in the black dress, that was obviously the sidekick, standing next to her let out a loud horse sounding laugh. "Gurrl, you so crazy. You know we on the VIP list. Reggie ain't gone let us sit out hea an' get all wet."

Terri caught her self staring at the pair and she just shook her head. She was from the hood but there was some places where *keeping it real* wasn't necessary. The black dress the sidekick wore was an obvious four sizes too small for someone of her size. Terri could see every one of the woman's love handles in deep detail when the lady turned to face her friend. Terri hurried and turned to face the front as the line before her began to move. She didn't want the ladies to see her staring. She had seen fights had broken out over less than that and she didn't want to get into a fight with two women and let Cedric see her get beat up before she got a chance to know him good.

The bouncer began letting people inside in floods, so Terri shuffled toward the front of the line. She glanced up and the huge historic movie theatre style sign that hung above the entrance. "Reggie Jenkins-Live for two shows," the sign read. That was obviously the "Reggie" the women were speaking of.

"That figures," Terri said aloud with a snort. "Those women are groupies from head to toe."

Once she passed the bouncer, the large man outstretched one of his muscular arms to signal the end of the flood. The ladies that were behind Terri were not on the favorable end of the signal.

"Naw, honey. You got me messed up. I need ta git in dat club," red dress erupted.

"Sorry, Miss, but I-..." the bouncer trailed off as red cut him off. Terri looked around and the sidekick was trying to calm her down.

"Whurr is Reggie? I'm through wit' you. You ain't nobody no way. Go git him. That's all you can do fo me."

Terri didn't see or hear what happened next because she continued into the club through the vestibule. She looked around and the place was a lot classier than she had suspected from the outside appearance. She was taking back by the classy look that the room had. The first thing that caught her eye was the huge crystal chandelier that hung from the ceiling. It was beautiful and she decided that when she got the home of her dreams, she would have to get a smaller replica.

The next thing that caught her attention was the 50's style of the room. There were huge round tables with white table clothes topping them, spread throughout the room. At nearly every table, there were guests seated. The room was nearly packed to capacity. In the center of the room was a rounded stage on which the MC stood speaking on an old style microphone.

"It's time for the main event," The announcer, a tall man with dreads that appeared to be in his mid-twenties, was saying. "You've seen this man on all the major comedy shows across the country. He's the funniest man I personally know. Out of Brooklyn, New York, put your hands together for the hilarious Reggie Jenkins!"

Wangsta by 50 cent started playing on the speakers as Reggie ran onto the stage. He was a skinny light skinned man that wore a New York Yankees baseball cap and matching navy blue t-shirt. He complemented the outfit with light colored blue jeans and wheat colored Timberland boots.

Once he reached the microphone, Reggie threw both of his arms up into the air like he had just won a championship fight. He wore a huge smile across his face like all comedians do. Once the applause stopped, he made a slashing motion across his neck to signal the DJ to stop the music.

"What's up, Naaaashviiiiiille? Reggie yelled into the microphone.

Everyone in the crowd began ranting and raving, including Terri. She found herself stopped along the back wall of the club. She had never been to a live comedy show, so even though she had just gotten there she was already enjoying herself.

"It is good to be in the South, I'm tellin' ya," Reggie continued. "I love it down here. Yesterday, I was jus walkin down tha street and a man jus walked up ta me and spoke. Even shook my hand ya'll. See I'm from New York. I aint used ta dat. Last time somebody walked up ta me and spoke in New York, I gave him my wallet and jus ran, I aint lyin."

The crowd erupted in laughter. Terri was laughing harder than anyone standing around her. Comedians were funny on TV, but she never knew how funny they were in person.

"And the women down here. Oh my God. I aint neva seen nuttin like it in my life. See in New York, everybody is all petite and skinny. Ya'll know. Anorexic. Down here, the women are thiiiick and I mean dat in a good way. It must be in da water, I aint lyin. What ya'll drinking? Pork enhanced water? I need ta take me a bottle of dat home, I aint lying. I'm gone be sprinklin that in my girl's food from now on."

Terri was laughing so hard, she didn't even see Cedric walk up beside her. When he tapped her on the shoulder, she looked at him through teary eyes from laughter.

"Funny, huh?" Cedric asked

"Yeah, hilarious," Terri said still having fits of laughter.

Cedric leaned down so he could whisper in her ear. Terri guessed that it would be rude to talk aloud since there was only one person talking now. If he spoke too loudly, he would have been heard all over the club.

"Follow me," he said,

Terri followed him along the back of the club and then down the side. As she did she admired Cedric's looks. *This man truly is fine*, she thought. *He's even good looking from the back.*

She admired the cut of the suit he wore because it fit him perfectly and accented his sculpted frame. His curly hair was lined so perfectly that it seemed as if someone drew the line by hand. And when he turned briefly to smile at her, she admired his perfectly placed white teeth.

They continued down the side of the club until they came to the front. Terri froze. "What are you doing?" she whispered loudly.

Cedric didn't respond he just waved his hand telling her to come along. They walked right into the front of the club and took a seat at the table closest to the stage. Terri looked around and all eyes were on her.

When, they were seated, she decided she would just make the best of it and enjoy the show. When she looked on the stage, she saw Reggie's eyes had also diverted to them.

"Oh, man. Look who it is," Reggie said interrupting his whole routine. "What's up Cedric, man. I know you told me you were coming out tonight, but man, you didn't tell me who you were bringing. She's got to be *tha* finest woman in here."

Terri blushed heavily and as she looked around she noticed the envious looks on all the women's faces. To them, Terri assumed, she was stealing the show. Reggie continued on with his show like nothing ever happened, but Terri still felt eyes on the back of her head.

When the show was over, the jazz band took the stage and Reggie came over and introduced himself.

"What's up, frat?" Reggie said when he came over.

"You got it," Cedric said as he stood to embrace Reggie.

"And who is this fine lady?" Reggie said looking at Terri like she was the entrée of a full course meal.

"This is Terri," Cedric said with a smile. "And I see you lookin'. You can forget it though, because she's all mine."

Terri let loose a giggle that she hadn't meant to let escape.

"Nice to meet you, Reggie." She said. "How do you know Cedric?"

"First of all, he my frat bruh. Q Dooooog," Reggie said while throwing up a half Omega sign with one arm. "Then he's part owner of this establishment we're sitting in right now."

"Is that right," Terri said briefly eyeing Cedric. She knew he was a doctor but she didn't know he was an entrepreneur as well.

"Well, you know, a brother does what he can," Cedric said humbly. "How long you in town for?"

"I leave back out tomorrow. I got a show to do in Chocolate City."

"That's too bad. I wanted to hang out for a while tomorrow, but I'll have to get with you the next time you're free."

"Oh, okay. I get the hint," Reggie said still stealing looks at Terri. "I'll let ya'll be alone. Besides, I see a little thang I invited here tonight," Reggie said as he stood shook Cedric and Terri's hand one last time and left the table.

Terri looked around and saw the woman in the red dress sitting across the room and assumed that's who Reggie was talking about. She didn't understand what he saw in the woman. Even though Reggie was a little too thin for her taste, he was still attractive and could do better than that. She guessed a man would sleep with any woman willing.

"Would you like something to drink?" Cedric asked when they were alone.

"I don't know. What do you have, Mr. Owner?"

"Cedric will be just fine," he said jokingly.

"Okay. In that case I'll have a club soda."

"How about we make that a Siroc and we go dance."

"I usually don't drink, but I guess I can make an exception," Terri said still smiling from ear to ear. The longer she spent with Cedric the more intoxicated by him she became.

"Let me get two Sirocs on ice," Cedric said stopping the nearest waitress. He didn't wait for an answer as he grabbed Terri's hand and led her to the dance floor.

The band played a jazz version of *Fire and Desire* by Rick James and Tina Marie. Once on the floor, Cedric pulled her in to dance. Terri inhaled his masculine smell. At first he acted as if he didn't know quite what to do. Then as they danced, he slowly pulled her closer. At first Terri wanted to resist, but as she became more comfortable with him she let down her guard. Cedric's hands began to roam wherever they pleased and she didn't mind. For just that moment in time it seemed as if no one else was there but them.

"I didn't know you could move like that," Terri said once they returned to their seats.

"I know I'm a little older than you, but slow jams are still my thing," Cedric laughed.

"I can see. I thought you wanted to talk about business."

"This is business. Right now my business is all about you," Cedric said with a sly grin.

Terri just let out a small giggle. She had a brief disapproving thought about Mark, and then she just pushed it into the back of her mind. She was sure he wasn't worrying about her at that moment.

"You're just so beautiful. I can't wrap my mind around it."

"Yeah, I'm sure you say that to every woman you meet."

"No, don't get me wrong. I've seen some beautiful women, but none like you. You have to promise me this won't be the last time I get to see you."

"Well, that's up to you. I really don't mind."

The rest of the night went by uneventfully. They just made small talk as they finished off a couple of more glasses of liquor. Terri was not used to drinking so she was starting to feel a little tipsy. She looked at her watch and noticed how late it was getting.

"I really got to get out of here," Terri said as she stood and grabbed her purse.

"Let me take you home," Cedric said. "I can tell you're not that used to drinking and I wouldn't forgive myself if something happened to you."

"No I think I can manage."

"Please, just let...."

"Really I can manage," Terri said cutting him off.

She turned to walk off and Cedric grabbed her arm and spun her around. He placed a gentle kiss on her cheek and released her with a smile. "Be careful," He said.

Terri turned to leave and all the other women were still looking at her. She guessed that was how it felt to be with a man that every other woman wished they could have. She deeply wished the night didn't have to end but it was getting late and she knew she had to go with Mark to church the next day. The only other option was to let Cedric take her home and no matter how much she had to drink, she was not about to let that happen.

Chapter 9

Mark tried to creep into the church as quietly as possible. They were always running late no matter where they went, but it didn't bother him as much as when church was their destination. St. Paul Missionary Baptist Church was so small that whenever someone walked in after the service started everyone turned around to see who it was. They all had the look on their faces as if they were saying, "Look who's coming in late again. They may as well have stayed home."

He looked over about middle ways on the left side of the church and saw Austin and Julie sitting next to one another. Julie briefly waved and turned back to face the choir. Austin couldn't be that civil because he always had to play the fool. He had a big, fat grin on his face. He pulled his sleeve back and looked at his watch and started shaking his head. He silently mouthed out, "Late." Mark grew so frustrated with him. If he wasn't trying to be a better Christian and standing in the house of the Lord, he would surely have cussed him out, punched him in the stomach, or something.

Quincey was sitting in the pulpit next to Pastor Lewis. He had been sitting there in recent services. Since he had announced his call into the ministry, the pulpit would be his permanent place in the church. Kim was seated on the front pew next to First Lady Lewis and was looking as gorgeous as ever. Quincey was his friend, but Mark had to admit that Kim was one of the finest women he had ever seen, next to Terri of course.

They walked in and took a seat near the back. Even if he was on time this Sunday, he would have picked a seat as far back as possible. When you sat near the back, there seemed to be no expectations from anyone in the church. You weren't sitting near the deacon or mother's board and you didn't have to feel like a hypocrite. On top of that, he felt so bad about the argument he and Terri had over her going to the club the night before that he nearly stayed home. He didn't feel like sitting in church pretending that everything was fine.

He watched his two children take a seat beside him. They looked so beautiful to him. They both wore matching pink and white dresses with little matching pink shoes and even had little white purses that matched their outfits. They couldn't wait for that Sunday morning because he allowed them to pick out their own clothes for church the night before. The girls had their mother's sense of style already at an early age.

Terri looked amazing as well. She wore a designer dress from some company. Mark couldn't think of the name but he knew it was expensive. She had just purchased it the weekend before when she went on an all day shopping trip. When Mark questioned her about it, she said that she felt the need to treat herself for all the hard work she had been putting in. Mark couldn't find any problem with that because Terri usually took care of the finances and if she thought they could afford it, he believed it.

They still were not really on speaking terms and Mark hoped that this would soon change. He didn't know how much more of her attitude he could stand. She was biting his head off about everything and she was always leaving the house for some reason. There was a little voice in the back of his head that was telling him that there may be someone else, but he didn't think that Terri would ever cheat on him. They had their problems but she had to still love him. That's why she was still there.

The choir was on fire that day. Mark couldn't help but stand and join in as they sang his favorite Kirk Franklin song.

"There's something about the name Jesus, There's something about the name Jesus, It is the Sweetest Name I know," the choir sang.

The entire church was moved as the song came to an end. The spirit was so high that after the song Pastor Lewis tried to get up and go into his sermon but couldn't. The congregation would not be seated. Then, the musicians broke out into praise music. Everyone was dancing and swaying back and forth to the up tempo. Even Stephanie and Jessica were on their feet clapping.

Mark was so moved that he couldn't help himself. He just allowed the tears to flow. Pastor Lewis now had the Microphone and began to minister during the praise service.

"Look, I don't mean to interrupt the praise, but God gave me something to say," he was saying in his deep, raspy voice. He had the distinct sound of a typical southern preacher. "He wants me to tell you that if you praise him right now in the midst of your turmoil, pain and trouble, that your breakthrough is on the way. If you can bless him right now, when you come out of this situation, your life will never be the same. Your future will be better than anything you could have ever imagined."

The tears were now streaming down Pastor Lewis's face. He was hugging himself and rocking from side to side. "I don't know who I'm talking to, but God wants you to know that even though your situation is tough, hold on. It may not seem like it but better days are on the way. Don't lose the faith." He put the microphone down and just lifted his hands to praise God.

Mark began to verbally praise. "Thank you, Lord! I receive my blessing!" he kept repeating over and over. He repented within himself for his recent actions at APS and for the first time since it happened, he knew he was forgiven. He just cried out for all the trouble and pain he had been through. He cried for all the problems in his marriage and believed that they were about to be over.

After he was done praising and calmed down enough to sit, Stephanie hugged him around the neck.

"Are you okay, Daddy?" she said obviously a little worried since she had never seen him cry.

"I'm okay, sweetie. Daddy was just crying because he was happy. It's okay to cry when you're happy."

He looked over at Terri who avoided eye contact with him. During the entire praise service she just sat there and he could not believe that she didn't feel moved at all. He touched her on the arm to get her attention and she glared at him with a look on her face as if to say, "Don't touch me."

How could she be acting this way in church? Its okay, he thought, *even if she didn't get that word from God, I did. Maybe it wasn't meant for her and only for me.*

Chapter 10

Austin felt wonderful. His business was doing better than ever and his sex life was doing even better than that. He was seeing Monica about three times a week and she always took care of his needs. On his off nights without Monica, he could always count on Julie to be eager and willing. *It's nothing like getting some seven days a week to give a man great self-esteem*, he thought.

He was just about to lie down on his bed, when he heard his phone vibrating against the dresser. He usually kept it on vibrate when he was home because whenever it rang aloud Julie usually came snooping around. He reached over and picked it up.

"What's up, bruh?" Austin said when he saw who it was on the caller id.

"What's up with you, man?" Quincey responded on the other end. Austin knew whenever Quincey called they were probably going somewhere.

"Nothing, just about to take a nap, since there's nothing else to do. What are you getting into today?"

"Take a nap? Man, you getting old too soon. There's a men's conference going on at the church. It would be cool if you could go. Mark's already in and it'll be fun for all three of us to kick it afterwards."

"Brotha, I'm not old and don't forget I'm younger *and* better looking than you. If you don't know, you better ask somebody. Anyway, I don't know about the church thang. It's Saturday and you know ya'll be in church all day."

"Whatever," Quincey said with a laugh. "It won't last more than a couple of hours. It's just one speaker tonight and he's not known to give long sermons."

"I guess. But, man, I'm telling' you if this lasts more that two hours, I'm gonna be out like a light."

"That's cool. Just swing through and pick me up. I got something to talk to you about on the way to the church. Mark's meeting us there because he has to wait for Terri to get home to watch the kids."

"A'ight, but what do you need to talk about?"

"Look, man, I'll talk to you about it when you get here. We don't have time to get into it right now.

"A'ight, I'll be there in about twenty minutes."

"Cool." Quincey said and hung up.

He wondered what Quincey could possibly have to talk to him about that sounded so secretive. He passed it off because he figured it couldn't be too serious. After all, Quincey was Mr. Responsibility.

Austin jumped up and got dressed. He threw on his yellow Armani shirt, a cream pair of slacks of the same name, and his tan Armani dress shoes. He looked at himself in the mirror and thought Tyson Beckford himself wouldn't look any better. He had to make sure he looked good, because there might be some fine ladies at church and he had to impress them.

He grabbed his keys off the nightstand and the Armani shades that he had just purchased. On his way to the front door he passed by the living room where Julie was watching T.V. Before he could turn the doorknob, she was in the hallway behind him.

"Where you going, Babe?" she said standing with her hands on her hips.

"Q invited me and Mark to some men's conference at the church."

"Yeah right. Since when do you go to church on a Saturday?"

"I know it's unusual, but I really am. Besides, I don't think I need your permission to go anywhere."

"I'm not saying that you need to ask for my permission," Julie said sounding like she was beginning to get mad. Austin knew a shouting match was not far off. *I need to think more before I speak*, he thought making a mental note.

"It's just that you didn't get home until after midnight last night and it's been like that a lot lately."

"I was working. I already explained that to you."

"It seems like you've been working a lot more than usual over the past few days."

"So what? Do you want me to start slacking on the business I've worked so hard to establish? Then how could we afford the nice things we have now?"

"It's not about that. I don't want you to stop working hard. I want you to be honest with me. What's going on?"

"What do you mean?"

"What I mean is things have changed. You're starting to go back to how things were before I caught you cheating the last time."

Austin sighed loudly and rolled his eyes toward the sky. "Is this what I'm going to go through every time I leave the house now?"

"Probably so," Julie said moving in closer to Austin. She was standing so close to him now that he could feel the warmth of her breath on his face.

"If that's the case, then this relationship is just about over. I'm not gonna be held hostage in my own home. Furthermore I'm not gonna be treated like a child. I'm a grown man."

"Well, you should have thought about the consequences when you were out with someone else."

"See that's the reason we're not married yet. You got too many issues and it's not like my cheating is to blame for all of them."

"You know that's one of the first things you've been right about in a long time. You aren't to blame for all of my problems," Julie said sounding like she was about to start crying. "My major problem is that the man that claims he loves me, acts like he wants every other woman but me and is not there to help me *deal* with my issues."

"Look, the issues you had before I met you are not my problem," Austin said raising his voice. He had reached his limit of arguing for the day.

"I guess not," Julie simply said.

"Look, I don't have time for this. I gotta go," he said and started opening the door.

"A'ight, you can keep walking, but these same things were happening the last time I caught you cheating. If I catch you cheating again, Austin, I swear I'm outta here."

Austin didn't even respond. He just got into his Bentley and drove off. He was so tired of hearing the same thing every other day. She had only caught him cheating once and he could not understand why she just couldn't trust him again. It was her, he reasoned. She was insecure about her weight and that wasn't his fault.

Instead of being down on me all the time, she should be happy. A woman her size should be happy to have a man like me, he thought as he sped down the interstate towards Quincey's house.

Austin got off on Quincey's exit without breaking his speed. He knew that Quincey would complain about him taking so long, so he did everything in his power to not make him wait any longer than he had to. He nearly had a wreck when he took his eyes off the road to find his cell phone which was vibrating in the back seat. Once he had it in his hand he got excited when he saw the ID read *Marty*.

"Hey, baby. I've missed you," he said when he opened the flip. "I haven't been able to stop thinking about you since we got back from Atlanta."

"I've missed you, too," Monica said on the other end. *Marty* was a name he put in his contact list in case Julie started searching through his phone.

"Austin, we have to talk. I have something really important to tell you. Do you have time right now?"

"Man, everyone has something important to talk about today. But go ahead. I've always got time for you."

"What are you talking about? Who else had something to talk to you about?"

"Never mind, don't worry about it. I'm all ears."

"Okay. You may want to sit down for this one. I don't know exactly how you'll take it."

"That's a problem because I'm driving right now." Austin said starting to get a little irritated. He hated when people told him he needed to sit down to hear some news. He was a man and he could take whatever it was.

"Well, then you may want to pull over."

"Look, why don't you just come out and say it."

"A'ight, here goes. I don't know how to tell you this but....," Monica said and let out a long sigh. "Austin...... I'm pregnant."

Austin pulled over to the side of the road. He couldn't believe his ears.

Chapter 11

Quincey hugged Kim as tightly as he could. He had always been taught to let the people you love know just that before you left, because you never knew what might happen. He walked over and ran his fingers over the golden picture frame encasing their wedding picture.

"Seems like yesterday," Quincey muttered slightly under his breath.

"What," Kim asked while pulling Quincey's grey overcoat from the coat closet.

"Our Wedding. It just doesn't seem like it was five years ago. Time is moving so fast. I guess it has that tendency when you're enjoying yourself," Quincey said with a smile.

"That's why we should spend more of it together," Kim said while handing the coat to Quincey. She pulled him in for another hug.

"I'll only be gone for a little while. This is a really big conference and Pastor Lewis is really showing me the fundamentals of being a good minister. I'm so amazed at how many things you have to do besides preach," Quincey said and placed a soft kiss on her cheek.

"I'm happy you're learning a lot, but I wish you would just stay here with me today," Kim said playfully wiping Quincey's kiss from her cheek. She looked at him blinking heavily and pouting.

"Kim, you know I can't. I already made a commitment to be there, so I can't back out now. Besides, I already invited Austin and Mark. We're gonna hang out after the service."

"It's funny how you can find time for everyone and everything else but me, your wife."

It was obvious now that she was getting mad. Everyone called him Q except Kim when she was extremely angry with him. He couldn't process the reason behind her anger because everything he did was to give them a better life.

"Baby, where is all this coming from? I thought you were happy when I announced my call to preach."

"I was until you put me even further down on your list of priorities. I was at least *trying* to deal with you working so much. I thought that was the price I paid for marrying a lawyer, but now with you being at church all the time, I'm growing tired of being alone."

"How can any woman these days criticize a man for working? The bible even says if a man doesn't work then he doesn't eat."

"Don't you quote scriptures at me, Quincey. I've forgotten more scriptures than you will ever know. Don't forget my father was a preacher."

"That's the reason I thought you of all people would understand."

She just shook her head. "That's one of the qualities I enjoyed about you in the beginning. You were nothing like my father. He used to leave my mother alone for long periods of time to do church business and then they would argue all the time about this same thing. I promised myself I would never go through that, but here I am."

"What type of woman are you, to be complaining about me spending too much time at church? Some women wish their men would go occasionally."

"But it's really not about that. That's just the surface issue. There's more to it than you being gone all the time."

Quincey was so tired of all these back and forth issues. He was trying to be patient but it was wearing very thin. He was a good man and he never stepped out on her once. Not many men he knew could boast the same claim. The first one that came to mind was Austin. He was cheating with every woman he could get his hands on.

"Well, baby, please tell me what's going on? I know I've been out a lot but I'm doing it all for you."

"It's just that I thought by now we would be pregnant. I'm really anxious to start a family with you."

"Kim, I told you that I'll be ready to have children when my career is where it needs to be. In the mean time we can have plenty of fun practicing," Quincey said and playfully slapped her on the butt.

"I just can't help but think about the fact that you have a baby by Janet and she's hardly the type of woman that deserves to have your child."

"Oh, now I see. This has nothing to do with you starting a family with me, but everything to do with you still being jealous of Janet after all this time."

Quincey could see that Kim was fuming now. Every time they got into a discussion about children she had to bring up her dislike for Janet. It was not like he made a conscious decision to get her pregnant.

"Look you know that I was a teenager when Janet got pregnant and I really made a bad decision in not having protected sex. In spite of any of that, I love my son and I couldn't imagine life without him," Quincey said dropping down on the couch.

"You may have to get used to it because I don't think Jeff is yours anyway. You and I both know how promiscuous Janet is."

"How would you know and anyway you weren't there when *we* made him."

"I didn't have to be there because I can use the eyes God gave me and tell that he doesn't look anything like you."

Just then Austin pulled into the drive and blew the horn. He came just in time and Quincey didn't think he would ever be this happy to see him. He knew the argument was not going to end any time soon and he couldn't even describe how tired he was of defending the fact that Jeff was really his son. Sure Jeff wasn't a splitting image of him, but he looked a lot like his mother. He also had a lot of the characteristics of Quincey's family. He grabbed his keys off the shelf and hurried for the door.

"Why won't you just give me a baby, Quincey?"

"Because I'm just not ready yet," Quincey yelled while walking out of the house.

Quincey hopped in the car with Austin. Austin had his radio on blast listening to the latest Kanye West song, but as soon as Quincey got in the car he tuned in to 880 am, the gospel station in Nashville.

Quincey found it funny how some people listened to rap all week but listened to gospel on Sundays or when in presence of Ministers.

He looked around and admired the Bentley that Austin had just purchased. He had never been inside one and he liked what he saw. The interior was all white and it felt crisp and clean. It even still had the new car smell. No matter how much he liked the car, he would never buy one. He didn't believe in spending money on something that would depreciate in value as fast as a car could.

"Man, you took forever to get here. I started to think you bailed out on me."

"Whatever. I told you I was coming," Austin said obviously preoccupied with other thoughts.

They rode about ten minutes without speaking another word. Quincey just bobbed his head to the gospel music playing on the radio. It had a way of soothing him when he was troubled. He looked over at Austin who had a frown on his face. Quincey could tell he wasn't the only one with troubles. He reached over and turned the radio down.

"Man, don't you ever touch a black man's radio," Austin said reciting a line from the movie *Rush Hour*. It was the most Austin had said to him since he had gotten into the car. That in itself was strange since Austin usually would not shut up.

"What's up with you, bruh? You okay? I know I pried you out the house on a Saturday for church, but I promise it'll be worth it."

"It has nothing to do with church. I was actually in the mood for going, but some things came up."

Oh man, him and Julie are into it again, Quincey thought. He didn't understand why he insisted on staying with the woman if he wasn't going to treat her right. There was bound to be some brotha out there that would love her the way she needed. A man like him only got involved with someone like Julie because he felt she has low self-esteem.

"What are you talking about? Have you and Jules been arguing again?" Quincey said less than concerned.

Austin shook his head. "Normally that would be a great assumption, since all we do is argue, but no not this time. I just got a bit of bad news, depending on how you look at it."

"What? Is everything a'ight? No one died did they?"

"No, but maybe I'll be departing soon if I don't handle this business. It's actually something that might change life as I know it."

"Man, just spit it out. Stop speaking in these riddles."

"You know that girl from the coffee shop that day?"

"Yeah, the one you went out to the bathroom to talk to."

"That's the one. I've been seeing her about three times a week. It's been going on since that day.

"What? Man I knew you went out to do a little hard core flirting, but that's ridiculous. Why do you keep stepping out on your woman?"

"Look I don't need any lectures from you. I know what I'm doing. I'm a grown man."

"Whatever, someone needs to tell you how wrong you are. So......what's the bad news you heard?"

"Look before I tell you anything else, you gotta promise me you won't go running your mouth to Mark. The last thing I need to hear is that brotha whining about *Jules' feelings*.

"A'ight, just tell me what's up."

"Well, her name is Monica. She called me when I was on my way to your crib to tell me she's pregnant."

Quincey just shook his head with a look of shock on his face. He thought he had problems. His wife was begging him to get her pregnant and here this fool was getting women pregnant he didn't even know. He didn't know how Julie would take it and he actually felt sorry for her. No one deserved to be treated like that.

"So what do you plan to do?"

"I don't know," Austin said.

Quincey actually thought he saw a certain look of fear on his face. It only surfaced for a second, but he would recognize that look anywhere. He wore the same one himself when he found out that Janet was pregnant with Jeff.

"Well, you need to think long and hard about it because you'll have to break the news to Julie eventually."

"Not if I get this situation taken care of first."

"I know you're not talking about her getting an abortion. Don't you care at all about what God thinks about that? You don't consider him in any other area of your life. At least respect him when it comes to murder."

"Man, to tell you the truth, I'm more worried about what Julie will do to me if she finds out I got another woman pregnant. To top that all off, the woman I got pregnant is white."

"It probably won't be that bad," Quincey said. "I'm sure the woman being white will be the least of Julie's worries."

"Yeah, well you don't know her like I do. She's not real big on the interracial dating thing."

"Well, bruh, the only thing I can offer you is my prayers."

"I guess that'll have to do," Austin said as he pulled the car to a stop at a red light. "I didn't mean to take up all the time, but we're almost there. What did you need to talk to me about?"

"Man, it doesn't even matter. My problems are not even worth discussing after I just heard yours. We'll talk some other time."

The rest of the evening went off uneventfully. The service was great and as promised, they were able to leave at a decent time. Austin remained somewhat distracted during the service and instead of hanging out afterwards, he drove Quincey straight home. This deeply troubled him as Austin never turned down a night out. As soon as he was home, Quincey sent up a prayer that everything would work out for his friend.

Chapter 12

Terri pulled into the parking lot of Che Marche, which was a high class restaurant located in the heart of Nashville. Cedric had already taken her there before on their second time going out together and she had fallen in love with it. So when he asked her where she wanted to meet, she couldn't think of anywhere better.

She was sitting in her car waiting on Cedric to show up. When she saw his black Mercedes pull into the parking lot, the butterflies began to flutter in her stomach. It was the way she used to feel about Mark, but with all the things that had happened over the course of their relationship, things had just changed.

It seemed like it took an eternity for him to park and get out of his car. When he finally did, she gathered her purse and opened the door to get out of her own vehicle. She paused for a moment to take off her wedding ring. She had almost forgotten and that would have been a huge mistake, since she had never told Cedric that she was married, or that she had children for that matter. The less he knew the better.

She took one last look at her reflection on the side of the car. She looked and felt extremely sexy. She wore a yellow blouse and black skirt with a matching waist length jacket from Macy's. The skirt was form fitting and accented her curves nicely. Whenever she went out with Cedric she made sure she wore something that did so because it was very flattering when she caught him looking as she walked by.

Cedric was standing near the door waiting when she walked up. It seemed like he got better looking every time she saw him. He was dressed pretty casually that night, but he looked good even then. He wore a pair of khakis with a light blue shirt that was buttoned up the front except for the top three buttons. He was one of those men that it seemed the designer had in mind when he dreamed of the clothes he would make.

"Hello, sweetie, how are you?" Cedric said when she made it over to him. He planted a kiss on her forehead and embraced her gently.

"I'm doing a lot better since I'm here with you," she said with a smile. When she made that statement, there was no exaggeration included. She meant every word. Cedric gave her an outlet from every day life and he was her escape route when she was feeling entangled.

Cedric pulled open the door and waited for her to enter first. *He is such a gentleman*, she thought as she entered the restaurant. *I bet Mark doesn't even know it's polite to open doors for women.*

Once inside, the host led them to their seat. Terri sat down and soaked in the jazz music before picking up her menu. She didn't have much experience with such but she knew she liked it. The live band was one of the reasons she loved going to Che Marche and being there with Cedric just added to the experience. He introduced new things into her life and instead of going to low budget restaurants and listening to hip hop all the time, he wanted the finer things in life.

The waitress came around and brought over the starter glasses of water. "Are you guys ready to order?" she said while pulling out her memo pad.

"Sure," Cedric said. "I'll have the Lobster and she'll have the same. Also, could you bring out a bottle of *Miani Sauvignon Blanc*?"

"No problem, Sir," The waitress said while reaching for the menus. "Will there be anything else?"

"I think that'll do for now," Cedric said while handing over his menu.

Terri just nodded and placed her menu in the young woman's hand. She had never had a man take charge like that. Mark had always let her make all the decisions. She often craved a man that knew how to be in control and that was exactly the type of man Cedric was.

"So how was your day?" Cedric asked after the waitress was gone.

"It was okay. I could barely get anything done. I was so busy thinking about you and coming here tonight."

"Well, I was pretty excited too. I couldn't wait to lay eyes on you. As always, you did not disappoint. You look absolutely stunning tonight."

His eyes roamed over her body from head to toe. She knew her face had to be getting a little red with embarrassment. Cedric complimented her all the time, but she was still trying to get used to it. Even though she hadn't quite grown accustomed to receiving the compliments, she still loved getting them. It made her feel like she was still sexy.

"Thanks, you don't look half bad yourself," She responded.

The waitress brought over the bottle of wine along with their food. Terri was happy because she was really hungry. Whenever they went out, however, she just took small bites of food because she didn't want to look like a pig.

As they ate, Cedric just stared at her and listened intently as she described each detail of her busy day. That was something Mark never did because he was always preoccupied with some sport or some stupid reality T.V. show. She deeply missed the attention he used to give. He was guilty of the same thing most married people were: complacency.

After they finished eating and knocking back about half the bottle of wine, Cedric said, "Okay, how is it that a woman as beautiful and smart as you is still on the market?"

"Well, I just haven't found anyone that appreciates me the way I deserve. I need someone that's gonna give me everything I need."

"Oh, so you're looking for someone to take care of you? A *sugar daddy*?"

"No, that's not it," she lied. "But, I do need a man that's doing something with himself."

"Doing something like what?"

"Something positive….anything besides sitting at home."

"So….if a garbage man approached you, what would you do?" Cedric said with a smirk on his face.

"I don't know. What does he look like," Terri said smiling from ear to ear.

"Oh, and she's shallow too," Cedric laughed.

"Well, you know. A woman got needs to," Terri said joining in on the laugh.

"But in all seriousness, what would you do. Just for the sake of the conversation, a fine garbage man approaches you. What would you do?"

"How much money does he make?"

"I don't know, twenty thousand a year."

"That's not that much. My initial thought would be to turn the brotha away, but deep down I would think he could be a good man in spite of his job situation," Terri responded. She began to feel a little guilty. Even though it was a hypothetical situation, she wasn't affording that same benefit to her husband.

"That is so nice of you," Cedric joked.

"Okay, Mr. Goody Two Shoes. Why are you single then?"

"I just went through a bitter divorce. I'm just now getting back on the dating scene."

"I'm sorry to hear that," Terri said in a sarcastic tone. "What kind of woman would let *you* get away?"

"Ha, Ha. That's the funniest thing I've heard so far."

"I try," Terri remarked.

"Truthfully speaking, I think I lost more in the whole ordeal than she did. One day she up and left. She took my two girls away from me too," he said pulling out his wallet to show her a picture of two beautiful girls that wore matching yellow dresses. They both had long curly hair pinned up with yellow ribbons and favored Cedric heavily.

"Do you ever get to see them?"

"That's the problem," he said looking as if he was choking back tears. I can't find them. I've exhausted all of my resources. I'd give anything to see them again.

Terri found herself trying to keep from being emotional. Of course she didn't know the little girls, but she empathized with Cedric's pain. She couldn't imagine if those were her girls that had been taken away from her. She also hadn't seen any man reveal his feelings in that way. All the men she had been around except for Mark and Quincey acted like they didn't have feelings.

She reached out and grabbed his hand to comfort him. "It's okay," she said while stroking the back of his hand. There was an underlying thought that plagued the back of her mind about how a woman could just leave a man that seemed so perfect and never contact him again.

"Terri?" a male voice said from behind. She immediately snatched her hand away from Cedric's. She recognized the voice and was afraid to turn around. Cedric was looking at her with a puzzled look on his face and she could tell he was wondering why she looked so startled.

When she looked over her shoulder, she saw Austin walking up to her table. *What is he doing here*? She thought to herself frantically. She was so nervous that she could barely function. She wasn't too fond of Mark at that moment, but she still didn't want him to find out about Cedric. She had no desire to receive the reputation of an adulteress.

"Austin, how are you?" she asked emitting a nervous laugh. She wore a fake smile trying not to look suspicious.

"I'm great, actually. How about you?" Austin said never breaking eye contact with her. Terri could read in his eyes that he suspected something.

"I'm doing okay. What brings you here tonight?"

"I was just about to ask you the same thing," Austin said diverting his look to Cedric.

"I was just out having dinner with my friend and ex-professor," Terri responded while motioning to Cedric. You?"

"I'm just out having dinner with a colleague," Austin replied pointing to a white lady sitting over at a table across the room. The lady didn't seem to be concerned about where Austin was at that moment because she never looked up from her menu. Terri thought she was dressed a little too proactively to be out on a business date, but she wasn't in any moral position to judge right then.

"Did you just get here," Terri asked hoping he didn't see her holding Cedric's hand.

"Yeah, I haven't been here long. The hostess just showed us to our seats. Now, don't be rude, introduce me to your *friend*."

She didn't want to, but Terri went along because she didn't want to confirm Austin's unvoiced speculations. The last thing she needed was for Austin to start adding events together in his head. He would call Mark and tell him everything he had seen if Terri didn't play her cards right.

The entire time that Austin was at the table, Cedric just sat back in his chair with his legs crossed. His head went back and forth according to who was speaking, as if he were watching a tennis match. He took the occasional sip of wine from his glass.

Austin extended his hand and Cedric reached out and shook it as they exchanged formalities. They kind of eyed each other the way that men do. Austin clearly thought something was up.

"Terri, can I speak to you a moment. It won't be long," Austin said with a sly grin.

"Sure," Terri said and excused herself from the table. Cedric just nodded and didn't say anything else. She followed Austin to the restroom area.

"You bet not be stepping out on my boy," he said blatantly as soon as they were out of ear shot.

"I'm not and I don't see how you can accuse me of anything like that."

"I'm not *accusing* you of anything. You just have the look of a busted cheater. Believe me I know. I could recognize it anywhere."

"Don't worry, I got this," Terri snapped back.

"I hope so. If I don't know anything else, I know that your husband loves you and those girls with all his heart. It would be a shame if you were out playing him."

"The last thing I want to do is hurt Mark," Terri said feeling her patience running thin. She really didn't want to hurt her husband, but she couldn't help but put her feelings first for once in her life. Besides, Mark never had her best interests in mind.

"A'ight, nuff said. I'm not here to lecture," Austin said. He placed a kiss on her cheek and walked back towards his table where the white lady was still studying the menu.

Terri reluctantly started her walk back to her table. She couldn't imagine what Cedric must have been thinking. She would probably be offended had a woman interrupted their dinner like that. When she made it back, Cedric was placing the tip on the table.

"Is everything okay?" Cedric said when she took her seat. "That guy was acting kind of strange."

"Everything is fine. He just wanted to catch up since he hasn't seen me in a while."

"That's cool, as long as everything is okay," Cedric said flashing Terri that smile that sent shivers up her spine.

"Oh, so you were looking out for me?"

"You know I was. I didn't want to have to rough anybody up, but I would have."

Terri let out a loud laugh at the thought of that. She didn't mean to sound rude but she knew Cedric was not much of a fighter. He was good to look at but protection wasn't his thing. She imagined that if ever given the chance, Austin would have taken Cedric on with one hand tied behind his back.

"I feel really *safe* now," Terri joked. They both shared a laugh and let the joyful mood linger.

After finishing off their drinks, Cedric came around and pulled her seat out and helped her put on her jacket. As they exited the restaurant, Austin waved as if to remind Terri of their conversation. She was so relieved that he didn't make a big scene. She knew it was totally wrong, but she didn't want Cedric to think she was a liar as she wasn't ready to stop seeing him. She enjoyed what he brought to the table. She felt like a lady when she was around him and she was not about to give that up for anybody.

Chapter 13

Austin drove down the interstate, head full of thoughts, on his way back to Monica's apartment in Franklin. They had left the restaurant not long after Terri and her mystery friend left. He couldn't wrap his mind around how comfortable she was being out with another guy. Sure she had said that the guy was a *colleague* but he could sense the chemistry between the two of them. He was so tempted to call Mark and tell him everything, but he just didn't know how to. Mark was so in love with that woman that it would crush him to hear that Terri could be seeing someone else. Besides, how do you tell someone that the person you've been married to for the last ten years is cheating?

He finally pushed the thoughts aside. It really wasn't his problem to worry about. If Mark would have listened to him a long time ago, he would have had a heads up. Besides, Austin had two big problems of his own.

Number one was the issue of Monica. That night was the first time Austin had seen her since she told him about the baby and he still was confused on how it could have happened since he had used protection every time and it had burst only once. If she was indeed pregnant then how could he be sure that the baby was his? There was no guarantee that she was being exclusive to him.

Secondly there was the matter of the child. He still liked Monica a lot and Lord knows that he loved the intimate times they spent together, but he was not about to let a baby ruin his relationship with Julie. Even though he didn't quite treat her like he was supposed to, Austin couldn't stand the thought of losing her. He planned to tell Monica just that when they reached her apartment.

Austin glanced over at Monica who was riding quietly with a serious look on her face. The window was partially down so her long blond hair tussled in the breeze. Austin still admired her beauty even though she carried a seed that he didn't intend on planting. He looked her over from head to toe. The low cut black blouse that she was wearing left little to the imagination. He allowed his eyes to roam south as he studied the skirt that stopped prematurely to reveal beautiful, thick, tanned legs.

He wondered briefly what she was thinking. He shrugged the thought off and reached down and turned the radio up. The Quiet Storm was on *92Q*. It was his favorite radio station, when he wasn't otherwise playing a CD. The sounds of the Isley Brothers' *Between the Sheets* engulfed the car.

Monica spoke up for the first time since they had left Che Marche. "Could you turn that down a little? I have a headache and don't feel well."

"What's wrong?" he asked genuinely. He didn't like the sound of that. Her being sick would ruin the rest of his night. He planned on handling the business with the pregnancy first and then experiencing her pleasures one last time. Then he was going to cut her loose.

"Pull over, Austin," she said and covered her mouth quickly. "Hurry up!"

He quickly swerved to the right shoulder and Monica threw the door open. "Just don't get any inside my car!" he yelled.

She leaned out of the car and threw up all the dinner she had eaten earlier. Austin didn't know what to do or say. He wasn't taught how to deal with a pregnant woman.

After throwing up for what seemed an eternity, Monica leaned back in and shut the door. They both rode in silence the rest of the way back to her apartment. The incident was a horrifying ordeal for Austin. Before that happened he still had the hope that she might not be pregnant, but now he really had to deal with the fact that he might have a woman pregnant that wasn't Julie.

When they finally reached her apartment complex, Austin was glad the ride was finally over. He dreaded the conversation they were about to have because he didn't know where it would lead or how Monica would feel about what he had to say.

Once into the apartment, Monica just unbuttoned her blouse and went into the restroom to brush her teeth. She still hadn't said anything to Austin since she threw up so he decided to be the one to get it started.

Austin looked around Monica's apartment as he waited for her to return. Everything looked very expensive. Her windows were all covered with Venetian blinds. The curtains and drapes were a soft golden color. Austin walked over and fingered them and they felt like they were made from an expensive silk. He took a seat on her couch and nearly sank all the way through the soft leather. He had never sat on a couch more comfortable. He nervously hummed to himself as he studied the paintings she had hanging on the wall in solid gold frames. It occurred to him that he didn't truly know how she made her money.

As Monica walked out of the bathroom, Austin asked "What are you going to do about the baby?" He didn't want to waste any time. He believed strongly in getting straight to the point.

"What do you mean, what am I going to do? The question should be what are *we* going to do?"

"I didn't mean it like that, but if it makes you happy, then what are *we* going to do?" Austin said trying to contain himself but that smart quip really got under his skin.

"I don't know. This all happened so suddenly. I was kinda leaning toward keeping the baby. My parents always taught me that abortion is wrong," she said.

Austin couldn't believe that she was trying to pull this right and wrong act out of the bag. After what they had been doing in the bedroom, nothing should be wrong.

"Keep it? What are you talking about? You should have at least called me before you *kinda* thought about anything," Austin said not trying to hide his anger.

"Okay, I get it," Monica said with a little grin on her face. Even though she was smiling, Austin knew there was nothing funny about what she was thinking.

"You get what?"

"The fact that I'm good enough for you to sleep with every time you get a chance, but not good enough to have a baby with."

"That's not it. You know this was supposed to just be fun. We weren't getting serious and having a baby is definitely serious. Then there's my business– "

"Don't forget that some of that business you got because I helped you," Monica said cutting him off. "Maybe we should call Mr. Green and ask him what he thinks."

Austin didn't even respond. He was starting to get irritated. He hated when a woman did something for you and wanted to throw it in your face every time she got a chance.

"That figures. You're just like every other *black* man I've ever dated, running away from your responsibility."

"Look, we are not about to get into the race thing. You still don't know me well enough to make comments like that. Further more, what do you mean, *every other black man*? How many has it been?"

"First of all, that's none of your business. You just need to be a man about yours."

Austin was getting so mad. He knew he had to get out of there as soon as possible. He was feeling so irritated he didn't know how to act. He *was* being a man. He was just trying to help her make the right decision. Besides, he was not about to let Julie find out he got someone else pregnant.

"Look, you're going to have an abortion and that's the end of this conversation. I'll even pay for it," he said trying to be as stern as possible.

"So you want me to get an abortion? Why? You must don't want your fat girlfriend, Julie, to find out?" Monica said with a smile on her face.

She must have been laughing at the way Austin was looking. He couldn't believe his ears. He thought all along that he was being a player, but it turns out *he* could have been the one that was getting played.

"How do you know about Julie?"

"Just like I researched your business, I researched your personal life. It wasn't hard to find out anything about you that I wanted to know. When I saw you with her on the internet I couldn't believe a man as handsome as you would be with a girl as big as she is. I called your house a couple of times to see if she really lived there. When she answered the phone, I hung up."

"Well, I don't care what you know about me. You're still getting an abortion. I'm done with you." Austin tried to sound surer about what he was saying than he was. The truth was he was shook by what she had just said to him. He stood up and started walking to the door. The best thing for him to do was get out of there.

"Austin, sweetie, you're not done with me until I say you are and if you don't want your precious Julie to find out, we have some things to discuss."

Austin just sat down on the couch. He didn't want to submit to her, but he had no choice. She had him exactly where she wanted him and at that moment there was nothing he could do about it. He decided the best thing for him to do was listen to what she had to say.

Chapter 14

Quincey sat in his office at the church making some revisions to the sermon that he would be giving on Sunday. Pastor Lewis had given him an office at the church not long after he announced his calling to preach. Pastor Lewis seemed as if he was more excited about him preaching than Quincey was himself. He could understand the urgency because the church was actually in need of help pretty badly. Poor Pastor Lewis was working himself to death trying to keep up with everything that was going on at St. Paul and on top of that the church was growing at an extraordinary rate. There was no better time for Quincey to have announced his calling into the ministry and he was now taking on his fair share of the church's responsibility.

He was feeling extremely nervous about preaching. He was a great lawyer and it didn't have any affect on him whatsoever to get up in front of a jury. He didn't like to boast but he was one of the best there was at it, but getting up in front of a church was an entirely different feeling. He just prayed that God would direct him through it.

Quincey was hard at work when he heard a knock on his office door. He wasn't expecting anyone so it shocked him to hear someone stirring around the church that late in the evening. He normally came into the office late as to not be disturbed. *I must have left the lights on up front*, he reasoned.

"It's open," he said when the knock came again and jolted him from his thoughts.

When the door opened he was surprised to see Janet casually walk into the room. He was shocked to see her because he hadn't talked to her in a couple of weekends. They normally didn't speak to one another unless it involved their son Jeff, so it struck Quincey as strange that she would go out of her way to visit him at the church.

"What are you doing here?" Quincey asked passively as he looked back down at his notes.

"I was just passing by and saw your car in the parking lot. I was going to call you but since I was right outside I decided to stop in and see what you were up to.

"Humph," Quincey said without looking up. Janet was being too cordial to him. Usually she was the prime example of Baby's mama drama, so her being there more than five minutes meant she wanted something or she had some news he wouldn't find favorable.

"Where's Jeff. I *know* he's not at home alone," he said with suspicion in his voice. Not that she had ever left Jeff at home alone, but he didn't put anything past her.

"You know he's not at home alone. He's at my sister's house. He's been dying to play with his cousins all week."

"That's cool. I know you didn't come by here just to talk, so how can I help you?"

"Well, I was stopping by to let you know about the increases in cost to take care of your son."

Here we go, Quincey thought to himself. He knew she wasn't just stopping by because she had nothing better to do.

"What increases, Janet?"

"Well, the cost of Jeff's daycare is going up. I pay nearly two hundred dollars a week now for his after care. Also the cost of his clothes went up. He's a growing boy. It's like I'm buying a new wardrobe for him every other month."

"Well, first of all, I'm paying you more that five hundred dollars a week without a court order for child support. That's more that two thousand dollars a month. That's twenty four thousand dollars a year. You bring in more for Jeff alone than some people make in a year. Some women would kill to get half of that. Secondly, most of the clothes in his wardrobe I buy. If he needs more, I'll buy those too. Not to mention he's on my health insurance. You're saving all kind of money based on that alone."

Janet just sat there staring at him. He knew she was about to come back with some smart comment. Quincey was growing fairly used to it. It never ceased to amaze him how some black women felt the need to use their attitude like a defense mechanism. If the truth came out most of them were soft as stuffed animals on the inside.

"Look, if I took your trifling self to court, you would probably be paying more than that and you would still have to pay for his insurance. I'm the one doing *you* a favor, so don't get it twisted."

Janet's neck was in full motion now. Quincey thought if she swung it any harder, her head would fall off. She should have been happy they were sitting in the church, because he felt like getting real ignorant.

"If the only reason you stopped by is to argue, then I don't have time for it right now. I'm too busy," Quincey said attempting to defuse the situation.

"I bet if that pretty little wife of yours was asking for more money, you would give it to her. You can't even give the mother of your son more money to support him. Trifling," Janet mumbled. Quincey almost missed the last word because it was said under her breath.

"Obviously you still didn't get it. Of course I give *my wife* anything she asks for. That's one of the benefits of being married. I'm not about to give you more money to use on yourself than I already do each month."

With that, Quincey just walked over to the door and opened it. He waved his hand as if to say, *Show yourself out.* He walked back over to his desk, sat down, and continued reading over his notes.

"Okay, I'm done arguing. That's not the only reason I stopped by here."

"What else could there possibly be, Janet?" Quincey asked not trying to hide the fact that he was highly irritated. Janet's face softened as she thought about her next statement.

"I was looking at Jeff the other day and was just thinking how much he looks like you. It was even funny how his actions remind me of the things you do. Like the way you sweat a little on your nose when you get upset."

Quincey let out a long sigh and wiped off the moisture that was forming on the bridge of his nose. *Where could this conversation possibly be going*? He thought to himself. He felt like being rude and telling her to get out or maybe physically removing her would have been a viable option.

"I was just thinking to myself," she continued. What would it have been like if we stayed together? Do you ever think about that, Q?"

He was completely caught off guard by that question. He never would have thought in a million years Janet still remotely thought of him in that way.

"No. If you haven't noticed, I'm happily married."

"I know you're *married*, I just didn't know it was happily. Jeff sometimes comes home and tells me about the way you and Kim argue when he's there. I didn't think anyone could be happy with all that arguing going on."

"Well, first of all, you're listening to the words of a child. I know that it's not right at any time to argue in front Jeff, but the times we do are far and few. Either way you look at it though, that doesn't mean I'm unhappy."

"All I'm saying is that I don't know if I could be happy with someone that complains at me all the time."

Quincey was getting more and more exasperated with Janet. He didn't even know why he was indulging in such a foolish conversation. He and Janet had never really discussed anything regarding their relationship since the breakup and now all of a sudden here she was trying to get in his head, all while he was trying to prepare his first sermon. He knew it had to be the work of the devil.

"What are you talking about?

"Jeff just told me that he hears you two fussing all the time about you being gone a lot."

"Well, Jeff doesn't know what he's talking about. Kim is completely happy with our situation," Quincey lied. Of course he couldn't admit the truth. He would have to ask for God's forgiveness later for lying in his house.

"I was just thinking that had I known that you would turn out to be the man you are today, I would have worked harder on our relationship. Besides, back then I was young and dumb," Janet said sounding really sincere.

"You should have been thinking about that when you were out cheating on me. I was the same man back then that I am now. Maybe I didn't have the money I have now, but I was still the same at heart."

"When are you going to get over that? Like I said, I was young and dumb."

Janet leaned over to pick up her purse that was resting on the floor beside her chair and Quincey observed her briefly. He had to admit that she was still attractive. She had cut her hair into short curls recently, and it looked good on her. Her hair was jet black which accented her fair skin and cute round face. Even though she had a child, she still had an awesome figure. She was one of those women who really didn't have to work for it. He resolved that no matter how good looking she was though, he was not about to go there again. He just loved Kim too much for that.

"Never," he said sternly. "We are *never* going to get back together. This conversation was over before it started. Now if you please, I have a lot of work to do."

Janet looked a little angry but she didn't press the issue any further. She just got up and walked out. She looked back briefly before she shut the door. Quincey let out a sigh of relief. After Janet left, he lost all desire to continue working. He decided he would go home spend what was left of the night with Kim because he hadn't done that in a while.

Chapter 15

Mark excitedly went about getting dressed because he was anxious to get his day started. It was the first time in a long while that he had an entire day to himself. When he didn't have the girls during the week, he was out looking for a job. Then on the weekend, it was like Terri found any excuse possible to get out of the house.

That day, however, it was her turn to be stuck in the house all day. He had won tickets to the Titans game from a local radio station. They were playing the Dallas Cowboys and he wouldn't have missed that game for anything in the world. He had been a Cowboys fan since he was a little boy and it was the fulfillment of a dream for him to see them play.

He won three tickets so he split the prize with Austin and Quincey. It had been about a month since they all had hung out together even though he saw Quincey nearly every week due to the case against APS. It had been a month or so since he had last seen Austin, let along them going somewhere as a crew like they used to.

He was putting on his new Dallas Cowboys t-shirt when Terri walked into the bedroom. Mark saw her eyes roaming over him in the mirror as he finished dressing. He didn't even want to turn around and face the icy stare because he knew where the situation was headed.

"I don't know why you didn't just sell those tickets so we can get some extra money. You don't *have* to go to that game today," she said while glaring at him, hands resting on her hips.

I guess it wouldn't be right it there was no argument about it, Mark thought to himself. It was like she didn't want him to have any happiness in life since he didn't have a job. He had some promising job interviews and he felt like he might land one pretty soon. He even took her advice and applied to some of the fast food joints around town.

"Terri, do we have to start today? We've been arguing for the past few months straight and I'm tired. I just want to go out with my boys today and enjoy this football game. I've wanted to see Dallas play since I was a kid and I'm not giving up my chance to go."

"Well what about the things I've wanted since I was a kid. What are you doing to make sure those things happen?"

"I've been doing everything I can!" he yelled. He felt himself getting upset. He had made a promise to himself and God after the incident at APS that he wasn't going to let his temper get the best of him again. "You know what, Terri, this conversation is over."

"It's over? We ain't done talking till I say we are."

Mark didn't respond. He just put his hat on and started walking toward the door. Terri was just trying to bait him into an argument and he was not about to go there. He just walked past her so he could leave the house before it got too heated.

He could feel Terri's eyes burning a hole in the back of his head. All of a sudden he felt her nails scratch the back of his neck as she grabbed him in the collar of his shirt. She was pulling at his shirt with all her might. Not being able to handle the strain being put on it by them pulling in separate directions, the t-shirt tore right down the middle.

Mark was shocked. He didn't know how to respond to Terri's actions. She had never been violent with him before, so it blindsided him like a bus. It felt strange that it came after he had made a determination to control his anger. He guessed the old saying was true: *When you make a promise to God, the devil hears it too and he's going make you work to prove it.*

"What's wrong with you, woman?" Mark yelled. He had never felt more like slapping a woman than he did then. "That was a brand new shirt."

"You shouldn't have tried to walk out on me while I was still talking," Terri said looking like she had done nothing wrong.

Mark didn't even feel like looking at her anymore. It was one thing for him to be trying to take a little extra abuse from her because he wanted this relationship to work but it was entirely another if they were going to be violent with one another. For all he cared at that moment their relationship was over. He just took what was left of his pride and walked out the door. He could hear Terri yelling something about not coming back, but he didn't even try to make out what she was saying. He couldn't care less what she had to say at that moment.

***

Mark drove above the speed limit trying to make it to Quincey's house. They were all supposed to meet up there. He was originally ahead of schedule, but due to Terri acting foolish before he left, he had to make an unplanned stop by the mall to buy a new Dallas Cowboys t-shirt. There was no way he would be seen wearing just the wife beater that was under the shirt that Terri had ripped.

He pulled into Quincey's driveway and parked. He couldn't help thinking about what happened at the house. He was really ashamed that any of it took place. He looked in the mirror at the huge gash on his neck from her grabbing at him and he knew that it would be impossible to hide. It stung really badly and he couldn't even think about touching it. He had doctored it up as much as possible. Just thinking about the scratch made him mad all over again.

He walked up and rung the door bell. He stood there for all of two seconds before Austin threw open the door. Austin was dressed from head to toe in his Titan's apparel.

"Traitor," Austin said when he saw Mark was dressed in the away team's clothing. "How you gone be from Tennessee and not root for the home team?"

"We aint always had a team in Tennessee and I've been a Cowboys fan since I can remember."

"Whatever. Quincey's in the den with Kim. We've been waiting on you to get here. What took so long?"

"I got caught up," Mark said not wanting to reveal the real reason he was late. They headed into the den where Quincey and Kim were sitting.

When he walked in the room, he noticed Quincey and Kim looked happier than he could remember in recent history. She was sitting on his lap and they were kissing. Mark didn't know if he should give them a few minutes or not. It looked to him like they were getting pretty intense so he cleared his throat to get their attention.

Quincey glanced over at him out the corner of his eye and cut the kiss short. "What's up, man? I was wondering when you were gonna get here. We couldn't go to the game without you. After all, you've got the tickets."

"My bad. I just ran into a few issues today. If you can pry yourself away from Kim," Mark joked. "We need to get going so we can see at least some of the game."

Kim laughed. "I'm not trying to hold up this little men's day out. She gave Quincey one more passionate kiss and left the room. Quincey watched her until she was completely out of the room.

"It looks like ya'll are hot and heavy again," Austin said as soon as Kim was gone.

"Yeah, we've kind of rekindled our relationship. I realized I could give her a little bit more time. But anyway are ya'll ready to go?" Quincey said.

"Yeah, I'm ready," Austin replied now examining the back of Mark's neck. "First I need to know what the heck happened to Marks neck. Man, it looks like *Freddy Krueger* visited you in your dreams last night."

Mark really didn't feel like going into it because he knew that their opinions wouldn't be anything he wanted to hear at that moment. But then again he needed to talk to someone to get some of the anger off of his chest so he decided to go ahead and tell them.

He brought them up to date about how his and Terri's relationship had been on the rocks. He took them from that point through their recent episode and Terri getting physical with him. Quincey just listened intently. He had a serious frown on his face like he was hearing the worst news in his life. Austin just shook his head and looked like he was thinking heavily.

\   hat's so unlike Terri," Quincey said with that disturbed look on his face. "I knew you guys were having problems, but I didn't think it had gotten to the point of physical abuse. That would have been enough to get her locked up had you called the police."

"Yeah, man, but you know I wouldn't do that. I couldn't send my children's mother to jail. It was bad enough that they could have seen us fighting."

"I know it's a tricky situation. Well, have you ever thought about counseling?"

Mark didn't reply. He just sat there and contemplated sitting down with someone and explaining all of his personal problems. He just didn't think he could do it. How could someone else know more about his issues than him? Besides he didn't think anyone short of God could get through to Terri. He glanced over at Austin who was still just sitting there. He hadn't said anything since Mark revealed his marital troubles.

"What's wrong with you?" Mark asked Austin. "If anyone would have an opinion about this I thought it would be you."

"I don't know, man. I just have some news that I really don't want to tell you."

"What is it, man?"

"Well, I was out the other day with Monica and -"

"You were out with someone else?" Mark interrupted. "Man you gone always be the same. You got that good woman at home and you out cheating with someone else. I just don't get it."

"See that's your problem. You don't ever pay attention. Instead of lecturing me and worrying about who I'm going out with, you need to be worrying about where your wife's been."

Mark knew where this conversation was headed. He and Austin always got in an argument when he found out Austin had been cheating on Julie. "Since you know so much, where has she been?" Mark said not trying to hide his sarcasm.

"That was what I was trying to tell you before you opened your fat mouth. When I was out with Monica, she was at the restaurant with some other dude. Some pretty boy."

Mark was getting so mad at this foolishness. Austin was taking it too far with this nonsense about his wife. He knew they had been having some issues and she had a little bit of an attitude problem, but she was not a cheater. He would not sit there and let him attack her reputation like that.

"Austin, you don't know what you're talking about. If she was with some other man, how come you didn't say anything to her? I would have said something if it were Julie that I saw."

Austin shook his head. "I did. She just blew it off like he was a co-worker. I was gone tell you but I figured we would be having the exact conversation we're having now."

Mark stood up because he was getting so angry that he couldn't contain himself any longer. He just would not believe that Terri was cheating on him.

"That's the last I'm gone hear about that. My wife is not a cheater."

Austin now stood. He had a look on his face like he would not be bullied. Mark had about three inches on him in height and more that fifty pounds in weight, but these two had more than their share of fights. It seemed like growing up they were fighting every day.

"A'ight, ya'll need to chill. There ain't gone be no fighting in my house," Quincey said stepping in between them. "Mark, I know you don't want to hear it, but there may be some truth to what Austin said. Look at all the problems you and Terri been having lately."

Mark didn't answer. He just walked out of the house. He heard Quincey calling him, but he didn't turn around. If Quincey was dumb enough to believe what Austin was saying, then so be it. He didn't have to listen to it, though. He just pulled his vehicle out of the driveway and headed wherever his heart led him. He just forgot about the football game because obviously, that day it wasn't meant to happen.

Chapter 16

Terri gave both of her girls a kiss and walked out and shut their bedroom door. Both girls were sleeping deeply, so they didn't even notice her entrance or exit. They were both her little angels and she loved them with all of her heart. It had been ages since she had spent time with them and it was starting to wear on her conscience. In her mind she excused her absence from home life with her need to unwind after a hard day at work.

She walked back into the living room where her purse was lying unzipped on the sofa. As she picked the purse up, her wallet fell onto the floor. Terri scooped it up and went to stuff it back inside, but her eyes fell on the Wedding picture that was featured prominently in the front of her wallet. She briefly ran her fingers over the outline of the two happy people in the photo. The groom contrasted the bride in every way, from skin tone to their look and style. The man wore a black tuxedo with a crooked bow-tie and the bride wore a white hand me down dress. He was dark skinned and she was much lighter than he was, so much so that she almost looked like a white woman standing next to him. They were both smiling from ear to ear and the couple was completely oblivious to the heartache and pain that the future years would bring.

The picture of course was of her and Mark and she wished deeply that they could go back to the way things were in those days. They loved and cared for one another unconditionally then. So many things had changed since and Terri didn't know how to begin fixing the relationship.

No matter how she tried, though, she could not stop blaming Mark for their entire situation. She blamed him for everything from their finances to their failing marriage. If it were not for her being able to talk to Cedric about *almost* everything, she didn't know how she would be holding up.

She did take responsibility for one thing. The fight that they had earlier in the week was all her fault. Violence was not a part of her character. She hadn't so much as been in a fight when she was in high school so she didn't even know if she knew how to fight or not. Most of the altercations she was in were over before they started. She had always bluffed her way out of the fights with her attitude and mouth.

Cedric had called her earlier in the day and asked if they could meet that night. Of course she couldn't turn down a chance to spend time with him, even though he had invited her to his home. Since it would be the first time she'd gone to his house, she felt a few reservations about being alone with him in such an intimate setting. She hesitated before accepting but went ahead and agreed after some light begging on Cedric's behalf. He had been nothing but a perfect gentleman and they hadn't done anything more than share a friendly hug or two. She had to admit that she was starting to enjoy his company more and more.

As soon as Terri heard Mark come in the house and close the door, she tried to rush out before the questioning began. "See you later, babe," she said and patted him on the chest.

"Where is it this time?" Mark demanded.

"I'm just going to the mall with Shannon." Shannon had been her best friend since the sixth grade and Julie knew that Shannon would lie for her if need be. She had confidence that Shannon would never rat her out to Mark, even though Shannon was slightly partial to him.

"So that means you should be home around ten o'clock then. The mall shuts down at nine."

"Where is all this questioning coming from. I'm a grown woman. I don't have to explain anything to anybody. Especially someone who ain't paying no bills."

"Look. I'm getting real tired of you throwing that in my face every time you get a chance. As your husband, I have a right to know where you're going."

"Well, as the person paying all the bills I have the right to not tell you," Terri said angrily.

"I guess that gives you something else on the list of things you can do freely now. Must be nice," Mark said and threw his keys on the table by the door.

"What are you even talking about?"

"I'm talking about you going out on a date with someone else."

Terri got so mad she could hardly contain herself. *That stupid Austin probably couldn't wait to run back and tell Mark what he'd seen,* she thought. *He wasn't so quick to run back and tell Julie about that white girl whose face he was all up in.*

"I already know that it was Austin that told you that and I'll tell you just like I told him. That was a one of my teachers in college. I've introduced you to him before. You would know him if you saw him," She lied. "There was nothing going on."

"Well, there would be nothing wrong with that statement if I didn't have to find out from Austin. If nothing was going on, then why couldn't you tell me about it?" Mark asked his voice softening as if his anger was passing a bit.

Terri hated to admit it, but he was right. Maybe she was feeling Cedric a little more that she wanted to let herself believe. Maybe that's why she automatically wanted to hide her relationship with him from Mark.

"Mark, I promise you that I have never been with anyone else since we've been married."

"I was talking to Pastor Lewis and he said-"

"You talked to Pastor Lewis about our marriage. I can't believe you," Terri shouted. She wasn't mad that Mark had made an effort, but she didn't want Pastor Lewis to know what was going on in her house. She just knew that his next sermon would be about marriage and infidelity. "I don't think I can show my face in that church again."

"He just suggested that we go through marriage counseling at the church," Mark responded like he didn't hear what she had just said.

"Mark I don't know," she responded hesitantly. She knew that Mark was trying to be more serious about church and everything, but she didn't think she was ready for that at that moment. If God loved her so much then why did he allow her life to be so messed up? She always heard Pastor Lewis preach about no matter what situation you're in, there is someone in a worse one. Well, one thing she knew for sure was Pastor Lewis didn't know the hell she had been through lately.

"Just think about. That's all I'm asking," Mark said.

"A'ight," she said and then left the house.

Terri thought about going to counseling on the entire drive to Cedric's house. She was so deep in thought that she passed Cedric's drive. She drove to the end of the street and made a quick u-turn. She knew she must have been preoccupied with her thoughts because how could she miss the biggest house on the block?

She pulled into his driveway and stepped out of the car. She was amazed at how big the house was. It looked like it could easily be featured on MTV Cribs. It was the largest houses she had ever seen and it seemed as if Cedric would have an entire staff of maids and butlers on payroll. It reminded her of one of those medieval castles because it was made of that sort of stone. She walked up and rang the doorbell and even it sounded rich as it played some classical tune. She didn't know who composed the tune but she had heard it on a couple of television commercials.

After standing there for about a minute and a half the door swung open. When she saw Cedric she was reminded of what compelled her to come to his house. He was good looking as ever in his khaki shorts and silk crew neck t-shirt. She could see his chiseled frame as the shirt clung to him when he moved.

He walked out and hugged her tightly. She took in his manly smell. She didn't know what the fragrance was that he wore but it smelt heavenly and seductive at the same time. She couldn't decide if she wanted to let him go or not.

"I thought you had changed your mind," Cedric said when they had finally released each other. He flashed her that nice smile of his and she felt as though she might melt.

"You know I would never miss a chance to see you," Terri said letting a little giggle escape. She had to catch herself because she was acting a little too overjoyed to see him.

"Well, in that case, come right in," Cedric said while stepping aside to allow her room to pass by him in the doorway. He had his arm outstretched as if to welcome her home.

She followed him out of the foyer and into a large sitting room. Terri was astonished. She looked around and admired the way the room was decorated. If she hadn't known better, she would have thought it had a woman's touch. The walls were painted a golden color and had the most amazing African American art she had ever seen hanging from them. His curtains had a royal feel and they sprung to life with rich sage and golden swirls. His area rug even went along with the golden theme.

"Is there something wrong?" Cedric asked when he noticed her looking around.

"No everything is perfect. I've just never seen a man put so much effort into the look of his home. Shoot, I've never seen a man *clean* his home."

"Well I take pride in where I lay my head. It's like the saying goes, *a man's house is his castle*," Cedric said with a smile.

They sat down to dinner and she was even more amazed with the meal he had prepared. Her plate was adorned with lobster and broccoli spears. She had a half full glass of Chardonnay to drink. She had never had a man cook for her before so she didn't now how to react. She had yet to figure out the occasion for all the special attention but since he went through so much trouble, she figured she might as well enjoy it.

During dinner they just had light conversation about everything from politics to football. Most of the time she rambled off and Cedric just listened. She didn't mean to steal the conversation, but it felt so good for someone to listen to what she had to say.

After dinner she sat and watched as he did the dishes. He cleared every thing from the table and put all the food away. He rinsed everything before placing it in the dishwasher. The night was growing old, so she was thinking it was about time to go.

"You know what? I've really enjoyed myself tonight. But all good things must come to an end. I think it's about time for me to leave," Terri said while gathering her belongings.

"Wait, don't leave yet," Cedric pleaded with her. "*The Color Purple* is coming on next and I *know* you want to watch that. You told me it's your favorite movie."

"I don't know. It's getting pretty late and I have some business to take care of tomorrow," Terri responded. She knew if she stayed she would have a lot of arguing to do when she got home as it was already later than the ten o'clock time Mark had expected her to make.

"Look, I'll be completely satisfied if you just stay and watch half the movie," Cedric said and flashed that gorgeous smile. How could Terri say no to that?

"Okay, I'll stay but for only part of the movie."

Cedric led her into a huge Media room on the back side of the first floor of the house. She was even more amazed with that room. There were theatre style seats in two rows in the middle of the room. The main attraction was the huge flat screen TV that hung from the front wall of the room. She didn't think she had ever seen a TV that big or clear.

Cedric turned off all the lights and took a seat right next to her. "I'm glad you decided to stay," He said and placed a hand on her thigh.

"Me, too," Terri said and gently brushed his hand off her leg.

She absolutely loved the Color Purple and easily lost track of time. They didn't do much talking during the movie. They only briefly commented about what happened from time to time. She noticed that ever so often Cedric seemed to be getting closer to her. She didn't really pay much attention to it until she felt him reach over and place his arm around her.

Now her full attention was on him. She knew the signal she must have been sending since she was at his home so late, but since she had never tried anything with her before, she didn't see any reason for him to start that night.

Cedric looked in her eyes and said, "Terri you're an amazing woman. You really need someone in your life that will treat you how you need to be treated. You see everything I have and all that I did tonight. You could have that on a regular basis."

"Cedric, I have to be honest with you. I am …" her words trailed off because he grabbed her face and planted a kiss right on her lips. The kiss was so passionate that she lost all train of thought. She found herself letting her guard down and ready to submit to him and then Cedric's phone rang. If anything applied to the situation, it was the saying: *The Lord always provides a way of escape.*

"I have to go," Terri said jumping up off the couch.

Cedric didn't respond. He just grabbed her by the hand and pulled her in for another kiss. She fought him some but not enough to stop him from having his way. Her mind told her that she should resist, but it was as if her body was marching to a different beat. She felt the heat of his kiss pass from her lips to the sole of her feet. Before she knew what was happening, *his* kiss had turned into *her* kiss.

Cedric, still holding her hand, led her up the stairs toward his bedroom. She followed behind like a sheep headed to the slaughter.

She thought about whether she would regret the act she was about to do, but she did not have the will power to stop at that point. She had to admit now that her feelings for Cedric were stronger than she thought. *God forgive me* was the last thing she thought as he laid her across the bed.

Chapter 17

The church was packed. There were so many people at the service that the ushers started bringing out folding chairs to line the aisles. Even with the extra seating, there were still people standing along the back of the church and in the vestibule. The church probably hadn't seen this many people since it was established and the people who designed it probably never thought it would. So, as more people came in than could fit in the congregation, they started to be seated in the reception hall in the back. No one was turned away because at least in the back they could still hear the service.

Quincey paced nervously back and forth in his office. He paused momentarily to study the walls and decided that he needed some type of soothing artwork to place on them. At least they might have served as something to calm his mind at that moment. He resolved that it would be one of the first things he did when he got around to decorating. Being so busy with his normal life, decorating ended up being on the bottom of his to-do list.

He cracked the door and took a look out and then quickly closed it. His office was located on the second floor of the church so he could see most of the sanctuary from there. People hustled back and forth in each aisle and children were playing in between the pews while their mothers scolded them for acting up in the Lord's house. He couldn't believe how many people had come to hear him preach. He gathered that not all of them came because they needed to hear a word from God, but some came just to see if he could preach or not. He wondered when people would grow past things like that and seek God for who he really is.

Just then he heard a knock on the door. "Come in," he said trying to sound as cheerful as possible.

Pastor Lewis pushed the door open and walked in. He was wearing a black and white pin stripe suit with matching black and white shoes. As long as Quincey had been going to that church, he always remembered Pastor Lewis having an amazing wardrobe. Even as a fairly wealthy man, himself, Quincey sometimes wished he could go clothes shopping in the Pastor's closet.

"How's it going, Brotha?" Pastor Lewis said taking a seat in one of the leather chairs in front of Quincy's desk.

"Honestly, the last time I was this nervous was when I was standing at the alter about to marry Kim. Maybe this even has that beat," Quincey said managing a laugh. He walked over and took a seat in his chair directly across from Pastor Lewis.

"I know what you mean. I remember my first message. To tell you the truth, the crowd that came that day wasn't half as big as the one out there, but I don't think it would have mattered because I was just as, if not *more*, nervous than you."

Quincey just laughed. He couldn't imagine Pastor Lewis ever being nervous. When he preached, he did it with such a great authority. Quincey had seen some dynamic speakers in his life both secular and Christian, but Pastor Lewis had to be one of the best.

"One thing you have to remember is in a sense you are getting married," Pastor Lewis continued. "You are letting the world know today that you are making a vow to proclaim the gospel of Jesus Christ for the rest of your life for better or worse."

"I never thought about it like that, Pastor," Quincey responded now in deep thought. He hoped he was ready for everything that came along with being a minister.

"I just came in to let you know that I'll be praying for you and to tell you to just let God have his way when you get up there. You can never go wrong if you let God be in control."

With those last words Pastor Lewis rose shook Quincey's hand and walked out the office. Quincey sat down and felt like he was more nervous now than before Pastor Lewis came in. He knew that the Pastor wasn't trying to make him nervous but now he was *really* thinking about the great responsibility he was accepting.

He sat back and prayed aloud. "Father I come to you now asking you to give me strength to do what you have set before me. I'm going out there today with complete faith that I'm in line with your will and I know that you won't leave me alone. I sought you for a word and believe that you gave me just that. I know that this is a word that you have ordained for your people. I'm thanking you for the peace that you will give me and I ask that the words I say will be a blessing to someone out there. I'm thanking you in advance for these things, in your Son Jesus' name. Amen."

He felt a sense of peace come over him. For the first time since he announced his call into the ministry, he felt he was doing the right thing. When he opened his eyes, Kim was standing there looking at him. She had a soft smile on her face.

"How long have you been standing there?" Quincey asked

"Not long, but I didn't want to interrupt your prayer." She walked over and kissed him on the lips. Quincey thought about how beautiful she looked that day in her white dress and white high heel shoes.

"So what brings you in here?"

"I was just coming in to tell you how proud I am of you. I know it's not easy being married to a woman like me. I know I complain a lot about you not being home, but I'm really trying to deal with the fact that you're doing it for all the right reasons."

Quincey was impressed. Over the past months, she really was being more understanding about him being gone so much so he took her comments as confirmation from God that he was going in the right direction.

"Baby, you don't know how much it means for me to hear you say that."

He walked over hugged her. He hugged her as tightly as he could without suffocating her. He wanted to make her feel his love for her through his embrace. He then kissed her softly on her forehead being careful not to mess up her make-up.

"I love you so much. Not to rush you off or anything, though, I need to look over my notes briefly before going out."

"That's fine, sweetie. I'll talk to you after the service," Kim responded holding his hand for a few moments longer. She let his hand slowly slip from hers as she walked toward the door. She looked back and winked at Quincey as she exited the office and closed the door.

Quincey walked out into the sanctuary and took his seat next to Pastor Lewis in the pulpit. He glanced around and was struck again by how many people were there to hear him preach. He would've thought that Bishop J.W. Walker was the preacher of the hour. He looked over and winked at his mother who was seated on the front pew. She smiled and nodded in return to his gesture. It made him feel good that his mother was able to make it. She owned her own business and it was sometimes hard for her to make personal appointments.

He looked on the other side of the church and was glad to see all his friends had shown up as well. Mark and Terri were there with their two girls. Austin and Julie were seated directly in front of them. He hoped that some of what his sermon was about that day would inspire his friends.

"I'm so proud of this young man," Pastor Lewis said as he began his introduction of the speaker. I have known him since he was a little boy coming to church with his mother. So this truly brings truth to the scripture that says *Train up a child in the way that he should go and when he is old, he will not depart from it*. It seems like just yesterday that he was the youngest one that served on our junior deacon board. Now, he is about to start his journey as a man of God. Without further ado I want to present to some and introduce to others: Minister Quincey Jenkins."

With that Quincey nervously stood and walked over to the podium where he was to speak. He placed his bible down and briefly scanned the congregation and then quickly diverted his eyes back to his notes. He feared that if he looked out for too long it would make his nervousness increase.

When he had gained enough composure to continue, he looked up and began to speak. "I want to …." He began but his words trailed off as his eyes fell on the back pew of the church.

He paused because he saw a face he didn't expect to see. It was Janet. *What is she doing here?* He thought to himself. She had to be there to stir up some sort of trouble. The first thought that entered his mind was her trying to get back with him a few weeks ago in his office.

He didn't spend too much time dwelling on it. He went directly into the sermon that he had spent so many weeks preparing. He spoke from the topic "You cannot get to low for God to pick you up." As a text he used the story of Jesus and Mary Magdalene and how she was caught being an adulteress. The elders caught her in the act and brought her to stand judgment before Jesus and a large crowd. The law of the land at that time said she should be stoned to death. Instead of Jesus joining in and calling for her head, he instead uttered the famous words: *He that is without sin among you, let him first cast a stone at her.*

"My life is a testimony of this," Quincey preached. "There were times that I did things that I'm not proud of and I thought God had given up on me. I thought that just like the people around me, that He had condemned me for my actions. But I stand here before you today to let you know that there is nothing you can do to cause God to turn his back on you. When I was at my lowest point was when God reached down and picked me up. The point I'm trying to get all of you to see today, my brothers and sisters, is that if he can forgive Mary Magdalene or me, then he is more than able to forgive you."

"The best thing about it is that whatever you've done, no matter how bad it is or how shameful, he will forgive you for it. There's no catch 22 either. Once you're forgiven, that's it. The bible says that he *casts your sin into the sea of forgetfulness.*"

After that the church erupted into praise service. The musicians played an up tempo beat. Some people danced in the aisles and others in the church swayed back and forth while clapping their hands. Some people shouted and others cried. Quincey looked out and noticed all his friends were on their feet even Austin. Terri just sat there staring in one spot as if oblivious to what was going on around her.

"Okay, I don't mean to interrupt this spirit of praise, but there may be more to praise him for in just a few moments," Quincey said once the atmosphere began to calm down a little. "I want to open the doors of the church for anyone here today that does not know God for themselves. I want to offer you a chance for redemption of your sins. The same God that has forgiven others you see sitting right here amongst you today wants to offer you the same forgiveness. He already knows you and is just waiting for you to know him. So, if you will accept this invitation, we invite you to come to the alter now."

Several people in the church began looking around at each other as if they didn't know for sure what to do. He didn't know how many people would come, but he did know that someone had to be in attendance that needed to surrender their life to God. "Look, I know that someone is wrestling with whether to come down or not,"

Quincey said in a soothing tone. We all have been where you are and I'm not giving up on you. I know that there is at least one person that needs to be down here."

Quincey stood there for what seemed to be ten more minutes as the Choir sang. All of a sudden, everyone in the church started clapping and looking around. Just as Quincey thought, there *was* someone that needed to be down there. He looked over to where everyone's attention was focused and, as sad as it was to say, was shocked to see who it was. There were about fifteen people coming down the aisle and Terri led the way.

Chapter 18

Austin looked around the church and observed how everyone was standing up and clapping as the people went down to the alter for salvation. He made sure to blend in by clapping along with them. He personally enjoyed the sermon his friend had just given but he didn't quite get into the Christianity thing anymore. It was all good when he was a child, but in his mind he aligned it with still believing in the Easter Bunny or the Tooth Fairy. Those were beliefs that just didn't work when you became an adult.

Even more than that, he couldn't believe that of all people Terri was going down front to rededicate her life. He wasn't knocking her for trying to better herself, but with all the dirt she was doing he was surprised she didn't burst into flames when she stepped in the church. Of course he knew that he was living foul, but at least he wasn't cheating on his spouse.

Austin was so deep in thought that he nearly leaped out of his skin when he felt his cell phone vibrating in his inner jacket pocket. He hesitated before taking the phone out. He felt a bad vibe come over him all of a sudden and believed it was an indication of who was on the other end of the call. He looked down and the ID read "Marty" and he shuttered at the thought of answering it. He quickly put it back in his pocket. He was quickly coming to the realization that meeting Monica may be the biggest mistake he'd ever made.

He looked up and Julie was staring him right in the face. The last time he had noticed anything, she was standing and clapping along with everyone else. Austin guessed that even a move of the spirit was not enough to keep her from noticing he had received a phone call.

"Who was that?" Julie asked only moving her lips as to not make any sound.

Austin really didn't want to talk about it because if he could read her lips then there was some nosey person in the church that could read them too. The last thing he needed at that moment was more people up in his business.

"Business," he inaudibly lied back.

Julie gave him a smirk like she didn't believe him and then turned back to face the front. He knew that it was an argument waiting to happen. No matter what he told her she wouldn't have believed him anyway.

After the ones that went down to be saved were ushered to the back, the service ended pretty quickly thereafter. Austin went up front to congratulate Quincey. Even though he wasn't ready to get back into church at that moment, he was still proud of his friend for what he'd done.

He waited around for about fifteen minutes and grew impatient. "I'll just call him later," he said to himself as he walked off. He just couldn't find the time to talk to Quincey because so many *church* women were gathered around him. One of the women caught Austin by surprise, though. Janet was one of the first ones to run up to him after the service.

Just about everyone wanted to stop Austin and talk on his way out to the car. He tried to talk to each and every one of them because he knew what was coming when he made it to Julie. She was sitting in the car waiting on him and he just knew a huge argument would come from the phone call that he received during service. He wished so desperately that she had more self confidence.

When he made it to the car they hadn't made it out of the church parking lot when Julie started.

"So who was it, Austin?" Julie asked rolling her neck with her arms folded across her chest. Austin *had* thought she was cute in her peach dress, but that opinion was quickly changing with every minute she stared at him with a frown on her face.

"I told you, babe, it was business."

"Who does business on Sunday? You must think I'm stupid."

"I'm not calling you stupid. I'm just saying that it was nothing you need to worry about."

Julie looked at him like he had said something she had never heard before. "Anything concerning *our* relationship is something *I* need to worry about."

"What does *me* getting a phone call in church have to do with *our* relationship?"

"It's not the phone call that bothered me, Austin. It's the look you had on your face when you saw who it was. You used to have that same suspicious look the last time you had something going on."

Austin reflected on the exact moment that he had gotten the call. He knew that inside he felt an extreme sense of uneasiness, but he could only imagine how that must have translated on his face.

"Why do you always take it there? You know about the two other women I was with and I promised that I wouldn't cheat again. Since you believe so much in what you're taught in church, then where is my forgiveness?" Austin said with the irritation growing in his voice.

"I *know* you're not trying to throw church in my face. I had to drag you to church today and it was *your* friend's first sermon today."

"It's no secret that I don't particularly like going to church, even to hear Quincey preach. He would've been okay if I had missed."

"That's what I'm talking about Austin. You only think of yourself and never how your actions will affect the people around you."

"Look, Jules, I'm sorry. I don't have another woman. I promise you that it was just a business call. You're the only woman in my life," Austin reasoned.

Technically, he felt that he was telling the truth. Julie *was* the only woman that he was involved with at that moment. Austin had made a vow to himself. When Monica told him she planned to keep the baby, he promised himself that he would never cheat on Julie again. The difference in this vow and the one that he had made to her before was that this time he wasn't just saying it to get her to stay with him. He made this promise to himself and he was intent on keeping it. As a matter of fact, he became set on getting more serious about marrying Julie and actually setting a date for the wedding.

Austin stroked the side of Julie's face and she moved her head into the motion as if she enjoyed his touch. He looked at her with such passion in his eyes that it was as if he was seeing her for the first time all over again.

"The truth is, Babe, I love you and I'm very attracted to you. There's no other woman I would rather be with," Austin said in sincerity.

"Then, why don't you act like it?"

"I promise you from here going forward, I'm really gonna try," Austin said.

The women he cheated with all had one thing in common: they were all beautiful, but that's all they had. Julie had a good heart and that's what made her so attractive to him. It was just too bad that he didn't know how to stop breaking it.

They went through their normal Sunday routine that day. Austin took her out to a nice restaurant. The arguing they had done was a thing of the past and as far as he knew, it was over for at least that day.

When he pulled in to his driveway, the first thing he noticed was the silver BMW parked across the street. He couldn't see inside because of the dark tint on the windows, but he knew immediately that it was Monica's car. He hadn't known before that moment that Monica knew where he lived.

Austin hurried Julie from the car and rushed her to the front door.

"What's wrong, babe?" Julie asked with a perturbed look on her face. "Is everything okay?"

"Yeah I'm fine. I think the cheesecake I ate for dessert is coming back to haunt me. I need to get to a restroom fast," Austin lied. His stomach was in an uproar, but it was more from butterflies than cheesecake.

He fumbled nervously with the lock on the front door and even dropped the keys when he missed the keyhole completely. The cell phone is his front pocket started vibrating and he knew exactly who it was.

"I'll be back, Jules," he yelled out as he ran upstairs to the master bathroom. When he made it in, he shut the door and turned on the water for background noise.

"What?" Austin snapped when he flipped open his phone to answer it.

"I see you're out playing the family man today with your chubby little girlfriend," Monica said in a smart tone. "I still don't see what you could possibly see in her."

"Well, I can't possibly see what I saw in you," Austin said not trying to hide his disdain. "And how did you know where I live? I never told you that."

"I told you before. I know everything there is to know about you. It wasn't hard to find out what I needed to know."

There was a long pause. Austin wanted to say so much but couldn't string the right words together. He couldn't believe he was dumb enough to let himself get into this kind of a situation. Monica was the type of woman his mother always warned him about. She was the kind of woman that was always looking for a man with money that couldn't control his manhood.

"Well then I guess I'll get straight to the point, since obviously you don't know what to say," Monica said jolting him from his thoughts. "I don't like when I'm ignored, especially by the father of my unborn child. There could've been something wrong with the baby."

"Well, is there?"

"No, but that's not the point. What I'm trying to get you to see is that ignoring me may be a bad decision for you."

"First of all don't threaten me. Secondly I wasn't ignoring you. You knew that I would be in church today. I told you that this morning before I left."

"Yeah, well, I needed to talk to you because that money that you supposedly transferred into my account is not reflecting yet and I have some things I need to get."

"You know I put it in there. I gave you the receipt and everything. You should be happy that I'm even doing this because a thousand dollars a week is too much money for a child that I'm not sure is mine, anyway."

"You don't want to go there, playa. Trust me. I can ruin everything you have at the drop of a hat. You must've forgotten."

"Whatever. If you called me just to argue, I have much better things to do."

"Don't worry. I don't want to speak to you no more than I have to. This is all about business. I think we need to start exchanging cash because the money is not making it into my account fast enough and I need the money each week before the weekend begins."

"Well, I'm not giving you that money so you can support your shopping habit. I'm giving it to you so you can put it up for the baby. That was the agreement."

"I wonder who put you in charge of this situation. The last time I checked I was in the position of power. Maybe I should just ring the doorbell and ask Julie what she thinks about it."

Austin walked over and looked out the bathroom window and his mouth dropped open in pure horror. Monica was standing at his front door stretching her hand out like she was about to ring the doorbell.

"Are you crazy?" he yelled into the phone. What are you doing?"

"I'm letting you know that I'm serious and my rules will be followed. This is not a joke to me, Austin. You treated me like some whore off the street and wanted to drop me when you found out I was pregnant. So for that, you have to dance to my tune or I can take away everything you hold dear in your life."

Austin didn't respond because he couldn't bring himself to say anything. He had wanted to argue but seeing Monica that close to exposing his dirt to Julie took the fight right out of him.

"So have I made myself clear?" he heard Monica say on the other end of the phone. "I need the money in cash from now on and as a matter of fact meet me at my house in one hour. I need some extra cash for these shoes I've been dying to get from the mall."

"Okay," was all Austin could muster.

He felt like a fool. He hated to admit it but that day at the coffee shop, Mark was completely right. He should never have gone after Monica. As they say, however, hindsight is twenty-twenty and now his life was being taken away from him. He didn't know how he could get out of this situation. If he had not been so ashamed, right then would have been a good time to pray.

Chapter 19

Terri rolled over and groggily wiped sweat from her brow. The old box fan that sat in the window rattled as it tried to cool the room with no avail. Terri had hardly slept a wink the night before. It was more from nervousness than the room being hot. She was very excited about her new found relationship with God but on the other hand she felt incomprehensible guilt about her fling with Cedric.

It had been a month since she had rededicated her life to Christ. She was making a valiant effort to be more patient with her husband and at least trying to stick by his side. She and Mark were now attending counseling once a week and trying to get their relationship back on track.

Terri now even found more time to be with her children. She had forgotten how fulfilling it was to be around them. They brought more joy to her life than anything else she was involved in at that time.

Cedric had been calling her nearly every day since the night they were intimate and she had deliberately been avoiding him. He had even come by her job one day, but she had one of her co-workers tell him she was busy helping a patient. She was just trying to buy time. She realized, however, that if she didn't deal with her past it would one day come back to haunt her.

Mark had taken the girls out to get ice cream so Terri was home alone. She decided that it was overdue for her to see Cedric and break off the relationship. She had called him and asked him to meet her at a local bookstore around the corner from his home. It was a little inconvenient for her to drive all the way across town but it allowed them to meet in a quiet but public place to talk. She didn't know how Cedric would react when she told him that she was actually married and the relationship that he wanted so badly for them was never going to happen. He was a stumbling block on her path to reconciliation that had to be dealt with.

When she walked into the bookstore she saw Cedric sitting at one of the tables in the corner sipping from a white coffee mug. When he saw her walking towards him he stood with a smile on his face. He looked as good as she remembered, but somehow there was something about him that she hadn't noticed before. She couldn't put her finger on it, but he seemed different and she wasn't as attracted to him as before.

"Hi," Terri said with a smile that only touched her lips. She gave him a brief hug and Cedric tried to lean in for a kiss, but Terri turned her head so that his lips planted firmly on her cheek.

"Long time, no see," Cedric said when they were seated. He looked her over intently. "I was starting to think you were avoiding me."

She was waiting for him to laugh or at least smile, but neither came. Cedric's tone let her in on everything. His remark was not to be taken as a joke. He was being accusatory.

"I've been so busy at work that I haven't had time for much of anything personally. I completely lost track of the days," she said and laughed nervously.

"Yeah…Well, all that's beside the point. I'm just happy you decided to see me today. I haven't been able to think about anything else since you were last at my house."

"Well, that's kinda why I called and asked you to meet me today. I really need to come clean with you about a few things."

"Well, I hope that look on your face is no indication of what you have to say. If it is, then I'm in trouble," Cedric said sounding almost sarcastic. Terri hadn't realized how she must have been looking. She was so nervous about what the outcome might be when she told him her secret that she wasn't paying much attention to anything else.

"Okay…so what is it?"

"A'ight. There's no other way to put it so I'll just come out with it," Terri said and then paused briefly. She had never had to break up with anyone. Mark was her first and only real boyfriend, so she didn't have any experience in that area. She decided to just wing it and hope for the best.

"I've been keeping a secret from you since that day we met outside my job."

She waited for a response but when he didn't say anything she reluctantly continued. "Cedric, I'm married."

Cedric didn't say anything. He just stared down at his cup of coffee.

"I have been married for ten years to the same man that I dated when I was in high school. We also have two beautiful children."

Cedric still didn't respond. She thought she saw some sort of emotion on his face, but she couldn't tell what it was as his head was still down. It seemed as if he was concentrating more on the coffee than he was on her.

"Cedric, say something," Terri pleaded with him. The longer they sat silent the worse she felt. She really believed she was hurting a really great guy. Under ordinary circumstances they probably would have been great together.

"What do you want me to say? Would you like to hear that I was a fool? Or maybe you'd like to hear that everything you did will be okay."

"No, I don't *want* you to say anything specific. I just want you to say something so I don't feel like such a jerk."

"Well, I don't think there's anything I can say to do that because that's exactly what you're being," Cedric said now visibly upset.

"I deserved that."

"You're right. You *did* deserve that and whatever else you get."

"I know you're upset," Terri said sounding genuinely concerned. "I was having all kinds of problems at home and I was going through a very rough time in my life. You helped me through that."

"What? Is that supposed to make me feel better about this situation? The fact that you lied isn't so easy to overlook. Even if I could look past all that, I don't understand why you slept with me? There must have been something about me you liked other than me just being a shoulder to cry on."

"I never meant for it to go that far. I went into our relationship because you were so easy to talk to, but found myself getting more and more involved. Under different circumstances you would be a great man to be with."

"Don't give me that crap!" Cedric yelled. The bookstore was so quiet that his voice echoed off the high ceilings. People were now staring at them. Terri felt so embarrassed.

"You don't have to yell. I already apologized about what happened."

"That's not good enough," Cedric said lower but still in a loud voice.

"I don't know what else I can do. The one thing I'm sure of is this relationship has to end. I'm just doing what's best for my family."

She found herself no longer feeling sorry for him. She knew that Cedric was the victim, but she was not about to let some man yell at her in front of all those people.

The people next to her were looking at them like they were watching a talk show. She thought they would break out a bucket of popcorn at any moment. "What are ya'll looking at?" Terri yelled at them. They turned away but she knew they were still listening to every word.

"Well, sorry if I don't care more about your family than my own well being," Cedric said with a look of disgust on his face.

"Looks like I was wrong about you. You're a butt-hole like every other man."

Coming in, she didn't know how he would react. Never in a million years did she imagine him causing a scene like that because she thought people with money acted more distinguished.

"You ain't seen nothing yet," Cedric said and then jumped up turning over the table with a swipe of his arm. The people next to them jumped up and let out a low squeal. He started quickly walking toward the door. "You won't get rid of me that easy," he yelled as he exited the bookstore.

Terri was shocked. She heard the people around her murmuring and some of them were laughing silently. She felt a mixture of emotions as she tried to decipher the situation. She was so embarrassed that she wished she could just disappear. Then she felt angry that all these people were standing around gawking at her like she was some sort of side show attraction. Finally she felt an indescribable sense of fear of what Cedric had just said to her. She now knew what she saw in Cedric that she couldn't place earlier and what possibly made his wife run away with the children. The look was that of possession. She knew that Cedric believed that since they slept together, she now belonged to him. As with most men, she didn't think Cedric would give up anything that he believed he owned without a fight.

Chapter 20

Quincey walked out of his large walk-in closet and looked in the golden trimmed full length mirror as he finished tying his brown tie. He had plenty of suits but the black Armani one he had on was his favorite. He hurried with the finishing touches to his attire so that he could get his busy day started. He gathered that if he could get started early, he could make it back in enough time to spend the rest of the day with Kim. She had been hinting all week that she wanted to spend some time with him.

"Son, I have some important information to discuss with you," Pastor Lewis had said when he called Quincey the night before. "If you can, it would be great if you came to the church first thing in the morning."

"You know I can't refuse a chance to sit down with my Pastor," Quincey said.

Pastor Lewis didn't go into much detail but Quincey could tell that it was something important. He came to this conclusion because Pastor Lewis had requested to meet with him on a Saturday. One of the things Quincey had learned about Pastor Lewis was that he never did church business on the weekends unless it was important.

Quincey walked over and kissed Kim on her cheek. She opened her eyes and squinted. She then threw her hands up to shield her eyes from the light and smiled groggily.

"You leaving already, babe? Why don't you come back to bed for a little while?" Kim asked.

"I wish, but I have to meet Pastor Lewis at the church."

"I guess it's another day spent without you. Just don't forget that we're going out tonight.

Kim let out a sigh and turned over in the bed so that her back was to Quincey. He started to walk over to her and attempt to say something but decided against it. He knew that if he did, it would probably lead to an argument and he didn't feel much like arguing that morning.

When Quincey was in his car, he put his Bluetooth headset on and began the first thing that was on his agenda that day. He had a phone conference with APS' lawyers. They had been trying to settle with Mark out of court for the racial discrimination lawsuit that he had filed against them. The last thing a huge company wanted was to let a discrimination case go public.

He picked up the phone and dialed Phillip Blumenthal, the defense's leading attorney. Phillip was a hard nosed attorney that hated the idea of settling out of court but it was his client's wishes and he really didn't have any choice in the matter.

"Phillip Blumenthal's office," a young secretary said on the other end of the phone.

"This is Quincey Jackson. Mr. Blumenthal is expecting a phone call from me. I would appreciate it if you would put me through to him," Quincey said automatically switching into lawyer mode.

"No problem. I'll just have to place you on hold for a few moments."

As Quincey waited on hold he thought about the meeting that he had with Pastor Lewis. What could be so urgent that he needed to rush down to the church on a Saturday morning? He hoped that everything was okay. Pastor Lewis was like a father to him and Quincey couldn't bear the thought of anything happening to him.

"Counselor," he heard Phillip Blumenthal's nasal tone say over the earpiece. "I think I have some news that might be satisfying to you.

"That's good, because my client is becoming extremely impatient with all the red tape involved in this case."

"Well, he may not have much longer to wait. I think we can come to a settlement that would make everyone involved happy."

"That's music to my ears. What are we looking at?"

"Okay APS is willing to settle for seven hundred and fifty thousand dollars along with dropping the assault charges that are pending against your client."

"You're kidding me right?" Quincey laughed. "I'm not going to even call my client with such a bogus offer."

"Mr. Jackson, I think I should remind you that the accusation of racial discrimination is on the table but yet to be proved. Your client, however, *still* faces jail time for assaulting the two men in the office. That *is* one thing about this case that we know for sure. I think the money plus no criminal charge is more than enough to compensate."

Quincey took the argument from Phillip in stride. He knew that a big corporation would try and play hard ball. They always assumed that a person with no money would jump at the first offer made.

"I think that I should also remind *you* that while my client did commit a criminal act, the money that you would stand to lose when the judgment rules in favor of my client and from APS' customers pulling their business out due to them not wanting to be associated with a company found guilty of racial discrimination would be greater than any amount of money that my client would be seeking to settle out of court."

Phillip didn't say anything. Quincey could hear him tapping his fingers angrily against his desk. He knew that he had Phillip right where he wanted him and was not about to let up.

"So, counselor, I suggest you contact your client and have them reconsider their offer and then contact me when a real offer is ready to be made. Until then, have a great day, Mr. Blumenthal."

Quincey pressed the end call button with joy. He knew it wouldn't be long before APS finally broke and gave Mark some real money. He enjoyed having the upper hand in this case because it was long overdue for Mark to catch a break.

When Quincey pulled into the church parking lot he saw that Pastor Lewis had already arrived. It didn't even look as if Pastor Lewis' Cadillac had been driven. There was even dew settling on the hood of the car and Quincey wondered to himself how long the Pastor had been there.

After stepping out of the car, he entered the church nervously. It was odd being there on a Saturday morning. That day of the week was reserved for choir practice and even though he had been working out of his office in the church for a while, it still felt weird.

Quincey knocked lightly on the door to the Pastor's study.

"Come in," he heard Pastor Lewis' baritone voice say on the other side of the door.

Quincey entered the office and saw Pastor Lewis sitting behind his desk reading the bible. That was exactly what Quincey expected to see him doing.

"How's it going, Pastor?"

"Pretty good. Just waiting on you to get here. How's your morning been so far?"

"I can't complain, just taking care of a little business. What you reading?"

"Just reading the fourth chapter of Timothy and getting prepared for our meeting."

"Okay. Well, don't keep me in suspense. What's the urgent issue?"

Quincey still felt that nervous feeling in his stomach. He didn't know what to expect Pastor Lewis to say, but he hoped it wasn't anything bad.

"Well, you know that I've been working in the ministry for more that forty years now," Pastor Lewis began. "The fact of the matter is that as much as I'd like to think differently, I'm not getting any younger."

"You don't act as if you're a day over thirty," Quincey interjected.

"I appreciate the flattery but I won't lie to myself and pretend that I'm not getting on up in the years. With that being said, I've been seeking God about a good time to retire from the church. So-"

"You're thinking about leaving the church?" Quincey interrupted. He didn't mean to be rude but he couldn't imagine how the church would run without Pastor Lewis leading it.

"Yes, I've not only thought about it, but I've already reached a conclusion that gives my spirit peace."

"I couldn't imagine what could be peaceful about you stepping down. I don't know what we would do without you."

"I can do better than that. I'll tell you what you can do. The church *will* go on and God has shown me the direction in which he will be taking this church. It's going to move forward and become a mighty force for the kingdom of God. God has also placed it in my heart to ask you to be the leader."

"What?" Quincey asked. He didn't know how to respond. "I've only been preaching for a couple of months now. I don't think I'm ready for that type of responsibility."

"I think you're more than ready and I don't think that God would have placed it on my heart to ask you to do so without *Him* knowing that you're ready."

"I don't know, Pastor. That's a big decision. It would change my life as I know it."

"All I ask is that you consider it. If God confirms it with you and you decide to go forward with his calling then I wouldn't be stepping down as Pastor until the first of next year. That would give us plenty of time to get you up to speed with the day to day responsibility. It'll also give you time to get a little more experience under your belt."

Quincey sat in thought for a long moment. He didn't know how to answer. His first thought was to turn down the offer and get out of the office as fast as he could. Then after some deliberation, he decided that he at least owed it to God and to Pastor Lewis to think about it.

"I have no problem with that," Quincey finally said. "I'll definitely pray about it and speak with Kim. Whatever God has me do, that's what I'll do."

The rest of the meeting was small talk about things going on in the church. Quincey tried to pay attention to what was going on but he couldn't. His mind was flooded with thoughts of the offer Pastor Lewis had made him. He didn't know how Kim would react because she had told him not long ago that she didn't want to be married to a Pastor. All he could do was pray for the best.

Chapter 21

Kim sighed heavily as she sat in her car staring at herself in the make-up mirror that was underneath the sun visor. She dabbed smudges of runny mascara from either sides of her eyes with a balled up piece of tissue. The tears she cried were partly from nervousness and partly from joy. It was as if her inner self couldn't decide which emotion to display. She had been meaning to leave every minute since she had walked out of the Doctor's office but her limbs weren't getting the message from her brain. With just having received such life-changing news her body was in a temporary state of paralysis.

When she looked down and saw what time it was, she turned on the ignition with a hurry. She put the car in drive and sped from the parking lot. Kim was normally a speed law abiding citizen but that day she had almost totally forgotten about the dinner that she and Quincey had scheduled.

They had spent a lot of time together during the weeks leading up to his first sermon, but since then quality time was scarce. She was lucky to see him at all before she turned in for the night. That made it all the more important that she kept their dinner date that night, especially since she had such important news to discuss with him.

When she pulled into the driveway she saw that Quincey's car wasn't there so she figured he must have already left for the restaurant. "I'm running short on time," she thought aloud as she rushed into the house.

Once inside, she threw her purse onto the counter and then checked the answering machine. There were three messages recorded. One of them was from one of Quincey's law buddies. The second one was from Austin. She didn't really pay attention to either one of them.

She went ahead and started undressing while waiting for the third message to play.

The message quickly caught her undivided attention. It was from Janet. The very sound of her voice made Kim's blood boil.

"Quincey, I really need to talk to you," Janet said in her irritatingly high pitched voice. "It's important. Give me a call as soon as you get this. Oh, I hope you thought about what we talked about at the church a few weeks ago."

It took everything within Kim to not pick up the phone and dial Janet's number. *Why didn't Quincey tell me anything about Janet meeting him at the church?* She pondered angrily.

She found herself having to check her attitude. It was an important day for her and she was not about to let Janet spoil yet another one for her. Her mother always told her to make sure you wait until you have all the facts in front of you so that your reaction will be an educated one.

She went into the master bathroom and took a quick shower. When she was done there, she quickly put on the elegant black dress that Quincey loved to see her in. She couldn't blame him as it fit her petite yet curvaceous frame perfectly. She took one last look in the mirror to make sure everything was in place. She loved the way the dress stopped just short of her knees and showed off her gorgeous, ebony-toned legs. She spun around and admired the way it accented her curves without revealing too much. She had to be mindful of those things now because she was a minister's wife. She couldn't dress too scantily. She put on her final touches of make-up and ran out to the car. She sped away fast as she could to make up for the time she'd lost.

When Kim walked into the restaurant she saw Quincey waving to her from a table in the corner of the room. She walked over and kissed him on the cheek being careful not to smear her make-up. Quincey looked great as usual. She had heard that some people loose their attraction to their spouse after being married for so long. If there was anything she was certain of, it was that she was still as attracted to him as the day they met. He looked especially good in his black suit.

"How you doing, Babe?" Kim asked as she took her seat.

"I'm good. I started to think for a second you weren't going to make it." Quincey said laughing at his own joke.

"You know I wouldn't stand you up for anything in this world."

"I don't know. You *have* acting pretty strange lately," Quincey said still laughing.

"A'ight now. You may not find out what secrets Victoria has for you later."

"In that case, then let me change the subject. I'm really glad we got together. It's a treat to spend time with the most beautiful woman in the world."

"Well, I'm glad too because I have something important to talk to you about."

"I have something I need to discuss with you, as well. I don't know how you'll react to it, though. Depending on how you look at it, it could be really great news, but I can wait until I hear yours first."

When the waiter came over they went ahead and ordered their food and made small talk until their entrees arrived. Kim really enjoyed herself. It had become so hard for them to just find the time to enjoy each other's company. She wished very much that his news would be that he was cutting out some of his responsibilities so they can have more time together. She at least hoped that he would have a change once he heard her news.

While they talked she remembered how much she was in love with him. Sometimes it was easy to take a person for granted when you have them around everyday. There were so many women that would kill to have a man like Quincey, but she was fortunate enough to have him in her life.

"Okay, I can no longer take the suspense," Quincey said finishing the last bite of his steak. "What's the big news?"

"News?" Kim joked. "Why I don't know what you're talking about."

"Ha, Ha very funny. Now seriously, what's the big news?"

"Okay. Well, this morning when I knew you were gone, I got up and went to see my doctor. I bet you thought I went back to sleep when you left in such a hurry didn't you?"

Quincey didn't say anything he just smiled sheepishly.

"I've been feeling really sick in the mornings and the rest of the day I've been eating everything I can get my hands on."

"You've been eating a lot?" Quincey said obviously still amused and not catching any hints.

"Yes, I have," Kim said giving him an evil yet playful look. "So, anyway that's what I went to get checked out. I kinda had a feeling about what it could be but I wanted to confirm it with my doctor."

"I pretty much know I'm asking the obvious, but what did he say?"

"Well, he said to start getting that extra room ready for a nursery. We're pregnant!" Kim squealed.

The other couples in the restaurant looked at her smiling at the announcement that another life would be brought into the world. The older man and woman sitting right next to them started clapping and voicing their congratulations.

Quincey was just sitting there looking shocked. Kim really hadn't given much consideration to how he would react but she expected something more than what she was getting. She was trying real hard not to read too much into his actions.

"Aren't you going to say anything?" Kim demanded.

"How did this happen? I mean I know *how* it happened, but I thought you were on birth control."

"I was but obviously I ended up getting pregnant anyway. A pill is not what determines whether life is created or not. God is in control of that. *You* of all people should know that. What's the big deal, anyway? I thought you'd be a little bit happier than you are."

"It's not that. It's just that a lot of things are running into each other in my life lately. I'm starting to juggle too many things."

"Well, whose fault is that? Definitely not mine. I'm the one that's been begging you to drop some of the things you do."

"I may as well go ahead and tell you *my* news then. Any chance of you seeing it positively is out the window," Quincey said sounding defeated.

"What it is, *Quincey*?" Kim said angrily. She wasn't really feeling him at that moment. She was tired of him only thinking of how things in their life affected him.

"When I met with Pastor Lewis at the church today he hit me with a pretty big offer."

Kim let out a long sigh. "More responsibility, huh? What does he want you to do? Become the churches lawyer on call."

"Actually, no. He wants me to succeed him as Pastor of the church starting at the beginning of the year."

Kim was stunned. She was more than lenient when she didn't fuss too much about him becoming a minister, but she was not about to just stand by as he took more responsibility and took over the church.

"I know you told him no," she said not hiding the anger in her voice.

"Not exactly. I'm actually considering it. I figured you would see the upside to me becoming a pastor. It would mean that I would have to stop practicing law."

"Upside? What Upside? Like I told you before, my father was a Pastor and I know about the downside of it all too well. Pastors work just as much as lawyers and their hours are even more irregular."

Quincey didn't say anything he just sat there looking at her like he couldn't understand what she was saying. The more she looked at that blank stare, the angrier she got.

"Why would you even start the thinking process without talking to me about it first? That's a decision we need to make together."

"I don't know what you expect, Kim. I'm not gonna just write off the calling that's been placed on my life. It's my responsibility to follow it no matter where it leads. As my wife you have no choice but to stand by me."

Kim couldn't believe he was trying to pull rank. Where did he get off thinking that she had no choice in the matter? She did too have a choice, no matter how difficult of it was to make.

"Well, Quincey, I guess since as your wife I wouldn't have a choice in the matter. I would have to go along with anything you decide."

"I'm glad that you came to that conclusion. I didn't want to-"

"Wait. Don't get too far ahead of yourself," Kim said cutting him off. "There is another option that you didn't think of. Maybe I won't be your wife."

"So what are you saying? You'll leave me if I choose to take over as Pastor of the church?"

"Yeah, that's exactly what I'm saying. Quincey, I love you but I won't be plan b for you anymore," Kim said and then crossed her arms and gave Quincey a smug look to let him know that she was set on her decision.

"Well, Kim, I definitely don't want to loose you, but if you can't understand the way my life is headed then I guess you have to do what you have to do."

Kim had somehow thought that his reaction to her threat would go differently, so she was stunned when Quincey called her bluff. She had to prove that she had the guts to leave or he would think that he could walk all over her from now on. With that firm resignation, she got up and left the restaurant. She would show him that she didn't need him in her life because it wasn't as if he was completely there to begin with.

Chapter 22

Mark looked over at Terri as they sat in the waiting area of Pastor Lewis' office. She flipped through the pages of a home decorating magazine but he could tell her mind wasn't on what she was reading. She looked rather distracted and often just stared off into space like she was in deep thought. He gently touched her on her leg and she jumped as if she had forgotten he was there.

"You okay?" Mark asked her.

"I'm fine. Why do you ask?"

"You're staring a whole in the wall. I was just wondering what you were thinking on so heavily."

"Nothing in particular. I was just thinking about all the things I have to do when I leave here. I really wanted to do something with the girls tonight."

Mark didn't think Terri was being completely open with him about her thoughts but he didn't want to press the issue because he was afraid it would lead to an argument. He wanted to continue to make progress in the confines of their relationship. Since they had begun to undergo marital counseling, they were at least being cordial to one another and that was enough to give him hope.

"Mr. and Mrs. Baxter, Pastor Lewis is ready to see you in his office now," the receptionist said to them.

They entered into the office and Pastor Lewis was seated comfortably on the other side of his large mahogany desk. "I'm really happy you guys made it," he said.

"We wouldn't have missed it for the world. Its doing wonders for our marriage," Mark said excitedly.

"Most couples come a few times and just quit before we can get to the real meat of the issue. After only a few sessions you only scratch the surface. Today out goal is to dig a little deeper into the issues in your marriage and start the work towards resolving them.

"Well, I can't wait to get started," Mark said. He was really looking forward to getting his marriage back on track, so at the point he was game for anything.

"What about you, Mrs. Baxter?" Pastor Lewis asked startling Terri out of her dazed look.

Mark was really growing irritated with her not paying attention to what was going on. She acted as if she didn't know where they were.

"I am, Pastor. It was such a busy day today and I have so much to do. My mind is just a little preoccupied, that's all."

"Well, I wouldn't want to waist too much more of your time, so let's get started," Pastor Lewis said with a huge smile.

Mark couldn't tell if Pastor Lewis was referring to the way Terri was acting or simply being polite. Either way he was embarrassed that she could be so disrespectful.

"Communication is the number one breakdown in relationships. One thing we don't do well as men *and women* is communicate to each other what our feelings are," Pastor Lewis said as he motioned for Mark and Terri to sit in the two red leather chairs positioned on the other side of the desk. "So today your exercise is to express to your counterpart how they make you feel when they do certain things."

Mark didn't know what to think other than the exercise was going to open up a whole can of worms. One of the major issues he and Terri had was sharing and respecting each other's feelings. He had a feeling it was going to get real heated.

"In our exercise," Pastor Lewis continued. "I will name off different things that you both expressed as concerns in our individual counseling sessions and you will tell the other person how that makes you feel."

This brought a slight smile to Terri's face. Mark was already irritated and he couldn't understand what she found to be funny at that moment. It seemed as if she would enjoy that part of the counseling session.

"We'll start with you, Terri. You told me that you have a huge problem with Mark being out of work for so long. Tell him how that makes you feel."

Terri sat there thinking for a second like she really didn't know how to start. Mark was sure it was as hard for her to talk about this problem as it was for him to *hear* her talk about it.

"Well, I really don't know where to start."

"Just start with what you feel Mark *should* be doing," Pastor Lewis interjected.

"Well, I feel like a man is supposed to provide for his family. He's supposed to make sure his family is taken care of in every sense of the word. I've thought about it several times and I don't feel like I'm wrong for feeling that way."

"Terri, we're not here to say who's right or wrong. What we're here to do is find resolutions for these issues that work for you both," Pastor Lewis interjected.

"I understand that, Pastor. It's just that this situation is changing my perspectives on a lot of things. I've started to feel that I'm wrong for expecting for my husband to take care of me. It seems like more and more you see women in the workforce and men sitting at home. So it's starting to make me question some of my views."

"There's nothing wrong with you feeling like a man should provide for his family. That's what he's supposed to do. God put it in us to want to do that. When we're not fulfilling that role, we feel like we're less than a man," Pastor Lewis said. "What about you, Mark? How do you feel about this subject?"

"Pastor, I agree with everything you're saying. I enjoy being able to provide for my family. Nothing would make me happier. It seems like as hard as I've tried, I just cannot find a job. I'm at the point now that whenever she criticizes me, I just don't feel like trying anymore."

"Mark, I don't mean to criticize you," Terri interrupted. "It's just that I get so frustrated when I'm working so many hours and I get home and it looks like you've been lying around all day."

"I know, but most of the time I really have been looking for a job. One time I thought I really had one, but you know what happened with the APS thing. The only thing I can promise you is that I'll try harder in the future."

"That's good," Pastor Lewis said smiling from ear to ear. "Do you see how much better it is when you have a civil conversation? A lot can be accomplished that way."

"Mark, let's get your major issue on the table. It's a tough one to talk about sometimes, but we have to get it in the open to achieve a resolution. You have a problem with Terri refusing to be intimate with you. Why don't you tell her how you feel?"

Mark let out a loud sigh. He sat back in his chair and folded his arms across his chest. He struggled within himself to find the right words to say.

"The thing is that I really love you a lot. I would love to be able to express myself to you in that way and show you a physical expression of that love."

"Okay. Terri, do you have any response to that?" Pastor Lewis said.

"Mark, I really don't feel like it's just an expression of your love. I feel like it's more physical than emotional. I enjoy the physical aspect of it but I would much rather you show me your love by providing a decent living for me and the children."

"See. That's what I'm talking about. Why does it always have to go there?" Mark said now sitting on the edge of his seat plainly upset by Terri's last comment.

"I'm not trying to take it there. It's just that you having sex with me don't necessarily mean you love me. It just means that you have a need and I'm there to fulfill it."

"What we need to do is examine the different ways in which women and men view sex," Pastor Lewis interjected obviously realizing that the conversation was getting heated. "Men view it as being mostly physical. We see it as an outward expression of our love. Women, on the other hand, see it as emotional. To them it's an expression of how they feel on the inside. That's why a woman needs to feel that her other emotional needs are met in order for her to engage in a healthy sex life. Men really don't require any emotional maintenance to lead a healthy sex life. All they require is for the woman to be present and willing. It doesn't matter how she feels about it."

"What either side has to do is understand what motivates the other in this area. That's how you can come to a resolution. Mark, you need to be there for Terri more. Make her feel protected and loved. Terri, you need to let Mark know that you are still there on that physical level."

Both Mark and Terri sat back in their seats and intently listened to Pastor Lewis for the rest of the session. Pastor Lewis led them through some biblical examples of the principles that he had given them in the session. The time really flew for Mark. Before he knew it the session was over. It never seemed as if they had enough time and Mark wished that they could get more things resolved each time because he readily waited for the time when everything was back on track.

"Mark, if you have time, could you hang around for a few minutes longer? I have something to talk to you about," Pastor Lewis asked as Mark and Terri gathered their belongings.

"Sure," Mark said.

He then kissed Terri on the cheek and assured her that he would see her in just a little while when they both made it home. He watched her walk out and shut the door behind her before sitting down again.

"What's up, Pastor?"

"Mark, I know it's been hard since you lost your job. There was a time in my life when I had the same struggle. I didn't go without a job for that long, but I had to swallow my pride and allow the First Lady to take care of me financially while I searched for a job."

"What? I wouldn't think you would have ever been through something like this," Mark said surprised. Up until then he thought that he was the only one that had ever been through this situation.

"Yes, it's true. The main thing to remember is not to be prideful. The bible reminds us after all that pride goes before destruction."

"I've definitely heard that before," Mark said thinking of what Quincey had told him in the coffee shop so many weeks before.

"Anyway, that's why I wanted to talk to you. I know you've been struggling to find work. It just so happens that I have a position opening for an assistant. The position pays pretty handsomely and you would have the benefit of doing Kingdom work for the Lord."

Mark was so overwhelmed that he didn't know what to say. He had no intentions of getting a job when he came to the session that day. It was a huge blessing for the Pastor to offer him the position without him even applying for it.

"So what do you think?" Pastor Lewis asked flashing Mark a huge smile.

"It sounds great, but I don't know the first thing about being an assistant or working at the church for that matter."

"Don't worry about that. All you have to do is show up. You'll just be helping me with some things around the office and the best thing about it is I'll have all your responsibilities lined up just for you."

"I'll take it then. Thank you so much, Pastor. You don't know what this means to me. I feel so blessed."

"Don't thank me. Just be a blessing to some one else down the road. That's what blessings are about. We're blessed to bless others."

Mark left the office on cloud nine. He couldn't wait to get home and tell Terri because it would really make her day, no better yet, her year. After all the time he'd spent letting her down it would be good for once to deliver her some good news.

Chapter 23

Terri sang along with the radio on her way home from the church. She felt like she had made an incredible connection with Mark at the counseling session. She now understood why it was so important to him for them to be intimate and she also understood how she made him feel like less than a man when she talked down to him about not having a job. She promised herself that she would work on being more positive when she spoke to him.

She cranked the radio up a couple of notches when she heard *Looking for You* by Kirk Franklin come on the radio. It was one of her favorite songs and she found herself lost in it every time.

Her phone rang and she dreaded looking at the caller ID. In her gut she had a feeling about who was on the other end. She glanced at the small screen on the outside of her flip phone and recognized Cedric's number. She hit the ignore button and shuttered at the thought of him still calling her. She had made it clear to him on several occasions that it was over, but he just didn't seem to get the picture. She regretted the one time they slept together with all her heart. If she could pick one thing in her life to change, that would be it.

Terri prayed within her heart that this whole thing would just go away, but she knew it wouldn't. She decided that the best thing for her to do would be to tell Mark about the whole ordeal and maybe she could work toward moving on with her life. She resolved that when he made it home, she would tell him everything and beg for his forgiveness.

Terri arrived home and started preparing dinner. She decided she would cook a steak with a fully loaded baked potato on the side, which were two of Mark's favorite dishes. She next went up stairs and pulled the tight fitting, white and gold dress out of the closet that Mark loved her in. She thought that doing all these things would soften the blow of what she was about to tell him.

As she was putting on her make-up, she heard the front door open and immediately started feeling sick to the stomach. As terrible as she had been treating Mark over the past few weeks, she regretted doing anything that would destroy him. As far as she knew, he was completely faithful to her.

"Babe," she heard Mark yelling from the living room.

"I'll be out in a minute," Terri yelled back. She then put on her finishing touches of make-up and then slipped on the dress. She stopped to look in the mirror so that she could make some final alterations if necessary. The dress was perfect so she decided that there were no changes needed.

When she entered the living room, Mark's eyes roamed her from head to toe. He looked like he wanted to say something, but forgot and searched for the words that had slipped away.

"You like?" Terri asked trying not to reveal anything through nervousness.

"Of course I do," Mark said. "You look amazing."

"Thanks," Terri said with a smile.

"What's the occasion?"

"We just have some important things to talk about."

The closer it got to the time for her to reveal her secrets the worse Terri felt. *How could I have been so stupid?* She thought. *I had a good man all along, but was too blinded by my circumstances to realize it. Now I might lose him forever.*

"Okay, that's great because I have some things to tell you as well."

"Let's not talk about them now. We'll talk more about this after dinner."

"What....dinner too?" Mark said excitedly. It must be my birthday."

"No, silly, it's not your birthday. I just wanted to do something special for you. Is that okay?"

"It's more than okay. It's perfect."

She then walked past Mark into the dining room. He stood still and watched her pass. As she walked by he playfully smacked her on the butt and it made her feel good that he still looked at her the same as he did when they were in high school.

Over dinner they just made small talk ranging from the kids to Mark's friends. Terri remained as attentive as she could, but she couldn't help thinking over and over that in just a few moments she would be breaking his heart.

"So, what do you have to talk to me about that deserves all this special attention?" Mark asked when they had finished eating.

"Why don't you go first?" Terri said stalling for time.

"Well, my news is that I have a job!" Mark exclaimed.

"What? When did this happen?" Terri asked jumping out of her seat. She was so excited. This meant that she could start working regular hours and cut out some of her overtime.

"After you left the church, Pastor Lewis offered it to me. I'll be working as an assistant at the church," Mark said. He then recounted the conversation that he had with Pastor Lewis and filled Terri in on all the details.

"So what do you have to tell me?" Mark asked as Terri took a seat next to him. She had almost forgotten that she needed to tell him about her affair with Cedric. She had gotten so caught up in the fact that Mark had a job after months without one that nothing else mattered at that moment.

"You know what, I can't even remember," Terri lied. "I'm just so exited about your big news that I completely forgot what I was gonna say."

"Well, it's okay. If you remember later you can tell me then. It doesn't have to be over dinner."

Terri then leaned in and kissed Mark passionately. It felt good to place her lips on his. She couldn't remember the last time that they had an exchange like that.

"Come with me," Terri said and took him by the hand. Mark didn't put up a fight. He just followed her like a little puppy following his master.

Terri led him to the bedroom and made love to her husband for the first time in nine months. She had forgotten what it was like for intimacy to be in their marriage and at that very moment she felt more in love with Mark than she had in a long time.

The next day, Terri got up an hour early because she had to be at work earlier than normal. She got up and took a quick shower and threw on her work scrubs. She kissed Mark on the cheek as he lie in bed sleeping deeply. She felt an increased closeness to him after the night before. It seemed like their marriage was headed in the right direction.

She then peeked in on Steph and Jess. They were both sound asleep. She walked in their room and tucked both of them in again. She was extra careful not to wake either of them because she didn't want to have to explain to them why she had to go to work that morning, especially to Jessica. She was the youngest and still thought that her mother and father should both be home everyday.

She went ahead and got into the van and while she sat there waiting for it to warm up, she checked her phone for missed calls and messages. She realized that the phone had been left on vibrate throughout the night so she didn't hear any of the calls come through.

No one from the hospital had called her like they normally do, but she did have some other missed calls. She had fifteen missed calls and fifteen messages. They were *all* from Cedric. Terri immediately felt that sense of fear overtake her again. Cedric was really having a problem letting her go. She almost didn't listen to the messages because there was nothing else for them to talk about, but she quickly decided to listen to a few so she could know what her next move should be.

She opened the phone and dialed her voicemail number and entered her password when prompted to do so.

You have fifteen new messages. Message one is from: Cedric. It was received yesterday at 9:15 p.m., the electronically programmed voice counted off to her.

"Terri this is Cedric. I guess you know that because you're ignoring my calls and I don't appreciate that. Anyway, you *need* to call me back as soon as you get this message. Bye."

The next message is from: Cedric. It was received yesterday at 9:19 p.m. "Look I know you got that last message. It's in your best interest to call me back soon. Bye."

The next message is from: Cedric. It was received yesterday at 9:55 p.m. "Terri, okay, I've been trippin. I can't do anything but think about you ever since that night we spent together. If you think I'm gonna give up on our relationship just like that, you must be mistaken. We're gonna be together if it's the last thing I do."

The rest of the messages went on in that manner. Terri was terrified. She didn't really know what to do. One part of her mind thought that she should just meet with him. At least that way she could pacify him so he wouldn't wig out and do something stupid. The other part of her mind told her to just come clean with Mark and call the police to report Cedric for stalking her. She feared the second option more than the first because her marriage would surely end because of her infidelity.

She wasn't really sure about much of anything at that moment. One thing she did know for sure was that it would come down to her receiving help from a power greater than her own. So, the rest of the way to work she rode in silence and sent up a silent prayer to God. She prayed that, even though she didn't deserve it, he would give her strength to handle whatever situation would come her way.

Chapter 24

Quincey sat in his office at the church. His head hurt badly, so all he wanted to do was close his eyes and take a nap. He would have done just that, if it were not for the meeting that he had scheduled with some developers for the church. The church had experienced such growth in the preceding few months that new seats needed to be added. Pastor Lewis placed Quincey in charge of the development because of his background in law. He felt that it would be next to impossible to cheat a lawyer.

If it were not for the pastor asking him personally to do it, he would have turned the responsibility down. He really didn't feel up to the task and that was the way he had been feeling about everything as of late. It had been about two weeks since Kim left and went to live with her mother. He asked himself more times than he could count if it was all worth it. Why would he be meeting such adversity if he was doing the work that God meant for him to do?

He picked up the phone and decided to give her a call. He dialed her mother's number and waited patiently as it rang three times. Her mother picked up on the fourth.

"Hello," Mrs. Robertson said when she picked up the phone.

"Hi, mom, how are you doing today?" Quincey said.

"I'm blessed and that's enough for me," she said letting out a joyful laugh at the end. "What about you, baby? How have you been holding up?"

"I'm trying to hold it together. How's Kim? Is she doing okay?"

"She's doing fine. She's been having a lot of morning sickness the past couple of days. She's also been crying a lot. I've been doing what I can to keep her calm. I told her that stressing herself out like this isn't good for the baby."

"That's really why I was calling. I realize that a lot of this stress was brought on by me and I wanted to do something about it. You think I could speak with her?" Quincey asked but he really didn't think Kim would come to the phone. She had been rejecting his phone calls for the entire two weeks she'd been gone.

"Of course I don't mind. I'll see if I can get her to come to the phone. Hold on a second."

Quincey heard her mother set the phone down and walk away. He waited nervously and could hear some muffled talking in the background. He felt like he did when he was in high school and he called a girl for the first time. He wanted to talk to her so badly and hoped that she felt the same. He missed Kim desperately because they had not spent more than a night or two apart since they had gotten married. She was the love of his life and he felt empty without her. He just wished that she could see God's plan for his life.

After a few minutes of waiting, he heard someone pick up the phone. He sat up with hope that it was Kim.

"Sorry, she won't come to the phone," Ms. Robertson said on the other end.

"I don't understand it, mom. What did I do that was so bad?"

"Well to know that, you would have to know a little more about our family history."

"Why? What do you mean?" Quincey asked. He didn't really know how knowing the family history would affect his relationship now. Kim hadn't really elaborated on it except for the fact that her father was a pastor.

"As you know Kim's father was a pastor. Has she talked with you about any of that?"

"Yeah, she explained a little about that, but she didn't go into too much detail."

"Her father was a pastor for over twenty years. He was called to preach a few years before Kim was born. So his being a preacher was one of the first things she knew about him. On top of that, he came from a family of ministers. Most of the men in his family were preachers, including his father and brother."

"Okay," Quincey said. He didn't understand how that tied into his life, so he just continued listening patiently.

"When she was a child her father traveled a lot preaching all over the country. Of course to you or me there's nothing wrong with that, but Kim couldn't get used to him being gone so much. He missed a lot of events she had going on, like her dance recitals and some different things she had going on at school. There was one thing in particular. When she was about eleven, her school had a Father-Daughter Dance. Her father was out of town, but he promised her that he would be back in time. Kim was so exited. She got all dressed up. His plane ended up being delayed and he was not able to make it. Kim was so upset about it that she cried for days."

"That must have been rough on her, but I still don't understand why that makes her despise me becoming a Pastor."

"Well hold on, child, and let me finish," Ms. Robertson said. "One time it happened that I was out of town on business for some conference or another and Pastor Robertson stayed at home. I decided that I would come back a day early so that we could have some time together since we hadn't in a while. When I got home I noticed that his car was home but no one came to the door when I knocked. I twisted the door knob and it just so happened to be unlocked. When I walked into the bedroom, I caught him in the bed with one of the deacon's wives. Lord knows I beat that woman so ragged, I tried to send one of his children home to him that day."

"Wow," Quincey said holding back a laugh. He could not imagine Ms. Robertson fighting anyone because she didn't seem like she could harm a flea. "I would never have imagined that any of that went on. That explains a lot."

"That's not all. Not only did my husband cheat, but it came out later that most of the ministers in his family went through the same thing. As much as you try to hide this from your children they still find out. Kim eventually found out about that and all the other men in her family."

Quincey was shocked. Pastor Lewis had taught many times about generational curses. If there was ever any other example of it, it was this one. He really now understood where Kim was coming from but he just didn't know how he could help her through it.

"Did you leave him?" Quincey asked.

"No, honey. People splitting up wasn't something you heard a lot about back then. Besides, except for that time, the Pastor really was a great man and an even greater Pastor."

"Well, Mom, thanks for the information. It really goes a long way towards me understanding Kim's position on things. Tell Kim I love her and if she feels like talking to call me."

"I sure will, baby. You take care of yourself, you hear. Bye-bye," Ms. Robertson said and hung up the phone.

Quincey sat back and thought on the things he had just heard. He had to think of a way to let Kim know that he would never do that to her.

Quincey finished up with the meeting with the contractors and then locked up the church as he left. He had so many things on his mind that he could barely concentrate. He was just pulling out of the parking lot when his phone rang. He glanced at the ID and saw that it was Janet. He threw open his cell phone and answered it hoping that everything was okay.

"What happened?" He said when he put the phone to his ear.

"Is that how you answer the phone?"

"What do you want, Janet?" Quincey said trying to sound as contempt filled as possible. "Is Jeff okay?"

"Yeah, he's a'ight. I was just calling to check on *you*."

"What do you need to check on me for?"

"I heard what happened with you and Kim. I just wanted to make sure everything was okay and to see if you need *anything* from me?"

"I'm good. I don't need anything you're offering. You're a good mother to my kid and that's all I need you to do."

"Well, you don't have to get an attitude like that. I told you in the first place that pretty little wife you got don't appreciate everything you been doing for her. You wasting your time, Q."

Quincey let out a loud sigh. He didn't know what he had done to make Janet think there was even a small chance that they would get back together. He was married and on top of all that he was a minister. He had never once said anything out of the way to her. He guessed some women thought if they tried hard enough they could get anything they wanted.

"Look, Janet, I gotta go. I have a busy day ahead of me still and I really don't have time for this foolishness."

"I get the point, but when you get tired of playing around with her I'll be here waiting."

"Yeah, whatever," Quincey said and flipped the phone shut. It was excellent timing because as the conversation ended he pulled into his driveway.

Quincey walked in the house and just crashed on the couch. He was exhausted. He had so much on his mind with all the information he had been exposed to that day and then Janet was worrying him to death. She now hit on him just about every time they spoke. He had a lot of loose ends to tie up, but they would have to wait. It had been a long day and all he wanted to do was sleep.

Chapter 25

Austin sped through the paperwork left on his desk. He worked as quickly as possible but was sure not to make any mistakes. He was in a hurry because he had dinner and a movie planned with Julie later that evening and did not want to be late.

He depressed the intercom button on the speaker phone on his desk. "Have there been any important phone calls?" Austin asked after the long beep that let you know the speaker was engaged.

"There's been a couple, Mr. Barton," his secretary, Lynette, answered.

"Lynette, what did I tell you about that? Mr. Barton is my father and he's not here in this office," Austin said with a smile. "Call me Austin. Besides, I can't be that much older than you."

"Sorry about that, *Austin*," Lynette said through spurts of laughter on the other end. "Oh yeah, before I forget, this lady named Monica called you several times today. I know you told me earlier to hold all your calls, so I didn't send her through. She says it's really urgent, though, so you may want to get in contact with her as soon as possible."

"Thanks, Lynette," Austin said and ended the intercom session.

He just sat there at his desk and massaged his temples. His worst mistake continued to haunt him. He wished there was something he could do to just make it all go away. It was like waking up from a nightmare only to realize you were never sleep at all and the nightmare was reality. He had seen her number on his cell phone ID earlier but didn't pick up the phone. He began thinking that it may have been a mistake because whenever he ignored her, she came up with a way to make him pay.

Austin made a decision to just let it go. He didn't have time to worry about it anyway. He was really looking forward to the time that he and Julie would spend together. He was so busy looking at other women for his own selfish needs that he hadn't realized what he had at home. After his fling with Monica, he had found the saying, *Beauty's only skin deep,* to be completely true.

He finished signing the last few papers and briskly walked out of the office. He gave Lynette the rest of the day off and locked up before he left.

He drove as fast as he thought he could without getting a speeding ticket. While driving he admired the view of downtown that he had from the interstate. It was already dark and the city was lit up. A lot of people didn't know it, but Nashville was really a beautiful city at night. The lights from the buildings shone bright off the sky and the Cumberland River that ran right next to it. The Batman building towered brightly above the others. He thought that maybe after dinner, he and Julie would take a stroll down Broadway.

When he arrived at the restaurant he pulled right up front and hopped out. The valet driver eagerly took a seat underneath the steering wheel after him.

"Be sure you don't damage it, please," Austin told him."

"You don't have to worry about that, Mr. Barton," the valet driver said. Austin was really like a local celebrity. Most places he went, the people were familiar with him from his many appearances on local talk shows. He also did a lot of charity work. What better way was there to beat out some of the taxes rich people had to pay?

When he entered the restaurant, the host already knew who he was, so he walked Austin directly to his seat. The fact that Julie had not made it yet was great for him because he always believed that it made a woman feel important when you're early for a date with her.

His phone rang constantly and it was really starting to aggravate him. He knew who it was without even looking at it. No one else called him that much. He pulled the phone out of his jacket pocket and threw the flip open.

"I'm busy!" he yelled into the phone and slammed it shut. He laughed it off nervously when everyone started looking around to see what the commotion was.

After he had been waiting about twenty minutes, Julie finally showed up. She looked beautiful in her tan and black dress. It fit her perfectly. That was one of the things that he appreciated about her. She was a big woman that realized she couldn't wear those things that women half her size wore. She wore clothes that accented her beauty at her size.

When she made it to the table, he stood and kissed her on the lips. *She tastes just like strawberries*, Austin thought to himself as he pulled her chair out.

"I took the liberty of ordering you a drink. Do you mind?" Austin said once they both were seated.

"Of course not. I should hope by now you know my favorite drink," Julie said jokingly.

"I think I do, but we'll see when it gets here. We'll let it be a surprise until then."

"So what's the occasion? We haven't been out on a date like this in a while."

"Well, I just wanted to spend some quality time with you and also let you know what I'd decided about our wedding date. I know you said that you were willing to do it whenever and that you'll show up as long as I'm there."

Julie smiled from ear to ear. It was obvious to Austin that she loved him a lot and the more he looked at her the more he regretted what he had done with Monica and every other woman before her. He didn't know why he did the things he did. It was like he couldn't think straight when it came to beautiful women.

"And I still mean every word of it," Julie said. "I just need to know the date and time to be there."

"I've been thinking that we've put it off long enough. I know that you've wanted to marry me for such a long time and I continually come up with excuses, promising that we will do it one day. Well, I don't want to plan another time far in advance. I want to get married as soon as possible."

"Austin, don't play with me now. What are you saying?" Julie squealed.

"I'm saying that I want to get married two weeks from this weekend."

"Oh my God, I really didn't expect that. It sounds great to me." Julie said as she jumped up and hugged Austin around the neck. She placed a big kiss right on his lips. Austin thought that she was going to squeeze the life right out of him.

"I love you so much, baby. Are you sure this is what you want to do?" Julie asked once she had released him.

"Of course, it's what I want to do. I just regret it took me so long to come to that realization."

"This is so awesome. I have so much to plan. I really need to get started tonight."

The waitress brought over their meals and they settled in to enjoy the delicious looking food. Austin just mostly chewed and listened. He couldn't get a word in if he wanted to because Julie went on and on about all the things that she planned to do with the wedding. He didn't mind because for once he felt like he was making her happy.

When they finished dinner and left the restaurant, Austin decided that he would follow up on his previous thought and take Julie for a stroll down Broadway. The night was still young and she was so excited that there was no need to rush the night to an end.

They parked in one of the pay parking lots and Austin cursed because he hated to spend twenty dollars for parking when he would only be there for a couple of hours. He figured in the end it was probably worth it to have someone keep an eye on it, because if his Bentley was damaged he would probably have to hurt somebody.

As they walked, Austin couldn't help but notice all the beautiful women that were out that night. He had to make an extra effort to focus more on the conversation that he and Julie were having because that was the reason that he was in the situation he was in with Monica.

"Look at all the people in cowboy hats," He said to Julie laughing loudly.

"Shhh, you are too loud," Julie scolded him, but it didn't have any affect on Austin because she was laughing too.

"What? You know it's funny or you wouldn't be laughing. I guess that Nashville has been known for country music for so long that people don't realize there are actually other cultures here too."

As they rounded the corner on Second Avenue, Austin felt his cell phone vibrating against his hip. He had reached his limit on irritation for the night. His phone was ringing back to back and he decided something had to be done. He grabbed Julie by the hand and ducked into the closest restaurant.

"I'll be right back. I gotta get to a restroom bad," Austin said being careful not to let Julie think anything was up.

When he was safely in the bathroom, he pulled out his phone. Before he could flip it open, it rang again.

"What do you want, Monica?" He yelled into the phone when he put it to his ear.

"Where have you been? I've been trying to call you all night," Monica said.

"I've been out. What do you want?"

"Well, I need an advance on the money that you're going to give me next week?"

"Are you crazy? I'm not giving you any advance," Austin said getting angrier with every second that ticked by.

"First of all, you need to calm down. Secondly it's not like you weren't going to give me the money anyway."

"Monica, I just gave you a thousand dollars yesterday. I'm not about to give you another cent today. You're taking this too far."

"Was I taking it too far when you were laying on top of me and helping me conceive this baby?"

"You know what, Monica, I'm sick of this. I'm not gonna allow you to blackmail me anymore. If you want some money out of me, then come and see me when the baby is born and we get a DNA test."

"Wait..."

"No. You wait," Austin said cutting her off. "I'm sick of you and I regret the day we ever met. This is the last time we'll talk until that baby is born. So, don't you call me anymore, you understand?"

"I see how it is," Monica said in an even tone. Austin couldn't make out any emotion in her voice. He really didn't know how to respond, so he didn't.

"You'll be sorry that you ever had this conversation with me, but by then it will be too late. I hope you're satisfied with your decision," Monica said and then hung up the phone.

Austin finished up in the bathroom and went back out to Julie. He grabbed her by the hand and they continued their late night walk downtown. Austin felt a sense of freedom. With that freedom, however, was an underlying feeling of dread. A woman that could come to his house and attempt to confront his fiancé was capable of doing anything. He almost expected for her to jump out from around every corner. Luckily, that night she didn't but with the threat she had made earlier, who knew what the future held?

Chapter 26

"How you doing, girl?" Terri said to Shannon, her best friend, as she went around the front desk to log in her time. She was in a really good mood that day, so she wore her smile like a piece of clothing.

"I'm good. Seems like you're doing a'ight with that big cheesy smile on your face," Shannon said placing a hand on her hip.

"I'm okay."

"Looks like better than okay to me. It's been a while since I've seen you in a mood like this. So, what's going on?"

"Now, I'm not one to brag about the things that are going on in my life, but everything has been real good at home lately."

"That's good, girl. So you and Mark are working it out, huh?"

"Yeah, it's like ever since he got his new job, we've been doing better than ever."

Just then a loud beep came through on the intercom at the desk. They looked down and saw that it was coming from room 215.

"Girl, its Mr. Smith again," Shannon said laughing.

"What are you laughing at? Go on down there and see what he wants."

"I'm not going. It seems like I've been in his room ten thousand times already this morning."

"Man," Terri groaned. "What could it be?"

"Something probably got in his eye. You know how he is. He calls us in his room if he feels and unexpected breeze."

"I guess I could get it this time," Terri said and dreadfully walked down to his room.

When she was in his room, she cut the light on and everything seemed normal. "Is there anything wrong, Mr. Smith?"

"Yes. This TV doesn't get comedy central. I need to watch my favorite show tonight," Mr. Smith answered angrily."

"I'm sorry. We don't get that channel in the hospital. Maybe you could call and have someone tape it for you. That way you can watch it when you go home."

"There is no telling when I'm going home and I've been waiting a long time to see this episode."

"I'm really sorry you have to miss it, but there's really nothing else we can do to resolve it for you. You probably won't be in here more than a couple more days. If you have someone tape it, you'll be able to watch sooner than you think." She didn't really know when he was going home, but she prayed it was soon.

She stayed in with Mr. Smith for thirty more minutes trying to explain the issue to him. When she finally pried herself away from his complaining she all but ran back to the front counter.

"What took you so long?" Shannon laughed.

Terri didn't even answer. She just shot Shannon a nasty look to let her know she didn't find anything funny.

"Oh, yeah…That fine man sitting over there has been waiting on you since about the time you went into Mr. Smith's room. I tried to help him, but he wanted to see you."

"What man -," Terri asked freezing mid-sentence when she looked around the corner. When she saw that Cedric was sitting there reading a magazine, her heart began to race. *What is he doing here?* She thought terrified. She hadn't heard from him in a while because after the night that he left all those crazy messages, she had changed her phone number.

"What's wrong? Why you looking like that?" Shannon asked obviously seeing the look of terror that gripped Terri's face.

"It's a long story. I'll have to tell you later."

"Do you want me to call security?"

"No," Terri laughed nervously. It's not that serious. He just wasn't who I expected to see."

Terri then hesitantly walked out to the waiting area. When she walked in, Cedric looked up and smiled at her. Somehow that same smile that she had thought was attractive before now seemed sinister.

"How've you been, Terri?" Cedric said as he stood to greet her.

"What do you want? Why are you at my job?" Terri said looking around to make sure no one was listening.

"Well what do you suppose I do? It seems as if you've changed your phone number and I didn't get the memo about the change."

"Somehow, I thought you were smart enough to get the picture. I didn't want you to have the number. I don't want anything to do with you," Terri said hoping her words carried the fire that she intended.

"Well, I thought you got the picture. You are not going to be done with me until I say you are. I guess I have to start doing some things to make you believe that. Maybe I've been too nice and you're mistaking my kindness for weakness."

Terri tried to read the look on his face but she couldn't. He said every word with a blank look on his face as if he wasn't all there. Those words added with the expression sent chills up her spine.

"Look, I don't have time to keep playing these games. If you ever come by my job again, I'll call the police and have you arrested on the spot," Terri said hoping that threatening him with the police would scare him off.

"You'll call the police and what? Let everyone in on how loose you are by sending your boyfriend to jail."

"Don't you talk to me like that," Terri shouted and then had to take a look around again. "Also, you're not my boyfriend. I don't even like you."

"Oh, it's funny how things change. You weren't saying that when you were in my bed, now were you?"

"I know and I've regretted that moment every day since. I should have known you were too good to be true."

"Okay I'm sorry," Cedric said sounding pitiful. "It's just that I've fallen in love with you and I can't stand the thought of being without you.

"You can't love me. I already belong to someone else. I already told you that I have a family."

"If you cared so much about them, then you wouldn't have been out searching for something when you found me."

Terri let out a loud sigh. It escaped her before she knew it. Cedric was really getting on her nerves. They had only been together once and he acted as if they had a lifelong relationship.

"Cedric, I don't want to be with you and that's it. I trust you know how to get out the same way you came in." she said pointedly and walked off.

"That's not it," Cedric yelled. "It's not over. I swear it's not over."

Terri didn't turn around. She was so tired of dealing with his foolishness that she was ready for what ever came along. She decided that if it was the last thing she did, she would come clean with Mark. At least then she could handle this stalking situation the way it should be. She was working the overnight shift that night so she didn't want to call and wake him from his sleep. She decided that she would tell him as soon as she made it home the next morning.

Chapter 27

"What's up, Q? How've you been?" Mark said as he met Quincey on the front porch of his house. Quincey was sitting on his front step waiting when Mark pulled his car into the driveway.

"I've been good, man, considering."

"I feel you. Have you talked to Kim at all since she left?"

"No. She's still avoiding my calls. I'm tempted to just show up over there. She would have to talk to me then."

"I don't know man. That may not be such a good idea. You know how women are. Multiply that feeling by ten and you'll get how they are when they're pregnant," Mark said half jokingly.

Quincey gave him half of a smile. "I know what you mean. I really don't even know what's really wrong with her. I just wish she would talk to me."

"What were you doing outside?" Mark asked trying to change the conversation. It was growing quite uncomfortable for him.

"Getting some air and waiting on you."

"Well, I'm here now," Mark said while play punching Quincey in the shoulder. "No point in moping around. It's time to get our work out on."

They had made plans earlier in the week to meet Austin at the gym and get a work out in. Mark was looking forward to it because he hadn't been since he and Terri had been married. He figured with so many good things happening in his life, he needed to get his body back in great physical shape.

"You ready?"

"Yeah, man. It's been a long time since I lifted any weights."

"I know we been trying to get you in the gym for the longest time. I started to think you were allergic," Quincey laughed.

"Maybe not allergic, but a real strong intolerance for it," Mark said while joining in on the laughter. "I've been promising myself that I was gonna get back in there tomorrow for about two years."

"Well, it seems like tomorrow never came. Anyway now is a good a time as any to get back in there."

They got into Quincey's car and drove over to the local gym. Austin was already there. Mark hadn't spoken to him since the day they got into an argument before the football game. That sort of thing was typical of their relationship. Even though they were best friends, they seemed to be at odds with each other quite often.

When they had gotten out of the car, Austin came over to join them. He had on his workout clothes already. "What's up, ya'll?" He said and then slapped Quincey five on his outstretched hand.

"I'm surprised you beat me here," Quincey joked.

"You know I'm serious about my gym time. What's up, Mark?" Austin said

"Nothing, man. I'm just ready to get in this gym and get my workout on."

"Look, man. I just wanted to apologize for that day at Q's house. I should learn to keep my big mouth shut."

"I'm glad you finally realized what we've been trying to tell you all this time," Mark said with a smile.

"Whatever man," Austin said and gave Mark a playful shove. "That's about as good of an apology as you're gonna get, so take it or leave it."

"Nuff said. It was my fault too. I need to work on keeping my temper under control."

"Besides, You know we been friends too long for us to stop talking over something that stupid," Austin said.

"That's true and if we stop kicking it, who would stay on your back about all those women."

Quincey burst out with a loud laugh. "That's true, Austin. I know you been with a lot of women, but imagine if your conscience over here wasn't on your back," He said putting an arm around Mark. "You would've been with every woman in Nashville by now."

"Well, ya'll don't have to worry about that any more," Austin said. Me and Julie are getting married in two weeks."

Mark couldn't believe it. He didn't think that Austin would ever go through with it. "Congratulations," He said and gave Austin a congratulatory hug.

"That's good to hear," Quincey added.

"I was gonna ask both of you guys to be my best men, but since I can't seem to keep it in my pants, maybe I'll ask someone else."

"Whatever, you know we'll be there and it's nothing you can do to stop us," Quincey laughed.

When they got into the gym, Mark and Quincey went into the locker room to put on their gym clothes. Austin went ahead and started warming up for his workout.

Mark hadn't worked out in a while so the only clothes he had to put on were just an old t-shirt and sweats he had lying around the house. He felt embarrassed about them at first, but when Quincey didn't say anything about it, the feeling passed.

Once back out on the floor they joined Austin on the bench press machine. Mark took a look around at the other men that were working out. The guy right next to them seemed as if he had been lifting for years. He had muscles on top of muscles.

"Man, check homeboy over there out. It looks like he has every weight in the building on his bar," Mark said.

"Oh, man, that's Rueben. He was a member here before I was. He's a professional bodybuilder, so he's in here for hours everyday," Austin said and walked over to Rueben and slapped him five.

"It seems like I need to get on his program," Mark said while sliding under the bench press bar.

"Man, you don't need to get that big. Most women say that they just want a man that's lean and cut. They think someone that big is threatening," Quincey said now standing over Mark to spot him.

Mark and Quincey alternated doing reps. It made Mark feel good to get a workout in. He had let himself go in recent years and had gained about seventy-five pounds since he graduated high school and was looking forward to working on a new him.

He looked around for Austin and saw him still talking to Rueben. He wondered what could be taking him so long. He wanted him to hurry back over so there would be a third person in the rotation as to give him a longer rest period between sets.

When Austin finally came back over, he had a disturbed look on his face. Mark wasn't sure what he had talked to Rueben about, but judging from his expression it wasn't good.

"What's going on?" Mark asked.

"Man, I really don't want to be the one to put a damper on things, especially since we just got cool again," Austin said.

"What is it?" Quincey said with a concerned look on his face. "Is everything okay?"

"Look, Mark, I'm gonna tell you this because you my boy and I love you. Please don't find a way to get mad at *me*," Austin said sounding a little nervous.

"A'ight, man, just say what you gotta say," Mark said feeling himself growing irritated already.

"Okay. You see that guy over on the treadmill?"

"Yeah, why?" Mark said glancing over at the guy.

It was some guy that looked like he was about forty years old. From the man's appearance, he appeared to be a gym regular. Even though Mark had only laid eyes on the man once, there was a distinct arrogance about him that was apparent upon first sight.

"That's the guy that I saw Terri with at the restaurant that night. I recognized him as soon as I saw him. I asked big Rueben if he'd seen him around before. He said that he's a regular in here and that he thought the guy was a doctor or something."

Mark felt anger welling up inside him because Terri had lied to him. She told Mark that he would recognize the guy she was out with when he saw him. Mark wasn't always great at remembering names but he almost never forgot a face. He knew for a fact that he had never seen that guy in his life.

"What's up, Mark? You're not thinking about doing something stupid are you?" Quincey said realizing the look on Mark's face wasn't a good one.

"I think I'm gonna just go over and talk to him for a second. Terri said that she had introduced us before so maybe talking to him will jog my memory."

"Bruh, I don't think that's a good idea," Austin said with a pleading look in his eyes. "What if he says something you don't want to hear? You know you can't control your temper."

"I'm gonna be cool. I won't do anything stupid," Mark lied. If that guy said that he and Terri were together, he knew it would take God himself to keep him from beating the guy within an inch of his life.

Mark got up and walked over to the treadmill area where the guy was working out. He didn't notice Mark standing there at first, so he waved his hand to grab the man's attention.

"Can I talk to you for a second?" Mark shouted out because the gym was extremely loud.

The guy gave him a bewildered look but nodded and shut the treadmill down. Mark motioned for them to walk outside and the guy followed behind him. He looked over at Austin and Quincey. They both watched intently with concerned looks on their faces.

Once outside Mark said, "You look familiar. Have I ever met you before?"

"Look, man, if you're trying to hit on me it's not that type of party."

"Nah, it's nothing like that. I'm straight as an arrow. It's just that I think I've seen you somewhere before," Mark lied.

"I don't know. I can't recall ever seeing you."

"My name is Mark," he said and extended his hand. The man looked at his hand as if he had something strange in his palm, but after consideration shook it.

"Do you know someone named Terri Baxter?" Mark continued.

"Oh," the man laughed. "Yeah....I know Terri. I know her real well."

Mark felt a twinge of anger hit him. He knew at that moment that Terri's relationship with that guy was more than what she had divulged to him. He tried to remain calm so that he could get as much information out of the man as possible.

"What do you mean by that?" Mark said trying to mask his anger.

"Nothing, I was just thinking out loud."

"Well what's your name, bruh?"

"Cedric. Why are you asking me so many questions about her?"

"She's my wife and I was just wondering how you knew her because I still can't remember where I've seen you."

"Oh, so you're her husband. I've heard about you a couple of times," Cedric said sounding a little too smug for Mark's taste.

"Good things I hope."

"Not exactly," Cedric said with a little smirk on his face that was driving Mark crazy. "From what I can tell, you're about to be replaced."

"With who?" Mark said now at his boiling point.

"With me. When I made love to her, she told me that I'm more of a man than you can ever be."

"What?"

"You heard me. I can treat Terri like she deserves. You, on the other hand, are some chump just pretending. When you learn how to be a man, then you can come and talk to me," Cedric said and then turned to walk back in the building.

Mark couldn't contain himself any longer. He grabbed Cedric's shoulder and spun him around. When Cedric was face to face with him he punched him with all his might. Cedric fell to the ground and Mark climbed on top of him and pounded him. He was trying to pound that smug look from Cedric's face as well as the picture of it etched in his memory. He must have been fighting for five minutes when Austin and Quincey snatched him up.

"They called the cops," Austin yelled. "Come get in the car with me and I'll take you to get your car."

He hopped in the car and Austin sped away. Mark cried hysterically. He knew it didn't look good for a man of his size to be crying like that but he couldn't help it. His very soul ached with the thought of Terri being with another man.

Austin tried to talk to him and calm him down, but Mark couldn't really comprehend anything at that moment. He was so mad and hurt at the same time. He wanted to fill Austin in on everything Cedric had said and apologize for getting mad at him when he tried to tell him about Terri before, but he couldn't. All he could think about was how ready he was to get home and confront Terri about everything he had found out. She couldn't deny anything anymore.

Chapter 28

"Thank God," **Terri** said when she pulled into the driveway of her home. She saw that Mark wasn't there and sent up a quick prayer of thanks. She was intent on telling him all of her secrets but she was thankful for every minute that she didn't have to.

When she walked into the house she saw a note with her name on it. Mark had left the note informing her that he had gone to the gym with Quincey and Austin. The kids were at his mother's and would be there until the late evening. She was glad that the kids wouldn't be home when she had her talk with him. She didn't know how he would react, so it was good that they wouldn't be there to see the fallout.

She thought about getting in the shower but decided against it as she wanted to be ready when Mark came home. She plopped down on the couch and grabbed the remote. She determined that maybe some TV would take her mind off of things.

When she turned the TV on it was already tuned in to a show called *Caught Slippin*. It was a show where people, who suspected their spouse or significant other of cheating, could call the show and get help catching red-handed. The producers would send out their private investigators to follow the accused. When they came back with evidence, the person that called the show would confront the infidel on camera. Terri really hated shows of that nature. She hated to see people acting fools on TV.

She flipped through the other channels a couple of times and couldn't find anything else worth watching, so she resigned to watching the show. This particular episode was about Latisha. She had reasons to suspect that her boyfriend, Mick, was cheating on her. She had noticed lately that he'd been staying out late and getting phone calls on his cell phone that he couldn't answer in front of her.

"I know it ain't nothin' important," Latisha said. "He ain't got a job, so it gotta be somebody he ain't got no business talking to."

"I love him. I just wanna know if he's foolin' wit somebody else. I'm so tired of him lyin' to me. It makes no sense. I want to marry him, but this is somethin' I need to know before we go any further."

The scene then cut away to the camera the private investigators were using. They followed Mick around for about four days. Of course he was cheating like all the people who made it on the show were. He was with another woman on every night that he wasn't with Latisha. She went to work at night, so the other woman showed up every night like clockwork. She was even spending the night in Mick and Latisha's home.

The producers presented Latisha with the evidence and were just about to go confront Mick, when Terri heard a car pull up in the driveway. She ran over to look out the window and her heart sank when she saw that it was Mark. He was home a lot sooner than she expected. Her stomach began to feel queasy. She wasn't mentally prepared at that moment. She thought she would have at least a couple of hours before the time came.

Out of nervousness, she started pacing the floor. She waited for what seemed an eternity and Mark still hadn't come in the house. She walked back over to the window to see what was taking so long. It struck her as strange that he was still sitting in the car after so long. She opened the front door just wide enough to stick her head out. He looked up at her and then looked back down. She was tempted to walk over to the car, but decided against it. She almost felt like putting it off for another day or two, but realistically she knew that couldn't happen. With Cedric stalking her now, she had to tell Mark as soon as possible.

She started pacing the floor again and then decided to grab a seat until Mark came in. She sat on the couch and picked up with the Mick and Latisha drama. The two women were now fighting and Mick was trying to break them up. *I don't know what she saw in him anyway. He is butt ugly*, Terri thought.

Terri heard the door to Mark's car slam shut outside, so she turned the volume down on the TV to listen for him coming into the house. The TV volume didn't matter whatsoever because she heard the front door slam loud and clear. Next she heard glass breaking and she jumped up with a panic. She ran around the corner to see what had happened. Mark was just standing there breathing heavily. She looked around and saw that the family portrait that was hanging in the hallway had fallen and the glass broken into a thousand pieces.

"What's wrong, baby?" Terri asked terror running through her veins.

Mark didn't respond. He just stood there with a blank look on his face as if the situation wasn't registering with him. She was almost scared to say anything else.

"Mark, please talk to me. What's wrong? Did you and Austin get into a fight again?"

Mark stood there about fifteen more seconds before he said anything. "I've been in tons of fights with Austin and I've never been as mad as I am today," he said in a voice that was barely audible.

"What are you mad about?"

"I think you know, so I'm gonna give you one last shot at decency," Mark said staring a hole through her.

"I don't know what you're talking about. Mark, baby, you have to talk to me," Terri pleaded.

"Don't call me baby. I gave you your last chance and you blew it."

"What are you talking about?"

"I ran into *Cedric* at the gym today," Mark said emotion running deep in his voice. "We had a real interesting conversation."

A million thoughts flooded into Terri's mind at that moment. She saw flashes of her life as she knew it pass before her eyes. All the happy times shared right there in that house were about to be erased and there was nothing she could do to stop it. The wheels had already been set in motion and the brakes had failed. Her head began to pound and the room started spinning. She had to grab the wall in order to stabilize herself and keep from fainting.

"I'm sorry, Mark," Terri said feeling the tears well up in her eyes

"Oh, so now you know what I'm talking about."

"Yes, I do. I'm very, very sorry."

"I think it's too late for sorry. I can't believe you did this to me. How could you do this to our family? And what about the girls? How did you think they would feel?"

"I guess I didn't."

"Of course you didn't. You were too busy thinking about how much of a loser I was for not having a job," Mark said and slammed his fist into the wall.

Terri shuttered with fear because she had never seen him that mad before. It was the first time she could remember being afraid he would do something to her physically.

"Mark, please. I'm so sorry. I didn't mean to hurt you," Terri said and moved toward him to grab his hand. He pulled away from her and she nearly fell to the ground from the force of the sudden action.

"You......Don't you touch me. Those are the same hands, you used to touch him."

"I know there is nothing I can do to make up for what I did, but I promise I'll do everything in my power to," Terri said now sobbing uncontrollably.

"There's nothing you can do. I trusted you and you betrayed that trust by sleeping with another man. The worst thing is that we went nearly a year without being together and you had the nerve to be with another man. I don't think I can ever get over that."

"I'm not asking you to now. You deserve to be mad, but please allow me the *chance* to try and make it up," Terri pleaded with him.

"You know one thing that sticks out in my mind?" Mark continued as if she hadn't said anything. "He told me that you said you were leaving me for him, because he was more of a man than I could ever be."

Terri felt sick to her stomach. She couldn't believe that Cedric lied on her like that. When they were together, the experience was anything but earth moving. She felt hurt to her soul over this whole situation, but she couldn't even fathom how Mark must feel. She would have given her right arm if she could to make it better.

"I promise you I never said anything like that. We were together only once. I told him I couldn't see him anymore right after that, because I felt horrible about what I did. He's been stalking me ever since."

"Oh and I'm supposed to start believing you now? I don't know if I can ever believe anything you say ever again," Mark said sadly and then sat on the arm of the couch with his head down. Terri couldn't see exactly what he was doing because his back was to her. When Mark emitted a low sob, she could tell that he was weeping softly.

She walked over and embraced him in her arms. He laid his head on her bosom and began to cry loudly. "Oh, God," he said through spurts of tears. "Why me?" He cried loudly for a few more moments before relaxing. Terri held him tightly and stroked the back of his head. She didn't know what she could do or say at that moment.

"Mark, I promise I'll make it up to you."

Mark pulled away from her. Terri could tell from the expression on his face that the sorrow that was there for only a few moments was now replaced by the anger that was there before. "Not now. I need some time away, because right now I don't think I can be in this relationship anymore."

"What? Please don't leave me."

"It's for the best," Mark said in a fleeting statement as he stood and rushed out the house.

Terri fell to her knees and screamed at the top of her lungs. She was sure anyone standing outside their home could've heard her but she didn't care. She let out all the frustration she had with herself for getting in this situation. She listened to see if Mark would change his mind and come back, but when she heard him peel off she knew that wouldn't happen.

She was devastated. She had just run off the only man to ever truly love her. She had never known the love of a man before Mark because even her father was a deadbeat. She couldn't think of anything else to do but pray. She prayed a prayer of forgiveness for what she had done. She also prayed that God would soften the effects of what her infidelity had done to Mark. She then prayed an undeserved prayer that God would preserve her marriage and protect her from the threats that Cedric had made.

Chapter 29

Austin sat on the back pew of the church and stared a hole in the wall as he reflected on all the things that had occurred over the past two weeks. *It's amazing how things change over such a little amount of time*, he thought to himself. Today was supposed to be a happy one for him, but his mind kept traveling to all the drama that had transpired in Mark's life. Austin had only talked to him a couple of times since the incident at the gym and it didn't seem as if he was doing any better.

Austin looked around the church and examined all the elaborate decorations. They had cost him a small fortune. He laughed silently to himself. It was his wedding day and he was too busy thinking of someone else's problems to enjoy himself. The whole situation was on the forefront of his mind and he couldn't shake it. Mark was supposed to be one of his best men and he hadn't even spoken to him all week. He didn't even know if Mark would show or not.

Austin made sure that he was the first one to arrive at the church so that he could personally see to it that everything was perfect. He just wanted the day to be as close to what Julie had in mind as possible. It was the least he could do for treating her so terribly in the past.

He walked over to the wall and turned all the lights on in the church. It dazzled with gold and black decorations. Julie insisted that those be their colors, since they were the colors of his fraternity and the gold represented royalty. He walked up to the front of the church where the arch stood and tried to prepare himself to give up his freedom.

"It's too late to reconsider now," a male voice said from over his shoulder.

"Mark, what's up bruh?" Austin said when he turned to see his friend walking up behind him.

"Nothing....just got here a little early so I can be as cool looking as you. You know I can't make the wedding pictures look bad."

"I ain't mad at you either. You know a brother does look pretty good in this tux," Austin laughed while fingering the lapel on his black tuxedo. The golden silk shirt with matching tie he had on underneath was the perfect touch. "I was a little worried you weren't gonna to show up."

"You know I couldn't miss my best friend's wedding," Mark said as they shook hands and embraced.

"How've you been?"

"I've been cool, just trying to deal with things one day at a time."

"I feel you. Have you talked to Terri?"

"Nope, she's been calling around the clock, though. I just haven't really felt much like talking."

"Man, I hope ya'll work things out. Deep down I really feel like Terri is a good woman," Austin said. He really felt that Terri would not intentionally hurt Mark. Besides, Austin of all people understood how you can get sidetracked.

"I don't know about all that. If she was so good then why did she jeopardize our family?"

"I couldn't answer that for you, man. Only she could."

"Well, whatever. Just show me where to get dressed," Mark said looking around and obviously not wanting to discuss Terri any further.

Austin showed him to the lobby area where the men were dressing. Just then Mr. and Mrs. Perry, Julie's parents, came into the church and looked around as if making sure everything was in its proper place.

"What are *you* doing here so early?" Mrs. Perry said with an attitude.

"And how are you guys doing, mom and dad? I'm glad you guys made it safely, too," Austin said sarcastically.

"You ain't my son-in-law yet," Mr. Perry told him. He face wore a smile but his voice was buried in condescension. Austin could read right through the facial expression and tell that her father meant exactly what he had said. He hadn't had the best of experiences with her parents considering he was always the cause of Julie being hurt.

"That's true but it will only be so for the next couple of hours. Then I'll be family."

"Okay, you two. That's enough. Austin, you have to go hide. Julie's waiting in the car and you know its bad luck to see her before the wedding," Mrs. Perry said while shoving him into the men's waiting area.

Man, no turning back now, Austin thought to himself as he grabbed a seat on the sofa in the lounge. Quincey walked in shortly after that. Austin enjoyed the time spent with his two friends chatting about the past and everything in between to pass the time. No matter what he did, though, Austin couldn't stop the butterflies from fluttering. It was the most important day of his adult life and the one that would change it forever.

The time had come and Austin stood before the church awaiting his bride. Austin and Quincey both stood by his side. He felt good about the wedding but nervous at the same time. He wasn't nervous about pledging his life to Julie because he felt that he owed her that much for putting up with him for so long. It was the dark cloud of Monica that continued to hang over his head. She hadn't even called in the past two weeks and Austin thought that was very strange.

He scanned over the church and every one he knew was in attendance. Also a lot of people he had never seen in his life. He figured either they were friends of friends or there for the food. He noticed his biggest client, Mr. Green from Black Pride Beauty Products, was in attendance. They had made each other lots of money since they started a business relationship in Atlanta.

He saw that Terri wasn't there. He didn't figure she would show up considering everything that had taken place. She was probably too embarrassed about what had happened between her and Mark.

The first person to walk down the aisle was Kim. She looked stunning in her golden dress. He was shocked that Julie could get her to be in the wedding since most pregnant women were self-conscious. She was showing a little pregnancy bump, but somehow pregnancy went well with her.

Next was the matron of honor, Julie's sister Valerie. She was a very attractive woman that Austin had only met once. She was a tall, slender, fair skinned woman with the body of a model. Valerie was the most eye appealing of the two sisters, and Julie had told Austin numerous times how people had favored Valerie over her. As far as Austin was concerned, Julie had what counts on the inside and that was all that mattered.

The ceremony didn't take long because they decided purposely to keep the wedding party small. Austin didn't feel there needed to be tons of people in the wedding to get the job done. It only wasted time and money. The bridal party was all in place and it was time for the bride. The wedding march music began playing.

The doors at the back of the church opened up to reveal Julie and her father arm in arm. Austin was taken back by the sheer beauty of his bride in her white dress with the long, flowing train in tow. He had never seen her look like that and it shined a new light on her for him. He actually felt the nervousness start to subside and a sense of excitement take over.

Julie and her father walked slowly down the aisle while the music played. Everyone smiled and took pictures. Austin almost lost track of them in the flashing lights. He knew those flashes must have come from media photographers. The wedding had been highly publicized over the last two weeks. The newspapers and magazines had read, *Local businessman, Austin Barton, to wed on this Saturday*.

When Julie and her father were finally at the alter, Pastor Lewis began the ceremony.

"Who gives this woman away in matrimony?" Pastor Lewis asked.

"I do," Mr. Perry said and placed Julie's hand in Austin's. Mr. Perry's gaze was still fixed upon Austin and it made him feel uncomfortable. He had a look of uncertainty on his face that suggested he truly didn't want the wedding to be happening.

"You look so beautiful," Austin whispered in Julie's ear when she had taken her place beside him.

"Thank you," she whispered back. Austin could see that she had already been crying. He hoped it was due to happiness and not from thoughts of everything that had gone wrong in their relationship.

Pastor Lewis began with a prayer. He prayed for what seemed to be an eternity to Austin. He didn't mean to feel that way. It was just that he had been standing in that one spot for a long time and he was ready to get the show on the road.

"We are gathered here today to witness the matrimony of Julia Renee Perry and Austin Alexander Barton," Pastor Lewis went on in his baritone voice. It shocked Austin out of his deep thought. He was zoning out until Pastor Lewis called his name. "If there is anyone among us that sees *any* reason why they shouldn't be joined, let them speak now or forever hold their peace."

A throat was cleared in the back and everyone turned to look in that direction. Austin's heart froze until he saw that it was one of the older ladies that attended the church. Everyone let out a laugh. Austin laughed but it was a nervous one. He really expected it to be Monica sitting back there waiting to ruin his wedding day. He loathed the fact that he was standing at the alter with Julie thinking about another woman. That in itself was proof of the power Monica had over him.

"Alright, if all throats are clear," Pastor Lewis joked. "Let's carry on."

Just then the doors of the church swung open and in walked a white man in his mid to late thirties. Austin spun around quickly. The man looked like some sort of celebrity and Austin could have sworn he was wearing make-up. The man looked rather familiar, but Austin couldn't place where he had seen him before.

"At the risk of being delinquent, I have reason that these two shouldn't be married," the man said.

There was a wave of gasps that echoed throughout the church followed by tons of whispering. Everyone had come to see a wedding, but now they were getting a show. Austin felt a burning anger growing inside him. *Julie was cheating on me*, he thought to himself. *That's why she's always accusing me of cheating on her. Her boyfriend must have found out she was getting married and came up in here to call her out.*

"Hold up, man. Who are you?" Austin demanded.

I can't believe Julie made me look like a fool in front of all these people, he thought silently attempting to show respect to Pastor Lewis by keeping it to himself. If they weren't in church it may have been a different story.

"My name is Max Krueger," the man responded with a slight smirk on his face.

"Now I know who you are," Austin said now sounding more like he was pleading than angry. "Please, man, right now is not the time for this."

"Oh, I think it is the time," Max said. "Besides, if not now, then when?"

The people in the church were still whispering amongst themselves. Austin figured they loved every minute of it. The cameras still flashed constantly but no longer were they trained on Austin, but now on Max. He couldn't imagine what was going through Mr. Green's head.

"What's going on?" Julie said with tears starting to well up in her eyes. It was the first time she had spoken since Max burst into the church. She looked as if she had become fed up with everyone interrupting her wedding day.

"Julie, I know you won't be able to appreciate any of this today, but I'm saving you from making the biggest mistake of your life," Max said.

"Look, man, I'm begging you. This is my wedding day. Please don't do me like this?" Austin begged to no avail because Max had come there on a mission and was not leaving until it was done. Austin looked around at Quincey and Mark and they both had a look of bewilderment on their faces.

"For those of you who don't know who I am, I host a reality TV show called *Caught Slippin*," Max said.

There were more gasps and whispers from the congregation.

Then all of a sudden the doors burst open again and in ran camera men and body guards. Next came the moment Austin had been dreading for two weeks as Monica walked in behind them. She had a certain look of determination about her as she marched down the aisle. On her face, she wore the ugliest scowl that Austin had ever seen. He wished he could just disappear because he didn't want to face what was next.

"Austin, do you want to tell Julie who this is?" Max asked. Austin was having about all he could stand from him.

Monica just stood there with her arms folded waiting for Austin to say something, but he couldn't put any words together to say. He just stood there. All eyes were on him and he knew everyone expected an answer.

"Who is she, Austin?" Julie said pointing at Monica. "And I want to know now."

"If he's not going to do it, then I will," Monica said.

The camera men now moved around so that they could get a better shot of her. The producer's for the show would eat this up when they saw the footage.

"My name is Monica," she said reaching out to shake Julie's hand. Julie just looked down at her hand like she was holding something disgusting in it. "I know you don't know who I am, but me and Austin had an affair earlier this year. We were messing around for several weeks."

There were more gasps. Austin looked over at Pastor Lewis wondering when *he* would stop everything, but he seemed too dumbfounded.

"What? Austin how could you do me like this. I thought you loved me. You lied to me over and over about how much you've changed, but I can see now you're the same dog you always were," Julie said now sounding angrier than Austin could ever remember. The strange thing was that she wasn't crying. Normally she would have been a ball of emotion by then.

"I can explain," Austin said.

"Hold on. That's not it. Monica, why don't you tell Julie the rest," Max interrupted. He was now standing at the alter along with all the other parties involved.

"I'm also pregnant," Monica said followed by more gasps and whispering.

"You know what I don't even care," Julie said and threw her bouquet on the ground. "I was fooling myself thinking I could reform someone like you. This wasn't what God had for me. I just wanted it so bad that I was forcing it to happen."

"Baby, please. I'm so sorry," Austin pleaded.

"Julie, obviously you don't want to deal with a loser like this. You could do so much better," Max interjected.

Austin had taken about all he could stand from Max's mouth. He drew back as far as he could and punched Max with a loud smack. The congregation erupted with people letting out brief screams. Max fell to the ground and his security crew ran over to restrain Austin.

"I'm done, Austin. I told you if you ever did this again that it's over and I meant it. I just didn't imagine it would ever be on this scale," Julie said looking Monica up and down. She started off toward the exit with her mother and father in tow.

"Julie, please," Austin pleaded trying to free himself from the guards. They wrestled him to the ground and he struggled until Julie was out of sight. Monica followed Max as he left nursing his bloody nose.

Even after the guards released him, he just laid prostrate on the floor of the church as the guests filed out after the bride. Through his frustration he had to admit that his relationship was officially over and there was no one to blame but him.

Chapter 30

Kim stared at the princesses that danced along the pink and white wallpaper on the walls of her former bedroom. Each time she visited, she wondered why her mother hadn't redecorated the room when she went off to college. The room was officially stuck in her childhood days. Her yellow dollhouse was still in the corner of the room and the shelves along the walls still held hundreds of stuffed animals.

Kim realized that she had been lying in bed all day but she couldn't shake the morning sickness that had plagued her since the early hours. She had also been having pains in her stomach all day. She heard from other mothers that it was quite normal to have pains from the baby moving and shifting around, so she didn't really read too much into it.

On top of all that, she felt bad about what Austin had done to Julie at the wedding the day before. She stood in the church in horror as the events of that day unfolded. She didn't know why men insisted on being dogs. It was ridiculous that Austin had a perfectly good woman at home and he had to go out and sleep with someone else.

She looked over at the phone and thought about calling Quincey. She hadn't talked to him since she left and, though she hated to admit it, was really starting to miss him. He had tried to talk to her at the church, but with all the commotion of the day, they didn't get to speak. She picked up the phone and dialed the first three numbers but then decided against it because she didn't feel like him begging her to come home again.

She got up and walked into the living room where her mother sat on the couch watching the morning soaps, that she had so adequately coined *her stories*. Kim plopped down beside her and sighed loudly and then looked over at her mother for a while. When Ms. Robertson didn't even look away from the TV, Kim let loose a longer more obvious sigh that finally got her mother's attention.

"What's wrong with you now, child?" Ms. Robertson asked.

"I don't know, ma. Just feeling a little sad today," Kim said sounding like a three year old.

"Why are you *sad*?" Ms. Robertson said and Kim couldn't tell if her mother cared one way or the other.

"Because I'm starting to miss my husband."

"Why don't you just go home then?"

"Because even if I'm at home, it's not like Quincey is gonna be there. He's thinking about being a Pastor and that means that's gonna be what his life is about now."

"You know," Ms. Robertson said like she just had an incredible thought. "We never have had the opportunity to talk about why you're so against him becoming a Pastor. That's the same profession your father had."

"That's just it, ma. I feel like I've been there and done that. The life of a Pastor's family is not as glamorous as it seems."

"Honey, I didn't know there was any glamour involved," Ms. Robertson laughed. "Here I am thinking all this time it's done for the Lord."

"Ma, you know what I mean. I didn't enjoy that lifestyle growing up. As a matter of fact, I hated it."

"I know it was hard on you. It was hard on us all, but your father did everything he could to be there for you."

"I just don't feel like he tried hard enough. There were so many key points in my life that he didn't get to see. To add to all that he cheated on you and every other minister in his family did the same thing."

"I can see how that could make you feel. But one thing you have to understand about him cheating is that he cheated on me as *my* husband. He was not your husband, but *your* father. Being a father was something he did an excellent job of."

"That's why I don't understand women like you," Kim said shaking her head and speaking in a condescending tone. "Why would you stay with a man that cheated on you with a woman in your own congregation? Now you're here defending him to me."

"See normally I would tell you that it was none of your business, but for the sake of saving *your* marriage I'm going to be completely open with you," Ms. Robertson said sounding a little irritated.

"I'm sorry, ma. I didn't mean to be smart," Kim said feeling bad for being short with her mother.

"It's okay, because you need to hear this. I stayed with your father because there were a lot of things you didn't know about me. Actually I was a lot like you."

"What do you mean?" Kim asked after such a shocking revelation. She thought all this time that she was nothing like her mother. That was one thing she had strived to be. She didn't want to be some helpless female that let her man walk all over her.

"I mean in the way that you are trying to hoard your husband's time. I was just like that. Even though your father was a Pastor and had a pretty large ministry, I still wanted him to spend all his time with me. Of course it couldn't be that way, so it led to big arguments."

"That didn't give him any right to cheat," Kim said refusing to let her father off the hook that easy.

"I'm not saying that it gave him the right, but I *am* saying it made it easier for him to do so. It's no way I could expect for him to want to come home to me every night and I'm turning that home into hell," Ms. Robertson said sliding to the front of the couch.

Kim didn't say anything in response. She just shook her head. She refused to accept the fact that she had to let Quincey run off and do whatever he wanted to. He was married to her and not anyone or anything else.

"You can shake your head all you want, but you will listen. I've lived a long time and I know some things about life that you can't see yet," Ms. Robertson said.

"I'm listening."

"I know that this is not easy to understand, but it was my calling to be married to your father."

"What do you mean?"

"Sometimes in life, especially in the black community, we're blessed with extraordinary men, unlike ones we've ever seen. They're called to do great things and to be a guiding light to many. Then, there are the women they're married to. These women have a calling that's just as, if not more so, important as the man does. Although it's a difficult one, it's still her calling none the less. And that calling is to share him with everyone else. It's hard to do because we want them to be with us at all times and because we see what great men they are, it's hard to share that with *anyone*, let alone people we don't even know or like for that matter. The problem with having that feeling is that he becomes so much to so many that we can't afford to deny the world his presence. He becomes a leader, father to some, a brother, a confidant, and any other role that needs to be filled. God put it in him to do so and it would kill him if he didn't."

"Imagine life for a second, if Coretta Scott King had denied the world Martin Luther King. Or better yet what if Michelle had denied us Barack Obama? Where would we be then? Your father had that very thing. I was just too young at the time to see it. I look at Quincey and I see the same thing that I saw in your father. That's why I'm being as open with you as I can. I'm trying to keep you and him from making some of the same mistakes that me and your father did. Kim, baby, you are married to a great man. You need to cherish him and let him be what he is designed to be."

"I understand that, mama," Kim said. "I just don't see how that constitutes Daddy cheating."

"It's not to excuse it. It's just to make you aware that there are some things I could've done better in my marriage, so that you don't do the same thing. Just think on it, honey."

They made small talk the rest of the evening. Kim helped her mother prepare a light dinner for the two of them. She thought heavily about what her mother had said and even though she didn't want to admit it, her mother made a lot of sense. She had spent so long hating her father because of what he had done, she didn't consider that he was still human and had made a mistake. She regretted the fact that they didn't get to talk about it before he had passed away two years before. They really were not on great terms when he did. It almost brought her to tears just thinking about it.

Kim awoke and immediately clutched her stomach. She felt a sharp pain surging in her abdomen. She was groggy but could make out that it was three o'clock in the morning. She couldn't imagine why her stomach would be hurting this way.

She decided that if she could walk to the bathroom and stir around a little, the pain would subside. She kicked her feet off the bed and tried to stand up. As soon as she did so, the pain intensified. It hurt so badly that she couldn't help but cry.

Kim fell back onto the bed. As soon as she sat down she felt wetness beneath her. She reached over and flipped on the lamp that sat on the nightstand. She lifted her gown and inspected her panties. There was a large red stain soaking through them.

"Mama!" she screamed.

About two seconds later Ms. Robertson burst into the room without her robe, which she always put on before leaving her bedroom.

"What's wrong, baby?" Ms. Robertson said sounding out of breath like she had been running. "You scared me half to death screaming like that."

"The baby," was all Kim could muster in between sobs.

"What? What about the baby," Ms. Robertson said rushing over now that she saw Kim was crying.

"I'm bleeding, so we have to get to the hospital. I don't want to loose my baby."

"A'ight, just calm down. Can you get dressed?"

"I don't think so. It hurts so bad when I stand up," Kim said.

"Okay, I'll help you get dressed and then we'll head to the hospital."

"Mama, can you call Quincey?" Kim asked trying to remain calm. Since she was going to the hospital, she really wanted him to be there.

"Sure. I'll call him from my cell phone when we're on our way."

Chapter 31

Quincey heard the phone ringing and looked over at the clock. It read 3:25 a.m. He felt like he had just closed his eyes. He stayed up late looking over some sermon notes because it was his Sunday to preach. He also had a few cases that he needed to finish up. He planned to take a much needed vacation after those cases were done. He had a lot of things to think about, especially when it came to accepting the position of Pastor at the church, so he didn't want anything causing a distraction when he did so.

"Hello," he said wondering who would be calling him so early in the morning.

"Quincey, I need you to get over to the hospital as soon as you can."

"What?" Quincey said. He went straight from sleepy to fully alert at the sound of Ms. Robertson's voice. "What's wrong? Is Kim okay?"

"She's as good as can be expected, but in a lot of pain," Ms. Robertson said.

"Is it the baby," Quincey said now speaking hurriedly. He felt a sense of fear begin to take over him. He jumped out of bed and started throwing open drawers to look for some clothes to put on.

"We don't know. I need you to calm down though. I know it's early and you probably were asleep. So, listen to me. Get dressed and meet us at Baptist Hospital."

"A'ight, I'll be there in about twenty minutes," Quincey said and hung up the phone. He resigned on the blue sweat suit that was in his top drawer. He was dressed two minutes later and out the door within five.

He called Mark and Austin and filled them in on the information he had. They both told him that they would be to the hospital in a matter of minutes. He also called his parents and told them as well. He was so worried that it just helped for him to have someone to talk to. His mother offered him comforting words and told him they would come to the hospital as soon as possible.

Quincey drove as fast as he could. He was so tempted to turn the emergency lights on and floor it. He tried over and over to remain positive, but couldn't find any positive thoughts. The only thought that played over and over in his mind was the way that he treated Kim when she told him she was pregnant. He had acted as if she had given him some bad news, but what he should have done was celebrate that God had blessed him with another child. Kim really didn't deserve that sort of treatment. The only thing he could think to do was pray.

"Dear Heavenly Father, I come to you today humbled. I don't know any formalities to say right now, so I'll just be me in this prayer. God I don't know what to do. I treated Kim horribly when I found out she was pregnant and I apologize for that. I don't want her to loose the baby. I realize now that it was a blessing from you, because there are so many people out there that cannot conceive. If it is in your will, please spare this child. I've definitely learned my lesson. No matter which way it falls, I know that it will work out for good. I thank you in advance, Amen."

By the time he had finished praying, he was at the hospital. He parked in the emergency parking lot beside Ms. Robertson's car and ran into the ER and looked around the waiting room. He didn't see Ms. Robertson or Kim, so he assumed they had already went back to see the doctor.

He walked over to the receptionist who was already engaged in a conversation on the phone. She glanced over at Quincey and put up her index finger to say she would be over in a minute. From the way she was laughing and giggling, Quincey could tell that she wasn't on a business call. He stood there looking for a few more minutes then lost his cool.

"Miss, could I please get some help?" Quincey said trying to be as assertive as possible.

The lady looked over at him and rolled her eyes. She muttered a few words into the phone and hung it up. She walked over to the front desk, her eyes intently trained on Quincey.

"What can I help you wit, sir?" she said with her hand on her hip and rolling her neck.

"I need to know where Kimberly Jackson is," Quincey said.

The receptionist looked through some papers. It seemed to Quincey as if she was taking her time on purpose. She finally stopped on a page and read some information.

"Are you her husband?"

"Yes," Quincey responded.

"She's in with her doctor. We have a waiting area inside those doors with the big emergency sign above it. I'll buzz you in and you can wait in there."

"What's going on? Has the doctor said what's wrong with her?"

"Mr. Jackson, of course you know, the doctor doesn't reveal that to us and if he did, I'm not at liberty to reveal it," she answered sounding unconcerned.

"If I had time I would talk to whoever's in charge. You definitely need an attitude adjustment," Quincey responded angrily. "Just buzz me through so I can check on my wife."

After what seemed like forever she buzzed the door open and Quincey walked back to the waiting area that was described to him earlier. When he rounded the corner, he saw Kim's mother sitting there with her eyes closed. He walked over and touched her on the shoulder. She jumped.

"Hey, mom, how's Kim doing?" Quincey said trying to soothe her.

"I don't know yet. The doctor went back with her and he said he would let me know something as soon as possible."

"What happened?"

"She had heavy vaginal bleeding and abdominal pains," Ms. Robertson told him and filled him in on everything that had happed that morning.

Quincey was so nervous. He didn't know what to expect. He was the type of man that liked to know everything, so not knowing what would happen with Kim bothered him.

After about thirty more minutes, both Mark and Austin had joined them in the waiting area. Quincey's parents arrived not long after that. Believing that prayer is the answer to all life's problems,

Quincey decided that they should join together and pray. He led a heartfelt prayer of supplication.

When it was over they all sat in their respective seats and waited quietly. About thirty more minutes passed before the doctor came out. Quincey was the first to see him, so he jumped up and rushed over to him. The doctor wore a blank expression, so Quincey still didn't know what to expect either way.

"Doc, is Kim okay?" Quincey asked sounding out of breath due to sheer anxiety.

"Kim is doing fine."

"What about the baby? Please tell me the baby is okay?" Quincey pleaded.

"I'm sorry, but we lost the baby," The doctor said sounding sincerely upset.

"No," was all Quincey could say.

"I'm sorry. Kim is sleeping right now, but you can go back and see her one at a time if you want to. You have my condolences," The doctor said and walked away.

"No, I won't accept this," Quincey said. He felt angry. He was doing all that God had asked him to do, so why was he being punished in that manner? He made a mistake. He didn't appreciate the baby when Kim told him about it, but he didn't deserve that punishment. He was so angry that he couldn't feel any other emotion.

"It's okay," Ms. Robertson said coming over to comfort him. She obviously saw the way that Quincey was looking. "It's okay to be angry. Sometimes we don't understand the reason things happen and I can't say that we ever will. The one thing I do know is that God will have some good come out of this."

"What good could come out of this, huh? I didn't even get the chance to cherish this baby. I was selfish. I wasn't even happy with Kim being pregnant," Quincey said.

Mark tried to come over and place a hand on his shoulder. He threw the hand off.

"I don't need any condolences. I'm fine," Quincey shouted.

"Quincey, baby, it's okay to mourn. It's also okay to cry. If you want to, go ahead and let it out," Quincey's mother said now trying to say something to calm him down.

She reached out to hug him and he resisted at first. Then starting to feel the first pains of his loss, he began to cry. He laid his head on his mother's shoulder and cried softly. He let out all his frustrations about life in general. He was trying to do all the right things and all the wrong results continued to happen. Through all his thoughts of guilt, frustration, and pain, he was resigned on one thing. He was not accepting the position at the church. If God couldn't do this one thing for him, why would he spend his life working for God?

Chapter 32

Terri heard a car door close outside, so she hurried over to look out the window. It turned out that it was not in her driveway, but in her neighbor's. She couldn't help but feel a little disappointment, but that was something she had come to terms with over the past few weeks.

She was hoping that she would look through the blinds and see Mark returning home. The longer that dream went unfulfilled the more apparent it became that it may not come to pass. She hadn't even spoken to Mark since the day he left. She had tried calling him several times everyday, but had not been successful in reaching him.

During the first couple of weeks she had found out that Mark was at least still alive and healthy from Austin or Quincey. They were like his brothers and she knew that if anyone had contact with him, it was them. Recently, however, she had not even been able to speak with either of them about Mark because they both had their own personal tragedies. It made her feel selfish calling them to whine about her problems.

Just thinking about the events of the past few months made her feel like the walls were starting to close in on her. She felt an overpowering shortness of breath and her lungs struggled to pull in enough oxygen.

She decided she just needed to get some fresh air, so she grabbed her beige sweater off the coat rack. She slipped it on and stepped outside. It was the middle of November so it was a cold and breezy night. The wind whipped across her body and she finally started to feel a little bit more relaxed.

With each and every free moment she had, she tried to sort through the mess that had become her life. She missed Mark terribly and felt like she was in the world alone. She hadn't heard from Cedric since Mark left, but she knew he hadn't forgotten about her. Her eyes started to moisten from the tears that began to form. Just then the front door opened.

"Mama, what you doing?" Stephanie as she poked her head out the door.

"Nothing, baby. Mama just needed to get some fresh air," Terri said drying her eyes. "Aren't you supposed to be sleep?"

"I was but it woke me up when I heard the alarm thing beep," Stephanie said. "I thought it was Daddy coming home."

It cut Terri deeply to hear that Stephanie was still waiting constantly for Mark to come home. She felt worse for the kids than she did for herself.

No one deserves to be punished for this but me, she thought to herself. *I'm the only one to blame for this family falling apart.*

"Sorry, Steph. It wasn't Daddy. I told you he's out of town, but he should be back soon," She lied. She didn't know if the girls were old enough to know what had really happened, but she knew that she wasn't ready to tell them.

"Okay," Stephanie said with a disappointed look on her face.

"Let's get you back in the bed," Kim said and opened the door. The alert that let you know when someone entered the house beeped again. That had been what woke Stephanie up. Terri had just recently had it installed so it was still fairly new to all of them. She couldn't take any chance of Cedric doing something stupid considering there was not a man in the house. Besides she didn't really know what he was capable of.

Once in the girls' room she tucked Stephanie back in and kissed her on the forehead. "Goodnight. Get a good night sleep. We need you to grow big and strong."

"Okay," Stephanie said and was sleep before Terri reached the door.

Once she was back in the living room she heard another door close outside. She walked over to the window and it was in *her* driveway this time. The widow was fogged so she couldn't make out whose car it was. She was just about to walk around and look out the other window when she heard someone knocking on the door.

Terri walked to the door and peered out the peep hole. It was Shannon. She swung open the door and gave her girlfriend a big hug.

They hadn't spent much time together since Terri took some time off work. She was using an overdue vacation to get her mind and her spirit together before going back to punching the clock.

"Hey, girl." Shannon said stepping into the house. She had a pizza in one hand and a rented movie in the other. "I thought we could make this a dinner and a movie night."

"Sounds good to me," Terri said smiling from ear to ear. "I've really missed you since I've been on vacation."

"I know. You can't just disappear. I'll find you no matter where you are," Shannon joked.

Shannon sat the pizza down on the coffee table and started to put the DVD into the player. Terri ran into the kitchen to grab a couple of plates.

Once back in the living room, Terri grabbed a slice of pepperoni pizza. It was her favorite so she knew she was going to pig out. Once she grabbed her seat she settled in to watch the movie.

When she saw what movie it was, she immediately started crying. She jumped up and ran into the kitchen. Shannon was right behind her.

"What's wrong? I thought *The Color Purple* was your favorite movie," Shannon said while wetting a towel so that Terri could clean her face.

"It was, but now every time I see that movie, I think about….," Terri said trying to fill Shannon in on the night that her and Cedric had spent together, but became too choked up to continue.

\   "Terri, you need to be honest with me. You need to tell me what's been going on with you. We have never kept secrets from each other since we were kids, but lately it's like you've been a different person," Shannon said looking genuinely worried. Shannon was a gossip queen, but Terri could tell her friend was really concerned. Shannon appeared to be really taken back by the way she had been acting.

"It's a long story. We should go and sit on the couch," Terri said motioning to the other room.

Over the next hour she filled Shannon in on everything that had been going on. Shannon never interrupted her. She just sat back listening intently. Just taking in everything Terri was saying.

When Terri finished speaking Shannon sat there for a minute just thinking.

"How could you be that stupid?" Shannon finally said flatly.

Her words stung Terri. They hurt her deeply. She hadn't expected for Shannon to say anything like that. She half expected for Shannon to sympathize with her.

"What? Shannon, I can't believe you said that."

"It's something you needed to hear. I wouldn't be a friend if I didn't tell you how wrong you were. Mark is a good man and there are women out there that would kill to have a man that's half the one he is. Lord knows I would. He only has eyes for you, though. What do you do? You go out and cheat on him," Shannon said shaking her head.

"I know I was wrong, but that still doesn't fix anything. He's probably gone forever and Cedric is still out there somewhere."

"Just to see that man when he came up to the hospital, I didn't imagine he was anything like that."

"Me either. He only got like that after I tried to end it. I don't know what to do."

"I can't tell you what to do since I don't even have a man. I wish I could find one that would still pretend to be good. All the men I meet are dogs from the start. They let you know from the beginning that they aren't gonna be faithful. And if *they* don't let you know, then their ten baby's mamas will," Shannon said nudging Terri with her elbow.

"Girl, the men you date do be some dogs," Terri said letting out a low giggle.

"A'ight, I didn't ask for any feedback," Shannon said sarcastically. "What I *can* do is tell you what I would do. I would be on my knees praying every time I get a chance that God would bring my husband back and spare my family."

Shannon's words resonated with Terri. She took them to heart. She knew that she had lost all control over her life, so she had to turn to the only one that could be in control. She would pray and ask God to somehow bring her family back together. She was willing to do and change anything about her that was necessary.

Shannon stayed a few more hours. They just had some girl talk and caught up on some things that had been going on at work.

"Well, I guess I have to get going, some of us have to go to work tomorrow," Shannon said and grabbed her purse off the couch.

"Whatever," Terri said laughing. "Really, though, I appreciate everything you said. You always know exactly what to say, when I need to hear it the most."

"You my sister, girl and you know I love you. Nobody knows you better than me."

Terri walked Shannon to the car and hugged her tightly. She appreciated her best friend. Shannon was sometimes hard on her, but she told Terri exactly what she needed to hear. Shannon got into the car and reversed out of the driveway. Terri stood there and watched until she could only see Shannon's taillights in the distance.

She had forgotten to grab her sweater so the wind chilled her to the bone. She turned to run back into the house, but the car sitting across the street stopped her in her tracks. The black Mercedes Benz that had almost run her down that day at the hospital was parked across the street. She couldn't forget it because she had also ridden in it many times.

Cedric stepped from behind the big pine tree that was in Terri's front yard and started walking towards her. She turned and made a mad dash for the front door. She shut the door quickly and locked it. As soon as she did there was loud pounding on the front door.

Terri quickly hit the panic button on the alarm control pad and it emitted a loud, screeching siren. The pounding stopped, but she still didn't move. The terror had her frozen solid. When she finally gathered the nerve, she walked over and looked out the window. The car was now gone. She shut the alarm off and then leaned against the wall trying to gather her composure.

Stephanie ran into the living room with a terrified look on her face. Jessica obviously hadn't even heard what was going on. She could sleep through a hurricane.

"What happened, Mama?" Stephanie asked.

"False alarm," Terri lied and shooed her off to bed. She didn't want Stephanie to be awake in case the police came over. She decided it was past time to take out a restraining order against Cedric like she should have done a long time ago.

The phone rang and she ran over to it. She figured it was the alarm company checking on the alert, so she didn't look at the id. She just answered it.

"There was someone trying to break into my house," Terri said not even taking the time to say hello.

There was no answer on the other end. She thought she could hear someone breathing lightly into the phone.

"Hello, Is any one there? It's an emergency."

"Yeah, I know. I don't appreciate you calling the cops. I just wanted to talk," Cedric said.

"This is not a game, Cedric. My children are here."

"Oh, were you afraid they would find out that mama's been out being a tramp?"

"I have nothing else to say to you. This conversation is over," Terri screamed into the phone.

"That's good because I only have one more thing to tell you. Let your man know to watch his back," Cedric said and hung up the phone.

Chapter 33

Mark awoke and painfully stretched all the aches and pains from his joints. He knew he had slept but didn't really feel rested at all. He hated sleeping on hotel mattresses and the ones at Roberts' Motor Court and Inn were the worst. His back hurt terribly and he could tell that he had never really reached a deep sleep because of all the tossing and turning he had done throughout the night. On top of that the air condition didn't work, so he was soaking wet from sweat as if he had been working out all night long.

He got up and went into the bathroom to take a shower so that he could feel semi-clean again. He turned on the dim light and grabbed some of the dingy bath towels off of the rack. When he peeled back the shower curtain, he grimaced at the permanent dirt ring that circled the tub.

After taking a shower, he went to the lobby to enjoy the stale continental breakfast. The old bagel and flat orange juice could hardly qualify as food, but it was all he had. He was staying at the worst place in town, but it was the only one that charged a price per week that he could afford.

Mark hated living that way. Of course he could have just gone home, but he couldn't bear the thought of Terri being in the same room as him. She had been with another man and Mark felt betrayed on the deepest level. She gave away her loving to someone else when it was supposed to be only meant for him.

He went back to the room and contemplated calling her, but he couldn't gather the courage because he just didn't know what to say. His mental image of her had been tarnished and the entire scope of their relationship completely changed. She was no longer the girl that was out of his league, but the one that *he* was too good for.

Now matter how angry he was at Terri, he longed desperately to see his children. It wasn't fair to them, but he hadn't seen Stephanie or Jessica since he left. Mark had put off seeing them as long as possible because Terri had caused him more pain than he could ever remember feeling and he didn't know how he would react to being in the same room with her, even if it was to see them.

Grabbing his cell phone off the make shift desk in the corner, he decided that he would just go by and visit them. He reasoned that a drop in visit would be better because if he spoke to Terri first, he would be more likely to change his mind.

He checked his phone and a red battery sign was flashing on the LED, signaling that the battery was nearly dead. He saw that Terri had called him eight times just since last night. It made him feel bad because, as much as he hated her for what she did to him, he still loved her. That was something he couldn't just turn off so, in his opinion, it meant that his love was true. No matter what she did, he couldn't just fall out of love with her that easily.

He walked out the door and got into his car. When he was pulling out of the parking lot, he noticed a black Mercedes Benz parked in the parking lot beside him. There was nothing out of the ordinary about the car itself. It just seemed of out of place. The same way a black man would seem out of place in Omaha, Nebraska. It just seemed to conflict with its surroundings. The hotel was located in a poor part of town and was where you would never expect to see a car that expensive unless it was driven by a drug dealer.

Mark pushed the thought out of his mind. He didn't have any reason to be concerned with the car; it just caught his attention in a strange way. Resigning that it was none of his business, he gave the gas a hard press and drove away.

When Mark arrived home, he couldn't make it out of the car before Stephanie ran outside. She met him at the car with a hug.

"Daddy!" she shouted. "I missed you so much."

"I missed you too, sweetie," Mark said and planted a big kiss on her cheek. It rejuvenated his spirit to see his Daughter's smiling face. "Where's your sister?"

"She's in her room watching *Spongebob*," Stephanie said still walking beside him with her arms draped around his waist. She acted like if she let him go, he would leave again.

He walked into the house and saw Terri in the kitchen finishing up breakfast. The house smelled of bacon and eggs. He hadn't had any good food in a while so his stomach began to grumble violently.

"You hungry?" Terri asked when she saw him standing there.

"Hungrier than I've been in a long time."

Terri looked amazing. She wasn't fixed up or anything. Her hair was pulled up into a bun and she had on her glasses, which she hardly wore because she had abandoned them long before for contacts. She had on a pair of stretch pants that she worked out in and one of Mark's big white t-shirts. Mark guessed it was because he hadn't seen her in a while and he missed her a little more than he thought. He was still angry, though. He didn't care if she looked like Halle Berry, he still wasn't ready to let that anger go.

"I fixed more than enough," she said with a weak smile.

Mark didn't respond. He walked to the back room where Jessica was pasted to the TV watching cartoons. It was hard to pry her away when *Spongebob Squarepants* was on *Nickelodeon*.

"Hey, munchkin," Mark said when he walked in the room. Stephanie still draped around his waist.

"Hey, Daddy," Jessica looked up and said nonchalantly. She immediately went back to watching TV.

"I missed you, too," Mark said and lifted her face with his fingertips so that he could place a kiss on her cheek. Jessica moved her head quickly like he was blocking her view.

He walked back into the kitchen and grabbed a seat after Stephanie finally let him go. She didn't seem to think that he was leaving right back out, but she sat in the chair next to him so that she could keep an eye on him.

"Steph, go and get your sister. Breakfast is ready," Terri instructed and Stephanie got up and immediately ran into the other room. When she left there was an uncomfortable silence that lingered in the room.

"What smells so good?" Mark asked trying to break the silence.

"Oh, I just cooked oatmeal, eggs, and bacon. We have some orange juice in the refrigerator if you want some," Terri said as she brought over the plates.

Mark got up to help himself to some orange juice. He didn't really know what else to say to her. He resolved that he just wouldn't say much of anything and let the conversation go wherever she took it. He didn't feel that he owed her anything, because she was the reason they were in the situation they were in, so he would let her talk if *she* wanted to.

"I want some eggs," Jessica said as she came in and climbed up into a chair. Mark reached over to help her because she still struggled a little getting into the seat.

Terri placed a plate in front of both girls and one in front of Mark. She still didn't make eye contact with him, so Mark still felt the uncomfortable feeling. It seemed like not long ago the house was a home full of laughter and joy, now he could hardly see the remnants of what it used to be.

They ate breakfast without speaking a word to one another. The girls had plenty to say, though. Mark just listened to them as they recounted all the events in their life. It was funny to him the things that children thought about.

"I was at school and my friend Brittney hurt my feelings," Stephanie said. "She didn't sit with me at lunch. She sat with Keisha, the new girl."

"That's okay, Steph. I'm your bestest friend in the whole world," Jessica said twirling her pigtails around her finger. She had eaten her scrambled eggs and was no longer interested in anything on her plate.

"Jessica, you're just a baby," Stephanie said waving Jessica's comment off with her hand.

"Don't say that to your sister," Terri said. "You know she thinks she's as old as you."

"Well, did you try to sit with them?" Mark asked.

"No. They didn't invite me. I don't guess Brittney wants to be my friend anymore."

"I'm sure that's not it. What you should do is, when you go to school on Monday, introduce yourself to Keisha. Perhaps when you do that, you will grow to have two best friends like I do," Mark said filling his daily quota for advice.

"I'll try, Daddy, but I don't know," Stephanie said shaking her head.

"You can do it, honey. Everything will work out fine," Mark said his mouth full with his last slice of bacon.

Terri hadn't said much of anything during the meal. When they were done she started clearing the table. The girls ran off to the back to play.

"I'll do it," Mark offered.

"You don't have to, but you can help if you'd like," Terri said.

"That's cool."

They started washing dishes and the uncomfortable quiet reared its head again. Terri washed as Mark dried.

I wonder why teamwork in marriage isn't this easy everyday, Mark thought to himself.

"Where you been staying?" Terri said finally breaking the silence. She walked over to the counter to grab the rest of the dishes.

"Around. Why?" Mark questioned. He didn't mean to be so short. He just lashed out with attitude before he knew it. "I mean…. I've been staying in a by-the-week hotel."

"I've been so worried about you. It's like you disappeared off the face of the earth."

Mark didn't respond. He just listened as she continued.

"I did see you on TV though. I saw the episode of *Caught Slippin* that Austin was on."

"Really? I bet I looked like an idiot standing up there," Mark joked and cracked a half smile.

"Yeah, Kinda. You were just standing there like you were lost to the world," Terri said and let out a small giggle.

"I still can't believe that happened," Mark said as he was drying the last dish in the sink. He hated doing dishes before he left. Maybe that was something he could have done differently.

"I really miss you," Terri said now leaning against the counter with her arms folded. She had removed her glasses and placed them on the counter.

"Is *that* right?"

"Yeah, it just doesn't feel the same without you being around.

"Well, that's something you should have thought about."

Terri went and sat down at the table. She rested her head on her hands and sighed heavily before saying anything.

"Mark, I don't want to fight. If that's what you want to do, then why did you come over?"

"It definitely wasn't to see you. I needed to see my children because I missed them so much."

"Some part of you must miss me, too," Terri said as if she was searching for some sort of answer.

"You know what? Part of me does. I miss the way we used to be, when we were two people in love. Before we had any of the problems that complicated our relationship," Mark said and took a seat in front of Terri at the table.

"I know that we can get that back. Of course it won't be the same since so much has changed, but we can get our relationship back in the same ballpark as it used to be," Terri said reaching for his hand.

"I don't know...."

"Why don't you come back home and we can work on it together. At least give it a try."

"I can't," Mark said flatly.

"Why not?" Terri asked with an exasperated look on her face.

"I think we need more time apart. My heart's just not in the place to forgive right now."

Terri didn't respond. She just leaned back in her chair and covered her face with her palms.

"Anyway, I'm about to go. I don't want to have to say bye to the girls. I just might not be able to tear myself away from Steph this time."

Mark got up and headed towards the door. "Kiss the girls for me," He said as he walked out. He felt like he was leaving Terri all over again, but what was he to do.

She can't blame anyone but herself, he thought as he walked out and shut the door.

Chapter 34

Terri walked over and locked the door after Mark. She leaned back against the door and let out a long sigh. She wished she could go back in time and make different choices. If she could, she would have been more patient with Mark with his job situation.

She walked over to the window and opened the blinds so she could get a good view of him driving off. When she did, she saw the black Mercedes parked across the street and immediately knew who it was.

Mark drove past the car and he didn't even look over. Terri wondered how long Cedric had been parked there because she didn't notice the car when Mark had arrived. It was all becoming too strange for her. She decided she would call the police and press charges since she had gotten a restraining order placed against him and he couldn't come within 500 feet of her or her house.

She walked over to the base and picked up the cordless phone. Just then Stephanie came around the corner.

"Where's Daddy?" Stephanie asked after taking a look around the house.

"He had to leave," Terri said preoccupied with dialing the police.

"Man," She heard Stephanie say as she stomped towards her room. She normally would have gone after her to discuss her feelings, but that would have to wait. She had to make sure Cedric couldn't do anything to hurt them.

As she waited for someone to help her on the phone, she walked back over to the window. She couldn't believe they placed her on hold. What if she was dying? She supposed she would be dead when they came back from whatever they were really doing.

When she looked out the window she saw Cedric standing across the street staring in her direction. She knew he could see her through the open blinds so there was no need to try and hide. He took his thumb and slid it across his neck as if to cut his throat. He then jumped back into his car and sped off.

"What is his crazy behind doing?" Terri thought aloud.

Let your husband know to watch his back.

Cedric's words echoed in her head. She quickly hung up the phone. Cedric wasn't sitting across from her house to bother her, but he was following Mark.

She grabbed the phone again and hysterically tried to call Mark. She wanted to warn him about Cedric but the call kept going to his voicemail. Terri guessed his phone was dead. She cursed under her breath. She had to catch herself to keep her attitude from growing out of control. Getting mad wouldn't solve anything.

She tried Mark back one more time and left him a message this time.

"Mark, *please* call me back when you get this message. I need to talk to you. You may be in danger," Terri said and hung the phone up.

She paced back and forth across the room. She wished there was something she could do. After thinking a moment, she realized there was.

She gathered the girls and loaded them into her minivan and called Shannon from her cell phone.

"Can you do me a huge favor?" Terri said when Shannon picked up the phone. She skipped the formalities because she was pressed for time.

"Is everything okay?" Shannon asked obviously hearing the urgency in her voice.

"I have the girls in the car with me, so I'll have to tell you later," Terri responded. She merged onto the interstate driving as fast as she could. If Shannon couldn't keep them, it was too bad because she was already on her way.

"What's up? What do you need me to do?"

"I need you to watch Steph and Jess for a couple of hours for me."

"You know I will," Shannon responded. "I wish you could tell me what's going on."

"I promise I will, as soon as I can," Terri said and hung up the phone.

Chapter 35

Mark was headed back to the hotel. He reached down to turn the radio on and tuned in to *92Q*. *The Michael Baisden Show* was on, so he turned it up to get a listen. He really enjoyed listening to the show because Michael Baisden dealt with real life issues. The show today was about infidelity and if should you stay with someone that has cheated on you.

"I think if someone cheats on you once, then they will cheat on you again," one female caller was saying. "You should leave them alone and find someone that will appreciate you enough to be faithful."

Mark took the back roads home that day, because he wanted to avoid the normal traffic. He hated being stuck in car jams, so even if he had to go thirty miles out of his way to get home that's what he would do. He was so absorbed by the radio show and the interesting comments the caller's had that he didn't notice the black car speeding up behind him.

Mark glanced in the rear view mirror. "Why is this fool in such a hurry? It's not like he can pass me on this two lane street," He thought aloud.

The car then sped up as if he were about to pass. Mark got a glimpse of the Mercedes decal on the hood of the car. *That looks like the same car that was parked outside the hotel this morning*, he thought.

He stopped at a stop sign and the car had to slow down to stop behind him. Normally Mark would have only come to a rolling stop at an intersection, but he made sure this time to come to a complete stop. He turned around in his seat so that he could try and get a look at whoever was in the car. The tint was so dark that he couldn't make out anyone.

Mark waited at the stop sign a while and even turned on his emergency blinkers to see if the driver would grow tired of waiting and just go around. After about two minutes of sitting there, Mark reluctantly continued driving. The car moved right after him.

On the country road that Mark was driving on, there was no way for him to pull over to the side. There were no side lanes and barely any guard rails running along the road.

The car sped up again and tried to pass. This time the car was going fast enough to get along side Mark's car. He tried to slow down a little to let the car go by, but every time he slowed down, the driver of the other car slowed down too.

What are you doing, you idiot?" Mark yelled out after letting down his window. He then waved his hand in a motion to tell the driver to go ahead and pass.

The passenger's side window on the Mercedes finally let down and Mark's blood began to boil. It was Cedric and Mark would have tried to beat him to a pulp had they been parked.

Cedric was yelling something out of the window.

"I can't hear you," Mark screamed back.

"Terri is mine," Mark made out from reading Cedric's lips and the motions he was making with his free hand.

Just then Mark heard a horn blowing in the distance. He looked up in a hurry and a huge truck was headed their way traveling in the opposite direction. He grabbed the steering wheel with both hands and tried to steady himself. The truck couldn't have been more than one hundred and fifty yards away. He expected for Cedric's car to be obliterated by the truck.

All of a sudden, Cedric darted back into Mark's lane. Mark swerved and felt the car getting away from him. He struggled to straighten the stirring wheel and gain control. He pumped the brakes and they began to lock. There was a terrible screeching sound as the wheels slid across the pavement.

Mark completely lost control of the car and went off the side of the road. There was a loud bang and the eerie sound of crunching metal when Mark's car came to a stop after crashing into a tree.

Mark's body rested against the steering wheel and he fought to keep consciousness. He felt a dull ache all over his body. Surprisingly it was not intense enough to pinpoint it to one spot. He did feel a throbbing in his head where he had smacked it against the steering wheel.

As the darkness took over him, he thought about Terri and the kids. He thought about how much he missed them already. "God please don't let me die here," He prayed aloud. He felt so sleepy that he could barely keep his eyes open. Mark felt the warm blood begin to trickle down his forehead. When he closed his eyes, the last sound he heard was the sound of the car horn blaring from his body resting against it.

Chapter 36

Terri sped along looking for Mark. As she drove, she reflected on the many arguments they had gotten into over Mark's phone never being charged. No matter how many times she told him he never listened and passed it off as her nagging.

"What if there's an emergency?" She had said to him so many times.

"You can always get in contact with me if you need to," Mark had said in return jokingly. "If I'm not with you then you know I'll be with Austin or Q."

So she did what he had suggested and called Austin first. Austin assured her that he had not seen Mark since the wedding. She didn't know if she believed him but at that moment she didn't have time for assumptions.

She then called, Quincey. Quincey picked up the phone groggily like he'd just woken up.

"Hel-," he said.

"Q, have you talked to Mark," Terri said cutting him off.

"Who is this? Terri?"

"Yeah, it's me. I need to get in touch with Mark really bad."

"I haven't talked to him today," Quincey said.

"Well, do you know where he's staying? It's important. He may be in danger."

"Danger.... what's wrong?"

Terri sighed lowly. "I don't really have time to get into it right now. I just really need to know where he's been staying."

"He's been staying at Robert's Motor Court."

"Robert's? Why would he be staying in that dump?" Terri asked. If it were her, she would rather stay in an unhappy home than a seedy motel like that.

"Yeah, I tried to offer him to stay with me, but you know Mark. He wouldn't hear anything of it."

"Okay. Thanks, Q. I'll call you later if I need you," Terri said and shut the flip on her phone.

She was sitting at the light and flicked her turn signal with her left hand. She thought that the interstate would be a quicker way to get to the motel. She hoped with all her heart that she could find Mark before Cedric did.

Terri reached over and rolled the window down. It was a cold day out, but the sun beamed down on her through the clear windows of the van. The heat from the sun made the temperature a little bit hotter on the inside than it should have been.

The light turned green and as she was about to turn onto the ramp, she noticed how backed up the interstate was. If she knew anything about her husband, she knew how badly he hated being stuck in traffic. So she decided to take the back roads to the motel. Terri swerved back onto the road and nearly had an accident. Some woman in red Bronco blew her horn loudly and flipped Terri off. The woman yelled curses as she sped around to pass her.

Terri drove along the two lane roads as fast as she could. Her mind was consumed with thoughts of her marriage. She thought about the good times that her and Mark had shared together as well as the bad. She came to the conclusion that the good outweighed the bad by far.

Those thoughts took her back to the things her grandmother used to tell her as a child. *Honey, at the end of your life, God is going to take a look at all the deeds you've done in your life. If the good outweigh the bad, then he is going to say well done. If the scale falls in the other direction then he will turn you away.*

"If God is willing to look past my faults, then why couldn't I do the same thing for Mark and our marriage," she thought aloud.

Terri sped up a little. She came to a stop sign and looked both ways before continuing. No more than a couple of hundred yards after the stop, she thought she heard the sound of a horn blowing in the distance. The further she drove the louder and more distinct the horn grew.

As Terri grew closer to the area where the sound was coming from, she noticed a big truck pulled over on the side of the road.

I wonder what happened, she thought to herself.

As she drove pass, she strained to see over the embankment and found the source of the horn. A piece of scrap metal that looked like Mark's car was crumpled around a tree. If it weren't for the fact that she had seen it a thousand times, she wouldn't have known what it was.

She threw her car in park and jumped out. "What happened?" she yelled to the truck driver who was standing on the side looking terrified.

"I don't know, they just came out of nowhere," the guy said and removed his hat and started wiping the sweat from his brow.

"What do you mean *they*? Is there more than one person in the car?"

"No. There was another car. A black one. It swerved into his lane and ran him off the road."

"Oh my God," Terri said and started to run down the hill. The descent to the car seemed like it grew longer and longer. As she grew closer she smelled the scent of gasoline in the air. She had seen so many cars blow up on TV after an accident that the thought briefly crossed her mind. She pushed the thought out her mind because if Mark died, she wanted to die along with him. It was her fault any of this happened anyway. Why should he have to suffer alone?

"Miss, you can't go down there," she heard the driver of the truck yelling over her shoulder.

She didn't care about much of anything at that moment. She just needed to make sure Mark was okay. "Mark, can you hear me?" Terri yelled when she made it to the car.

No answer.

Terri walked around the driver's side and saw Mark lying unconscious against the stirring wheel. It looked as if he had injured his head because there was blood running down his forehead. Other than that it didn't appear as if he had any other injuries. *I am so happy we make it a point to wear our seatbelts*, she thought to herself. She could see that he was breathing, however softly.

"Mark, honey, if you're awake please say something to me," Terri said.

Still no answer.

Terri started seeing all the times they had together flash before her eyes. How could she be so stupid? Her temples started to throb. Her head was hurting worse than she ever remembered. Her breathing started to become labored and she felt herself begin to shut down mentally. Then came the tears. She fell to her knees and sobbed heavily. The only thing she could think to do was pray.

"God, please. If you've never heard my prayer before, hear me now. I know I'm not worthy to ask anything of you, but I don't know what else to do. I know this is entirely my fault and I'm sorry. Please, Lord, don't let Mark die because of my mistakes. If you need to take anybody, take me. It's me that messed up, not him. He's a great person and he is really trying to live his life for you now, in spite of me getting in the way. Please, spare his life."

Terri then sat there on the ground crying loudly. A hand touched her on the shoulder and she nearly jumped out of her skin. It was one of the paramedics that had just arrived on the scene.

"Were you in the accident?" he asked.

"No....but....my....husband...," Terri said in between chest heaves. She just pointed over to the car when she couldn't speak anymore.

"Okay, get back up the hill. The police have to get some information from you," he said and rushed over to the car to check on Mark.

Terri watched as the paramedic called his partners from his radio. The other guys came rushing down the hill with a gurney. Following close behind them were the firefighters carrying the Jaws of Life, so that they could cut Mark out of the car.

Terri walked back to the top of the hill and a cop was waiting for her. She answered the entire line up of questions he had and even gave him some extra information. She told him about Cedric threatening to harm Mark and gave the policeman a detailed description of him.

She walked over by the ambulance and waited as the paramedics strapped Mark to the gurney. When they brought him over to place him in the back, he was still unconscious and it appeared as if he had some swelling on his face. Terri couldn't help but cry. She felt horrible seeing him like that.

"Is he okay?" she asked the guy that had come down the hill first.

"At this point, I'm not sure." He said.
"What hospital are you taking him to?"
"To Southern."

When Terri arrived at the hospital, she parked in a parking spot on the emergency side of the building. The paramedics rushed Mark into the building. Without thinking, she jumped out the car and forgot her purse. After running about twenty feet she realized that she needed her insurance card and turned back to get it.

She gathered her purse and shut the door. When Terri turned around she was in such a hurry she didn't notice anyone standing behind her. She was full steam ahead so she almost knocked the person to the ground. When she gathered herself she looked up and saw Cedric reaching out for her. She fell back against her van with terror and ferociously shoved his arms away. Cedric then just stood there with a sinister grin on his face staring at her.

"Funny meeting you here," he said rubbing his hands together.

"I don't think it was a coincidence at all."

"Doesn't look like you're gonna have *any* excuse to not be with me in a little while."

"What are you talking about?"

"You know what I'm talking about. Your husband is just about outta the picture. I made sure of that," Cedric said and let out a little laugh. This guy was crazier than Terri thought. How could he stand there and brag about trying to kill her husband? She slapped his face as hard as she could.

"I like it rough," Cedric said still wearing that stupid smile.

"I wouldn't be with you for anything in this world. And I'll make sure the cops know everything you just told me," Terri said and tried to walk away.

Cedric grabbed her by the arm and began twisting it.

"You're hurting me," Terri whimpered.

"You know...I'm getting real tired of your junk," he said.

"Cedric, please let me go," Terri pleaded.

"Oh, so now you're begging *me*?"

"You can't do this out here. People are looking at us."

"You think I care about what people think. See that's your problem. You worry too much about other people. That must be why you wouldn't leave that loser you're married to. So I had to help you out."

"You're wrong. I didn't leave him because I love him," Terri said trying to sound strong. Maybe he would back off if he saw strength in her.

"YOU DON'T LOVE HIM!" Cedric yelled. He released her arm but kept her pinned between him and the car. "You love me."

"Cedric I'm sorry I didn't mean to lead you on. At the time we were having problems. You're a great-"

"Shut up." Cedric said cutting her off. "He doesn't deserve to be with you because he can't even provide for you."

"I had to realize that life is not all about money. I looked at wealthy people and thought that's exactly what I wanted for me. You know, the grass always looks greener on the other side. Now I see that I had everything I needed all along," Terri said. She couldn't believe those words came out of her mouth. She silently gave thanks for the growth she had experienced since getting saved.

"Well, if I can't have you then no one will," Cedric said and pulled out a gun. He placed the gun against Terri's head. She was so shaken she couldn't even move. Her body was paralyzed with terror from the sheer thought of her children losing both of their parents on the same day.

"I'm sick of women like you. You think you can just toy with a man's emotions and then throw him away. Men have feelings too," Cedric said. His face was so close to Terri's that the spit that spewed from his lips splattered on her face like raindrops.

"Cedric, please don't do this," Terri pleaded.

"It's too late for begging," Cedric said.

Terri closed her eyes and waited for him to pull the trigger. She never imagined her life would end like this. Not being shot by a stalker. But then again, who does?

"Put the gun down," Terri heard someone yelling in the distance. She felt Cedric remove the gun from her head. She opened her eyes and saw Cedric turn around. He was now facing the cop that was on the scene of Mark's accident.

"Sir, I'm ordering you to put the gun down," the cop said again.

Cedric didn't respond. He just stood there with the gun firmly in his hand now dangling by his side.

Terri didn't know how this was going to end, but with Cedric's back turned toward her she took her chance. She ran as fast as she could to the Emergency Room entrance. When she was safely inside, she went over to the window that everyone else was crowded around to view the scene. People were asking her if she was okay, but she just blew them off with a wave of her hand.

She saw the officer shout something else out to Cedric. He didn't respond verbally that Terri could see, but instead he started raising his gun to aim it at the police officer. Terri let out a scream as the officer fired upon Cedric. His body fell lifeless to the ground.

Terri was in disbelief at all the events that had transpired that day. As most people do in times of distress, she started praying again. She prayed that God would spare the life of her husband and she could return to some shell of her normal life.

Chapter 37

Austin walked into the waiting area right outside the emergency room. He had rushed over as soon as he heard what had happened with Mark.

He scanned the room briefly and didn't see anyone he knew sitting there, not even Quincey. He had spoken with him briefly before he left and expected him to already be there.

"What room is Mark Baxter in?" Austin asked the lady perched on a stool behind the window.

She looked over her charts for a moment and then gazed back up at him. "He's been moved to CCU. Unless you're immediate family or religious counsel, I can't allow you to go back there."

"I am family. He's my brother," Austin snapped back. Maybe they didn't have the same parents, but there was no rule that said family is only defined by a blood relationship.

"I'm sorry. I'll buzz you in and you have to take the elevator up to the fifteenth floor."

"A'ight," Austin said and walked to the door and waited for it to open.

Mark must have been more messed up than I thought, he thought. Austin knew that Mark had been in an accident, but he never imagined he would be in critical condition.

Austin heard a buzz, so he pulled on the door. When he rounded the corner, he was nearly mowed down by EMT's and a couple of emergency room doctor's as they rushed a young black man into the operating room around the next corner. The man had tons of blood on his chest and a couple of small holes.

Man, another black man wounded in the streets. When is the violence ever gonna stop? Austin thought to himself as he continued on his way to the elevator.

He stepped on and pressed the button labeled fifteen and prepared himself for the ride. He didn't know what to expect. Terri wasn't able to fill him in on much when she called because she was too distraught to go into any deep detail.

When he arrived on the fifteenth floor, he walked directly into the waiting room. He glanced around and saw a few familiar faces. Pastor Lewis and some of the church members were there. He also saw Quincey seated in the front with his arm around Mark's mother.

Austin walked over and placed a hand on Mark's mother's shoulder. "How you holding up, Ms. Baxter," he said.

"I'm doing okay. Just staying prayerful," Ms. Baxter said never lifting her eyes up from the floor.

"I'm sure he'll pull through okay. What's up, Q, man? You a'ight?" Austin said and reached out for Quincey' hand.

Quincey shook his hand and stood up. They embraced. "Yeah, I'm good. Just trying to stay strong. Seems like I just left this place."

"I know what you mean. I haven't gotten a chance to talk to you since…well, you know. How've you been holding up?"

"I'm good, considering."

"What about Kim? Is she doing okay?"

"Yeah, she's still living with her mother, though. I just can't help but feel like it's my fault she lost the baby."

"How do you figure that?" Austin asked shaking his head.

"I should have been more supportive when she told me she was pregnant. Maybe then she wouldn't have been so stressed out."

Austin led him out of earshot of Ms. Baxter so that they wouldn't upset her with talk of anything else. She had enough to worry about without having to hear about other people's problems.

"Q, you of all people should know that you don't have any control over that. Haven't you told me more than once that it's in God's hands," Austin said. Whether he chose to believe in *having faith* or not, Quincey of all people should.

"Yeah, but it doesn't seem like that philosophy worked for me," Quincey said. "Anyway, I've got to get back over to Ms. Baxter. It must be tough dealing with this alone."

"I know. Real quick though, what's up with Mark? Is he okay?"

"We don't know yet. Terri's been talking to the police all day and she's in the back with the doctor's now. We're all waiting on a report," Quincey informed him.

"The cops? What's going on? Terri didn't have a chance to tell me what happened."

"Well, Cedric ran Mark off the road and then followed Terri back here and threatened to kill her."

"What? Did they arrest him?"

"They did a little more than that. There was a standoff and the police had to shoot Cedric down," Quincey said sadly.

"For real? I knew something wasn't right about that brotha when I saw him at the restaurant with Terri that night."

"Yeah. I can't believe she couldn't see it. I thought Terri was smarter than that," Quincey said shaking his head.

"Me, too," Austin said. He couldn't believe that Terri was that stupid. Sure he had been on the cheating side of a bad relationship, but Mark was a good guy and he didn't deserve to be lying in some hospital because a jealous lover had tried to kill him. Austin had to bite his lip to keep from saying so.

"Let me get back over here," Quincey said and took his seat again next to Ms. Baxter.

Austin made his rounds in the room and shook hands. He spoke briefly with Pastor Lewis followed by the church members he knew and some he didn't. He thought it was real cool that all these people came out to check on Mark. He wondered how many would come if it had been him.

Probably none, Austin thought answering his own question. *They probably would think I deserve it after that big scene with Julie at the wedding.* He missed her terribly and wondered briefly how she was doing. He hadn't spoken with her since. He quickly pushed the thoughts from his mind. It wouldn't do him or anyone else any good to be thinking about that now.

A few moments later Terri came around the corner. Everyone stood to their feet. She was wiping her eyes with a handkerchief. It was obvious she had still been crying. Her eyes were puffy and her nose was shining red, so Austin figured she had pretty much been crying all day. So from judging the appearance of the situation, he braced himself for the worst.

"What did they say, Terri?" Ms. Baxter spoke up first.

"Well," Terri said her voice quivering. "Mark's in a coma. He had severe blow to the head. The doctor's said that it's touch and go at this point."

Ms. Baxter wailed at the news. Mark was her only son, so Austin knew the news had to be hard on her. He didn't have any children, but he assumed it had to be hard to hear you might lose someone that actually came from your own body.

"I'm so sorry," Terri said. She never looked up from the floor. At that moment she looked just like a child that had gotten in trouble for doing something her mother had told her not to do. Austin thought she bore a striking resemblance to her daughter Stephanie.

Austin walked over and hugged Terri. "It's okay. It's not your fault," he said. He masked his true feelings. He wished he could tell her that it was all her fault and now whatever the outcome, she'll have to deal with it the rest of her life.

"Yes, it is," Terri said. I shouldn't have messed around with Cedric. If I hadn't, none of this would have happened."

"You had no way to know. Who would have ever thought that a man intelligent enough to be a doctor would be so crazy?"

"That's something else I just found out," Terri said pulling away from Austin's embrace. "He hasn't practiced medicine in the last year. As a matter of fact, the cops said his license was taken away after he stalked one of his female patients. He wasn't even allowed to teach at the school anymore."

"What?" Austin said.

Terri was about to respond, but as soon as she opened her mouth, Pastor Lewis called for everyone's attention.

"I know that everything looks bad, but the way we see it is not how God sees it," Pastor Lewis said. "What we need to do is touch and agree and go before the Throne of Grace."

Everyone began to join hands. Austin grabbed Ms. Baxter's hand with one of his hands and Terri's with the other. Everyone formed a circle around the waiting room. There had to be at least thirty people in there.

"Why don't you go ahead and lead us in a prayer, Minister Jackson," Pastor Lewis said. Everyone was then looking at Quincey.

Some people began to close their eyes and start to mumble low prayers under their breath.

"I don't think so today," Quincey said. The low prayers that Austin had heard had now stopped. Now everyone was looking at Quincey again. "I….I'm really not up to it."

Austin thought it was real strange that Quincey had turned down praying for their best friend. He thought that if anyone would pray, it would have been him. If Pastor Lewis had asked Austin to pray, now that would have been an entirely different situation all together.

"Okay, I'll take it then," Pastor Lewis said as if unfazed by the situation. "Heavenly Father we come before your throne of mercy in our hour of need. Father, we know that you know the situation, so there's no need for me to lay it all out to you. What we ask is that you let your divine will be done. We know that what has happened, no matter how bleak it looks now, can be used for good. I know that sometimes it seems hard and we don't quite understand the things that transpire in our lives, but help us to see that you are still in control."

"I pray for your divine favor. I pray that you will give the family strength in this trying hour. I also pray that you will show yourself all the more. We know that when it's all said and done, this situation will be used as a testimony for the up building of your kingdom. I'm calling it done now, in your son Jesus' name. Amen."

They released hands and everyone embraced, many of them crying on each other's shoulder. Austin had to admit that he felt moved by the prayer. He didn't care to let it show because he was definitely not about to cry in front of all these people

Austin stayed a while longer and visited with some more people. He again hugged Ms. Baxter and Terri.

"I've got some work to get done. If there are any new developments, please call me. I don't care what hour it is," Austin said and then excused himself. Terri looked like she barely understood what he was saying. He was sure the shock of everything that happened would subside and Terri would get back down to earth.

Austin walked into his office and looked around for a moment. It looked like the office had been hit by a tornado. There were papers scattered all over his desk and empty Chinese cartons formed a line along the back wall of the room.

He had pretty much lived in there since the day of the wedding. There was no need to go home now. Julie wasn't there and all he had was a huge house to live in alone. Sure he could go out and cruise the local bars and meet some other women, but what would be the point?

Austin turned on the small TV that rested on top of the file cabinet in the corner. He turned it up when he noticed a picture of him in the background as the anchor lady spoke.

Recently one of our local business men was featured on the reality TV show Caught Slippin. Austin Barton's featuring on the show was not a favorable one. Barton was revealed as a cheater when his lover burst into his wedding with video cameras galore. The woman revealed that she was pregnant and that Barton was denying the baby. Barton, the founder of Barton Marketing, was unavailable for comments when we tried to reach him.

Austin turned the TV off and threw the remote on his desk. He had been getting such bad publicity since that show aired. He had also noticed a significant decrease in business since the airing. A lot of business owners liked to keep their distance from any bad publicity, especially when it involves a dead beat father.

Austin jumped when he heard the phone ring. He walked over and looked at the id. It read Black Pride Products, Inc. so he nervously answered the call.

"Mr. Green, how are you?" Austin said.

"Not too well, Austin. Not too well," Mr. Green said with a certain disappointment in his voice.

"That doesn't sound good. What's going on?"

"Well, for lack of a better way to put it, Austin, I'll just come right out and say it."

"Okay, shoot," Austin said and walked over and took a seat in his office chair. He leaned back so that he was looking at the ceiling.

"I'm gonna have to pull my business out," Mr. Green said.

"What? Why?"

"I think you know. I run a Christian based business. I cannot have my business associated with a company run by a ladies man and no less a man that's denying his child. The media would have a field day with that."

"Don't act so hastily, Mr. Green. All it takes is a little damage control. When the baby is born, my attorneys have already demanded that a paternity test be done the same day. If you can just hold out until then, I'm sure we can minimize the damage."

"I don't think so. My mind is already made up. You'll receive pay for what you've done in the past month, but effective immediately I'm pulling out."

"Well," Austin said. "I guess there's nothing left that I could say."

"I'm afraid not. I'm praying for you brotha," Mr. Green said and then hung up the phone.

Austin sat in his chair still staring at the ceiling. With him losing so much business and Black Pride pulling out, he didn't know what he would do to keep his business open. He was already falling behind on some of the expenses. He couldn't keep going when it was growing increasingly hard for him to generate revenue.

All over that stupid show, Austin thought to himself. His world was crumbling all around him and he was losing everything he had worked so hard to achieve.

"Okay, God, you got me," Austin said aloud. "I don't know what else to do at this point. I'm losing everything. I've already lost Julie. Now my business is going under. What do you want me to do? Whatever it is, I'm willing to do it. I won't resist any longer."

Austin had not been receptive to anything that had to do with God before. But now that he was at his lowest point, he found that there was still a void. One that could not be filled by any of the women he had slept with or any amount of money he had made. There was still something missing. Whatever it was, the emptiness had been there the entire time. He was just too distracted with his temporary fixes to see it. Austin picked up the phone to call Pastor Lewis. He would know exactly what to do.

The phone rang a few times before First Lady Lewis picked up. "Hello?" she said with sleep in her voice.

"Hi, First Lady, It's Austin. I'm sorry about calling so late, but is Pastor Lewis available to talk?"

"Its okay, Austin, it's still *early* for people to be calling. I'm quite used to it by now," She said with a laugh. "He's in his study, so hang on and I'll go get him."

She put the receiver down and Austin waited patiently for Pastor Lewis to get on the phone. He had tons of questions that he needed answers to.

"Austin, how's it going brother," Pastor Lewis said when he finally came to the phone.

"I don't know, Pastor. I've got a lot of things going on."

"I know. Seems like the devil's busy right now. But I'm confident that everything will work out fine. So....what do I owe the pleasure of hearing from you tonight?"

"Well, I guess my question is complex to me but simple to you. What can I do to be saved?"

"Well the bible says in Roman 10:9," Pastor Lewis began. Austin could hear the smile in his voice. "That if you confess Jesus with you mouth and believe with your heart that God raised him from the dead you can be saved. Do you believe that?"

"I guess."

"Well, guessing when it comes to you soul is not good. What is it you're not sure about?"

There was a long pause before Austin offered an answer. "I think it's that I've done so many things wrong, I can't see how God could love me or forgive me."

"Austin, I'm here to tell you that no matter what you've done, God will always forgive you," Pastor Lewis said. "The bible says that we have all have sinned and fell short of his glory. So if everyone has sinned, even those of us that are saved now, then you'll be in great company. Do you believe what I'm saying?"

"Since you put it that way, I do believe what you're saying. What can I do to be saved?"

"Since we've now established that you believe, pray this prayer with me."

"Okay," Austin said. His heart began beating rapidly because he didn't know what to expect. Even though he had gone to church his entire life, he had never actually been saved. The whole thing was a new experience for him.

"Lord," Pastor Lewis began. "I believe that Jesus was your son and he died for my sins. Through his resurrection I have redemption for everything wrong that I've done. I accept you as my God and Jesus as my personal savior. I have faith that right now, at this very moment, I'm saved."

Austin tearfully repeated every word that Pastor Lewis had said and with each syllable a weight was lifted from his shoulders. It was the first time in a long while that he felt fulfilled. Pastor Lewis explained to him when the new Christian classes met at the church and expressed his excitement for Austin coming to God. When he hung up the phone, Austin was ready to grow his new relationship with Christ.

Chapter 38

Quincey stayed with Terri and Ms. Baxter until everyone else left. He figured that it was the least he could do and he imagined Mark would do the same thing for him if he were incapacitated.

Ms. Baxter didn't say much. The few words that she *had* spoken had been to Quincey. She seemed as if she didn't even want to look at Terri. The tension was so thick that he could almost see it in the air, but he guessed that he would be pretty upset if that were his child lying in some hospital bed all because of an affair.

"Terri, you need anything?" Quincey said to her as she walked past him for the hundredth time. She had been pacing back and forth for hours.

"No, I'm good. I'm just anxious to get back in the hospital room. The doctors said I could even spend the night back there once they give me the okay."

"I understand, but you may want to rest for a moment. It's been a pretty stressful day for you," Quincey said. It silenced him when he heard Ms. Baxter grunt under her breath.

"A stressful day for *her*? I guess so. Her little boyfriend is dead. I guess seeing that was stressful indeed," Ms. Baxter said angrily.

Terri didn't respond.

"I think both of you should go home and get some rest. I'll stay here in case there are any new developments," Quincey said. "Besides, the girls are probably looking for their mother by now."

"Quincey, I know you mean well, but I'm not going anywhere. I'm staying right here, because I actually love my son," Ms. Baxter said taking another shot at Terri.

"Well, I'm staying too. I can't abandon Mark now. Besides I just talked to Shannon. She said the girls are just fine," Terri said still not responding to Ms. Baxter's comments.

The whole situation was crazy to Quincey. He didn't see the reasoning in it. He couldn't help but include his own personal struggles in his attempt to acquire understanding. He normally didn't question God, but he couldn't help it this time. *Why is it that God's people go through the most*? He thought to himself. *I dedicated my life to the ministry and look at what I've received in return. My marriage is falling apart and I lost a child that I didn't even get the chance to properly love or appreciate. And then there's Mark. What did he do to deserve this situation? As a matter of fact he was directing his life more and more toward the church. He was even working there. I'm just so confused.*

"Quincey," Ms. Baxter called out disturbing him from his thoughts. "You okay? You were just staring into space."

"I'm fine. I'm thinking I'm gonna get out of here for a few minutes, though. That's if you guys will be okay for a little while."

"I think I'll be fine, long as I don't have to say too much to *her*," Ms. Baxter said nodding in Terri's direction.

Quincey looked over at Terri who was leaning against the wall by the vending machine. It didn't look like she had heard what Ms. Baxter said, even though it was clear Ms. Baxter wanted her to.

"Ms. Baxter, I can understand how you feel but I know Terri didn't mean for any of this to happen. She wouldn't do this on purpose," Quincey whispered.

"Yeah, but the fact still remains that if she wasn't out with another man, my son wouldn't be possibly dying back there," Ms. Baxter said starting to tear up.

"We are not claiming anything like that. We're staying positive and we believe Mark is going to pull through this," Quincey said and reached out and caressed her hand.

"I know, forgive me. It's just a lot to deal with. Don't worry about me, though, you can go ahead and get going. I'll be okay."

"You sure?"

"Yeah, I'm sure. Now get out of here, boy."

Quincey walked over and told Terri he was leaving for a while. He gave her a hug and then left the hospital.

He thought about Mark and Terri the entire way home. The more he thought about their situation, the more he thought about Kim. He missed her terribly and just wanted to hold her in his arms. He wanted her to come home very badly. They had talked several times since she lost the baby and even though she never admitted it, Quincey felt like she blamed him for not being there.

As soon as he walked into the house he heard the TV on in the living room. *I could swear that I turned that off before I left*, he thought to himself. He walked into the living room and was startled to see Kim sitting on the couch, eyes trained on the TV.

"Hey," Kim said when she saw him walk into the room.

"Hey, how're you?" Quincey said in return. There was a strange feeling in the atmosphere. It was the first time Kim had been inside their home since she left.

"I'm feeling a whole lot better," Kim said as she picked up the remote and clicked off the TV. Quincey took this as a sign that they needed to talk.

"How did you get here? I didn't see your car out front."

"My mother dropped me off. She needed to visit a sick member from the church and I didn't feel much up to it. Besides we have some things we need to talk about."

"Oh do we?" Quincey said playfully. He walked around and took a seat on the couch next to her. He looked her over from head to toe. He had only seen her twice since she left the hospital. One of those times he visited her at her mother's house but didn't get a good look because Ms. Robertson loved to keep it dark to save on her electric bill. So this was the first time he had gotten a real good look at her since then.

She looked great considering everything she had gone through. He couldn't even tell she had been pregnant. She wore a fitted sweater with an oversized neck and a pair of jeans. Her hair looked like it hadn't been done lately so she had it pulled back into a tight ponytail.

"So what's up? What's on your mind?" Quincey said ready to dive into the conversation no matter what it was.

"You. I haven't heard from you in a little while and I was just wondering where you've been."

"Working. I think APS is about to break on the case with Mark. Other than that, I've been just trying to get my mind together."

"So you were at work just now?" Kim said noting the slacks and dress shirt he had on.

"No actually as soon as I walked in from work, I got a call from Terri to come to the hospital. Mark was in an accident."

"Oh my God. Is he okay?"

"Well, he's in a coma. The doctor's say it's touch and go right now."

"That is so terrible. I better call Terri. How is she holding up?"

"Not too well," Quincey said. He filled Kim in on all the events of the day including how the cops had to gun down Cedric.

"I'm so sorry to hear that," Kim said as she sat back on the couch and went into a deep thought. There was a long silence, before she said, "What about church? What have you been up to there?"

"Nothing, really. I haven't been to church since we lost the baby. I haven't really felt up to it."

"Haven't felt up to it? I can't believe that."

"Look if you came over here to take shots at me, then you can save it. I'm not in the mood to fight today."

"I'm sorry. I didn't mean it like that. I just thought there was nothing that could tear you away from something once your mind is set on it."

"I had a loss last month just like you did. Besides I'm not taking over the church after all. You should be happy."

"Why would you say that," Kim said actually looking surprised.

"Because you didn't want me to take it anyway. You wanted me at home all the time and that's how it's gonna be for a while. I'm not going to be pastor and I'm taking some time away from the law firm."

"Quincey, look, I know I told you that's what I want but now that's changed."

"That's a new development."

"Yeah," she continued. "Before I went to the hospital, my mother had a long conversation with me that made a lot of sense."

"What did she say?"

"Well I can't remember the exact words, but basically she helped me realize that I'm holding you back from your full potential. Instead I need to be supporting you in what God has called you to do."

"I'm speechless. I don't know what to say," Quincey said. He wasn't really expecting her to say anything like that. "What about the baby? I thought you've been blaming me for the loss."

"What? No…I've been blaming myself. I was so ashamed that I had been acting the way I was. I really should have been more grown up about everything. And on top of that, I lost a piece of you," Kim said and tears started trickling down her cheeks.

Quincey walked over and grabbed her hand and lifted her up from her seat. He pulled her close and hugged her tenderly. He took his thumb and wiped the tears from her face and placed a soft kiss where they had been.

"Babe, it was not your fault. I don't think it was anyone's fault. I actually think there is some good that we can take away from this. I believe that we can use this to bring us closer together."

Kim didn't respond she just continued to bury her head into his chest. He could feel her breathing softly.

"I want you to move back home. I'm not angry with you. I love you to much to be," he said.

"I will under one condition."

"What's that?"

"That you don't deny what God has called you to do and take the position at the church."

Before Quincey could answer he heard his cell phone ringing in his jacket pocket. "One moment, I have to answer this," He said.

Quincey walked over and took the phone out of his jacket. It was Phillip Blumenthal's number. He had been waiting on that phone call all day. It meant that there was possibly some good news in the midst of all the turmoil.

Chapter 39

Terri had never left Mark's bedside since the doctor had given her permission to go into the room. It had been three days since he was admitted and he still remained unconscious. Even though he wasn't responding, Terri felt an incredible sense of hope. She felt as though God really heard her, so she converted that feeling into action as often as she could by praying whenever she had the thought.

Ms. Baxter had gone home a few hours earlier to get some sleep. The chairs in the waiting room weren't that comfortable so she would not have been able to do so in there. It took a lot of convincing on Terri's part to get her to go. It was clear that Ms. Baxter hated Terri now and was not going to change her feelings.

The phone on the desk started ringing and Terri walked over and answered it.

"Hello," she said.

"Terri, is that you?" Quincey asked with unmistakable excitement in his voice.

"Yeah. Who else would it be?"

"How long will you be there?" Quincey asked ignoring her previous comment.

"I'm not going anywhere. I've been here since Mark came in and I don't have any plans on leaving. I don't want anything to happen and I'm not here."

"Well, I'm on my way to the hospital. I've got some big news to tell you and I should be there in about an hour."

"A'ight, I'll see you when you get here," Terri said and hung up the phone. She wondered why Quincey sounded so excited. He had been coming over to the hospital every day since Mark had been in there, so she couldn't imagine what big news could have happened since she last saw him.

While she was on the phone a nurse came into the room and checked Mark's vitals. Terri was used to that since she'd had the pleasure of doing it so many times herself. The nurse gave a casual wave as she left the room.

When the nurse was gone, Terri took her seat again next to Mark's bedside. "Sweetie if you can hear me. I wish you would hurry and come back to me. Me and the girls miss you so much. I love you and I know you're fighting to get back as soon as you can."

Terri took his hand and started stroking the back of it. She lifted it to her lips and kissed it softly. *It's amazing that you never actually realize how much you love someone until you stand to loose them*, she thought to herself.

She stroked her cheek with Mark's hand and started to pray again. She had prayed so much that she couldn't really think of anything else to say that she hadn't already. She just simply prayed, "Lord, please bring my husband back to me." Terri just repeated those words over and over aloud.

Terri jumped when she felt Mark's fingers start to bend. She didn't mean to be startled but it was totally unexpected. She looked over at his face and Mark's eyes were open and he was looking right at her.

"Oh my God," was all she could say.

His eyes looked weak, but he smiled softly at her.

"Thank you, God. I have to go get the doctors," She said jumping up from her seat.

She rushed from the room and ran down the hall to get the nurse. The nurse then called the doctor on the phone and rushed into the room with Terri right behind her. They checked on Mark for the next half an hour. "You are a very blessed man, Mr. Baxter," the doctor kept saying. "I've seen people die in accidents not half as bad as the one they tell me you were in."

Terri just listened but she knew it didn't have anything to do with luck. It was all God. She would not give credit to anything or anyone else.

While the doctors were working in the room, Terri slipped outside to the hallway and cried briefly and then took out her cell phone and started calling everyone she knew to tell them the news.

The first person she called was Shannon and begged her to bring the girls. Shannon had been keeping them ever since Mark had been in the hospital, and it would do the girls good to see their father.

She was so focused on calling everyone that she didn't notice the doctor come out of the room. Terri jumped when she felt him tap her on the shoulder. "He's weak, but it looks like he is going to be fine. If you finish up with what you're doing you may be able to talk to him briefly, before we move him to another room for observation."

"Thanks," Terri said as she headed back to the hospital room.

She opened the door and peered into the room. Mark's eyes were closed and he breathed lightly. Terri walked over and took a seat by his bed. She leaned forward and touched him gently on the chest.

"Mark, sweetie can you hear me?" Terri said softly.

Mark opened his eyes and smiled at her. "I always could."

"I'm so happy you're okay. I was so worried."

"You know me, I'm indestructible. It'll take more than a tree to kill me," Mark said still wearing his smile.

Terri laughed nervously. "I've been praying so hard for you. For the first time in a long time I feel like God was actually listening to me."

"I heard you. It's funny…I could hear everything you were saying and I wanted to respond, but I couldn't. I heard every prayer and every word."

"Well since *I know* you can hear me now, I have something I need to say to you. Maybe this isn't the right time, but I really am sorry…"

"Don't," Mark said interrupting her.

Terri's heart sank. She deeply hoped that Mark would somehow find a way to forgive her. That hope started to fade when he refused to hear her apology.

"You don't have to explain," Mark continued. "I forgive you for everything. I figure if God spared my life and gave me another chance, the least I can do is offer the same sentiment to you."

"Mark, I love you so much," Terri said and leaned down and gave him a hug.

Mark dosed back off to sleep shortly after that. Terri held his hand the entire time. She didn't ever want to let him go. She had almost lost him before and now she felt that if she ever looked the other way for just a second, then she might miss that one last moment to be with him.

A couple of hours later, the orderlies and nursing staff came in to move Mark to his new room. Terri still followed next to the bed holding his hand the entire way. He never woke up during the journey to the floor below them, but Terri watched his breathing intensely to make sure nothing went awry.

Just as soon as they were getting settled into Mark's new room, Shannon walked through the door with Stephanie and Jessica behind her. "Daddyyyyyy," they shouted in unison.

Stephanie hopped up on the bed and hugged Mark tightly. His face began to frown as he labored to lift his arm and hug her back, but he couldn't. Terri figured that he was still too weak to do anything. Jessica just walked around the room examining all the medical equipment. She was obviously too young to fully understand what was going on.

They were only there for a short while when Quincey walked in the room and to Terri's surprise Kim was with him. She hadn't seen the two of them together in months.

"How is everyone? Mark I'm so happy you pulled out of this. I was praying for you," Quincey said and walked over to give Mark a hug.

"Thanks, man," Mark said. "You know I can't go anywhere yet."

"Well, my coming down here has a dual meaning today. I know everyone is overjoyed about you still being here with us, but I have some news that everyone will surely find exciting."

"I had almost forgotten that you called earlier," Terri said. "With everything that was going on, it was hard for me to think of anything else."

"Yeah, I understand. Well, I received a call the other day from Phillip Blumenthal, which is the lawyer that represents APS. Over the past few days, even though I haven't said anything about it, I've been working closely with them on a settlement for the case. They have agreed to settle for two and a half million dollars as long as we don't go public with the lawsuit. I told them that for that amount, our lips are sealed. Also, the man that made those racist remarks was asked for his resignation, effective immediately. So, Mark, I believe all your prayers have been answered. And don't worry, you don't have to pay me anything. It was great to just help out a friend and this case just happened to be the perfect one to be my last."

"What do you mean your last case?" Mark asked.

"It's my last case because effective immediately, I'm resigning from the firm and I'm going to become the full time Pastor of St. Paul."

"That's real big, bruh. I'm proud of you," Mark said giving Quincey the weak smile he had given Terri earlier.

"That's good, Q," Terri exclaimed. "And, Mark, Why didn't you tell me about the case?"

"I kept it from you on purpose," Mark said. I wanted to surprise you…that is if we won."

"Well I *am* surprised, but now with everything that's happened, I don't feel right even thinking about it."

"Don't worry about it, I love you and it's my pleasure to share the money and the rest of my life with you," Mark said.

Epilogue

Quincey sat in the Pastor's study reading over his notes and studying the bible verses he had selected to speak from. After practicing over and over again in his head, he decided it was time for him to go and take his place in the pulpit.

He walked out of the doors located just on the side of the pulpit and everyone rose to their feet. He walked up and took his seat beside Pastor Lewis.

He scanned the congregation. As usual it was packed all the way to the very last seat. It still amazed him how much the church had grown over the past few months. When he first announced his call to preach, the church had a mostly black membership that consisted of about 200 people. Now as he scanned the congregation, there were at least 800 in attendance and there were faces of every race scattered throughout. They were adding on to the church soon because the membership was growing every week.

As the choir sang "Your Steps Are Ordered," by Fred Hammond, Quincey glanced over on the left side of the church. Mark sat with his arm around Terri and their girls were positioned right next to him. It had been about nine months since Mark had left the hospital and he was nearly back to full strength. Mark had even resumed his position at the church as an assistant to the pastor.

Mark and Terri's marriage was making large strides towards returning back to normal. They had just recently completed the marriage counseling sessions they had started with Pastor Lewis. Quincey could only judge from what he saw, but it appeared as if Mark and Terri were the happiest they had been in a long time.

The money that he received from the settlement didn't hurt. Aside from working at the church Mark was in the process of starting a janitorial business. He also was finally able to buy that house that he and Terri had been dreaming about and lived two blocks over from Quincey now.

Seated directly in front of Quincey, on the front pew, was Austin. He was standing and clapping. He swayed from side to side singing along. Quincey was very proud of Mark and Terri, but he felt a special since of pride when he thought about Austin.

Austin had made huge leaps when it came to his walk with God. After Black Pride pulled out their business, Austin had no choice but to close down his office. He had to take a job teaching marketing at a local high school. Even though Austin had lost everything he had worked hard to accomplish, it was only then that he realized that he didn't do it all on his own.

After the baby with Monica was born, Austin had a paternity test done. When the test results came back, they proved that the baby wasn't Austin's. As a matter of fact, there was never another person named as the father. Quincey assumed at the time that Austin would be bitter, but the situation actually made Austin's walk with God stronger and his relationship closer. When Quincey talked to Austin about it, "Sometimes God does things we don't understand in order to get our attention," was the only answer Austin gave.

None of them had seen or heard from Julie since the day of the wedding. Quincey guessed that when she said she was through with Austin if he cheated again, she was sincere about it. She left Austin and didn't show any signs of coming back.

Quincey looked over on the other side of the church and winked at Kim and smiled lovingly at her. He thought she looked more beautiful than ever. She was now eight months pregnant and looked like she was about to deliver any day. She joyfully smiled back and blew him a kiss. He couldn't believe that there was a time when he didn't even want another child.

He was very happy the second time around when he found out she was pregnant. They visited the doctor regularly and there were no complications. The doctor told them repeatedly that Kim was extremely healthy. As a matter of fact she was pregnant with twin girls that they had already decided to name Chloe and Zoe. It would be great for Jeff to have a couple of sisters to look after.

Quincey had stopped practicing law, as promised. His last case was Mark's against APS. He was now available to help Kim out and spoil her as much as possible and she loved every minute of it.

Quincey guessed Janet, Jeff's mother had gotten the picture. She had stopped trying to get back with him when she realized that if Quincey and Kim's marriage could survive the loss of a child, then she didn't stand any chance. She had moved on to her next man and was only showing Quincey attention when it came to child support or Jeff. Those were both circumstances Quincey could handle.

"I'd like to thank everyone for coming out today. I'd also like to thank you from the bottom of my heart for allowing me to be your pastor for the last forty years," Pastor Lewis began when the choir was done singing.

"Unless for some special occasion, this will be the last time I'll address you in this manner. That's okay, because my task today is to present your new pastor, the man that is appointed to take you to the next level in life and in the spirit. I hope that you will be as good to him as you have been to me. I trust that he'll truly lead you in the direction that God has selected for you. With no further ado I'd like you to give a warm welcome to your Pastor, Pastor Quincey Jackson," Pastor Lewis said and stood aside clapping his hands.

Quincey walked over and gave Pastor Lewis an embrace before walking to the microphone. It made him feel wonderful to receive such a warm embrace. He looked over at Kim and she was clapping harder than anyone else in the entire congregation and it meant a lot to him to have her support.

When the church quieted down, Quincey began. "I'd like to thank everyone for that wonderful display of love and support. Also, I'd like to thank my wife for being a support system for me and my friends for teaching me so much over the past few months. Finally, I want to thank Pastor Lewis for believing in me when I didn't even believe in myself."

"With the formalities out of the way, I'd like to get right to the reason we are all here today. So, if you have your bible, I'd like you to turn with me to Psalms 37:1-5," Quincey said and then allowed a few moments to pass by as he waited for the rustle of bible pages to stop."

"It reads: *1. Fret yourself not because of evildoers; be not envious of wrongdoers. 2. For they will soon fade like the grass and wither like the green herb. 3. Trust in the Lord, and do good; dwell in*

the land and befriend faithfulness. 4. Delight yourself in the Lord and
he will give you the desires of your heart."

"And for a few moments of your time, I would like to speak to you from the subject: The Grass always *appears* Greener on the Other Side."

About the Author

C.L. Johnson resides in Nashville, TN with his wife and two children. He is currently working on a Psychology degree and writing his second novel. You can visit his website at www.CLJohnson.com